## HE WAS FASCINATED BY... HE IMAGINED WINDING IT AROUND HIS FINGERS, OVER HIS HAND, AROUND HER NECK . . .

A frown crossed Donevan's face as he watched Mia slip on a red bra. She put on a blouse and buttoned it, then stepped into a skirt, looking in the mirror, making sure the garment was straight. She picked up a hairbrush and thoroughly brushed her hair. Then, taking a brightly colored scarf in hand, she tied it around her head like a headband, leaving the ends trailing down along the left side of her face. When she had slipped on the orchid boots, she walked back to the closet.

Donevan swiftly blended back into the clothes, his pulse racing, his throat tight. Again, Mia reached into the closet without turning on the light; when she had taken a purple jacket from a hanger, she closed the door.

Donevan stood there for a moment, thinking how cleverly he had hidden himself. He felt himself growing excited. Carefully making his way out of the bedroom he eased down the hall . . .

# THRILL KILL

## B. L. WILSON

POCKET BOOKS

New York   London   Toronto   Sydney   Tokyo   Singapore

An *Original* Publication of POCKET BOOKS

POCKET BOOKS, a division of Simon & Schuster Inc.
1230 Avenue of the Americas, New York, NY 10020

ISBN: 0-671-68418-3

First Pocket Books printing October 1990

10  9  8  7  6  5  4  3  2  1

For Linda Marrow, who was willing to help me grow as a writer; for John Scognamiglio, who enthusiastically and generously guided me through the refining of the book; for Kathy Davis, and for Michael—always!

Also for Alice, R.K., Sarah, Carmen, Ellen, and Pat. And especially for Dr. Ashby, who helped more than he can know.

# ~ CHAPTER 1 ~

Standing in the shadowy light behind the diaphanous green curtains at the window of her cottage, Mia watched from her vantage point atop the hill as a black truck wound its way toward her. While she concentrated on the man at the wheel, she was only vaguely aware of the sweet strains of classical music filling the room with a low, soothing serenade.

The aromatic oils mingling with the pine logs that burned in the fireplace lent a familiar perfume to the chilly, moist air. The spring evening faded as soft rain fell on the Oregon soil.

Ancient trees leaning protectively over the cottage were a glistening chartreuse umbrella which shaded the house from the scarce sun and the prying eyes of the people below. Flowers and trailing vines combined to create a beautiful barrier, adding to the illusion of a hidden world.

Lost in her thoughts, Mia was not aware of the stranger in the green hat and raincoat hunkered down in the damp, lush vegetation. He sat still, waiting, staring intently at the hazy figure of the woman at the window.

\* \* \*

At the bottom of the hill Emma Carson laid down her movie magazine and rushed to the window to observe the black truck as it passed her house. After she pulled back the curtains, she hastily adjusted her glasses. She didn't want to miss anything. Excitement caused her bony hand to tremble as she peered out the spotlessly clean window.

"Come look, Buck!" she told her gray-haired husband. "It's the black truck, right on time. Funny, I could of swore he went up earlier."

"Stop snooping, Emma," Buck scolded as he had a hundred times before. They had had this conversation for eleven months, ever since the mystery woman had moved to the top of the hill.

"What does she do up there?" the old woman wondered, her forehead furrowed in concentration as she boldly stared up at the distant cottage. "There's sin and secrets and strange goings-on, to be sure."

When Buck continued to read his paper, Emma put her hands on her hips and glared at him. Either he was going deaf or he was pretending to. She spoke louder and more shrilly to get his attention. "I say, Buck, do you think she's selling drugs? Or is it something else she sells?"

"Hush, Emma," he murmured.

"Well, *something* accounts for all those strangers who travel the road at all hours of the day and night," she said, pursing lined lips in distaste at the thought.

Without looking up, Buck replied, "They say she's a massage lady. You know that."

"Some say that, some don't," the woman noted. "Some call her the masseuse. Some call her the lady of love. Some call her worse. All of 'em are guessing."

Buck nodded and began to rock, the regular creaking of his maple chair the only accompaniment to their voices. "Just another crazy Californian is my guess."

"Where do you suppose she goes when she vanishes for weeks at a time?" Emma asked, still brazenly peering out the window, her thin body plainly visible. "She never tells a single one of her neighbors. I don't suppose she tells her friends, neither, but then maybe she ain't got none."

"Except Frank," Buck noted.

"Pshaw! *Friend!* Frank ain't her friend, for crying out loud. Lover is more likely!"

"Now, Emma, you know he's the caretaker. He goes up there and does his work and feeds that cat whether she's there or not."

"Huh! Caretaker my eye! He's as weird as she is. Sounds mighty educated, but ain't got no regular job, leastwise not the kind of job a man with schooling would have. Now, why do you suppose that is?"

"I really don't know, but maybe he just wanted to get away from the rat race. Folks do that, you know."

"Yeah, but them's mostly people from California, and I don't know that's their truthful reason for coming. Too many people are flocking to Oregon, clogging it up with their filthy ideas and their drugs. It's downright criminal what's happening here. California's sending all her freaks up this way."

"Drugs and freaks is everywhere," he noted.

"Maybe. Maybe not. I read it's worse here 'cause we're like the last frontier, and we've got them loose drug laws. Anyway, Frank ain't from California. He's got that real funny snooty talk, like them New England people."

"Boston, maybe," Buck commented.

"Boston? Why do you say that in particular?"

He shrugged. His tone was condescending. "Boston's in New England."

"Buck, do you remember that killer terrorizing people in Boston? I think Tony Curtis played him in the movie."

"Yeah. Why?"

"Well, maybe Frank's here with no decent job because he's done something so bad he ain't wanting to call attention to hisself."

"Emma, stop thinking crazy and close the curtain."

Emma gazed out the window again, murmuring to herself.

"He ain't friendly and he keeps pretty much to hisself, excepting with that woman, of course. I wonder how she pays him. More likely than not—"

"Stop prying and speculating, Emma," Frank ordered. "Close the curtain."

Emma turned around and glared at him. "I still say we ought to call the police. I'm telling you she's into something strange. She's selling *something.*"

"You called the police the first month she was here, remember? They didn't find nothing strange."

"Hmph, she fooled 'em into thinking she was on the up-and-up," the woman grumbled, adjusting her glasses again.

"They were fooled for a mighty long time," he noted. "They were there for almost an hour."

"I recall," she said sourly.

"Close the curtain," Buck repeated. "Mind your own business. The fire needs more logs. It's your turn to tend to it."

Her severe features etched with displeasure, Emma jerked the curtain back into place. Buck was a fool if he thought that woman was on the level. But then, wasn't that just like a man? See a pretty face and lose what little good sense he had.

As Buck glanced at the swaying pristine curtain, he, too, wondered what the mystery woman on the hill did. He secretly watched when Emma wasn't around, and he'd been lucky enough to see the beauty driving down the road in her car. He wished he had the nerve to go up and find out what it was she was selling. He might like some himself.

Mia smiled, the gentle movement creating the only lines on her serene face as she watched the man in the black truck turn into her driveway. The blue in her blue-gray eyes, accented by the teal color of her modified sari, deepened with a pleasant thought.

"You're going to have a very special evening, Garson

4

Hundley. You're going to enjoy it," she murmured in her silken voice. "You'll see."

Silently moving away on feet clad in soft shoes, she went across the hall to her study. There, in the rich wood-paneled room, surrounded by her numerous books, she studied the bulletin board on one wall, where her regular client list was posted.

She cleared her mind and system so she could focus totally on her next client, energizing herself until she could feel her own vitality. She could do swiftly now what had once taken lengthy, intense concentration.

When she was ready, she deftly wrapped her shimmering waist-length hair in a chignon at the back of her neck, choosing as always not to cover it with the long cloth of the sari. She slipped from the room, the sleek material of the garment whispering against her slender legs.

Garson Hundley gratefully parked in the driveway of the secluded cottage at the top of the hill where the masseuse lived. He'd been coming here for weeks now, and he savored his time with Mia. She hadn't been at all what he expected that first evening. She was less, and yet more. Of medium height, youthful, and tantalizing, she was a pretty woman; however, she wasn't the kind of woman a man came on to.

Not that he could if he wanted to, he reminded himself with a harsh laugh. But that was what he'd had in mind when he first heard of her. He had always considered masseuses as prostitutes with pseudo-careers. In truth, he hadn't cared, if only one could help him with his problem.

A retired military man from California, he had always been the epitome of masculinity. He didn't want to think that his identity was tied to the area below his waist, but now the two seemed inseparable. The doctors had said his problem wasn't physical. That had been a relief, but it hadn't altered anything. Obsessed with his impotence, he knew he had to get some relief somewhere. No matter what it took.

Peculiarly enough, a doctor was the one who had finally

put him in touch with Mia. What he had found in the masseuse was an enigma; she was distant, yet deeply comforting in a way he had never known. He didn't know how to explain it, even to himself.

He only knew that he needed her and she was there for him. Strangely, it wasn't a physical need. Hell, he didn't want to think that it was spiritual, either, but she touched him in a way no woman ever had. He had respect for her and her devotion to her work. He was eager to see her now.

Mia opened the door before he could knock. "Hello."

Garson's dark eyes were drawn to her sweet smile.

"Good evening," he said.

Mia's gaze flashed over him, and she noted once again how physically fit the man was. His years in the military were evident in his rigid bearing. She opened the door wider so he could enter the heart of the house.

Odd, Garson thought, but he felt at home here. He almost felt as if the woman herself had drawn him to her bosom when he entered the cottage. There was warmth and succor. He absorbed it the moment he walked in. It was as though he had entered some other world, separate and different from the outside, as if he had entered a sanctuary.

Mia didn't say anything else as she led him down the hall toward the massage room. A cat, silhouetted against a wall in the dimly lit room, warily observed Garson as he passed. As self-contained as his mistress, the animal remained unmoving when Garson met his green eyes.

Mia's sari rustled softly; Garson found himself watching, hypnotized by the slight sway of her shapely hips in the loose garment. He suspected that she wore no restricting underclothes. She seemed to be more sensual than usual, emanating a heady seductiveness that filled him with longing.

He felt a tightening deep within, though he couldn't—and wouldn't—follow through if he could. Mia was a sexy woman; he did wonder how it would be to make love to her. The man in him responded to her, even if it was only mentally.

When they entered the massage room, she indicated the

table which was covered by a forest-green sheet. Without another word she turned her back, readying her oils while he undressed in the bathroom that was part of the massage room.

When he returned with a towel wrapped around his hips, Mia smiled at him. "If you're comfortable enough with me, we'll no longer use the towel."

Garson barely arched a brow. "Fine with me."

He was extraordinarily comfortable with her, and it wouldn't bother him to be completely nude. Although he was growing older, he had worked out with weights for years. He was proud of his body. Even if some parts of it didn't work right.

"Good." Mia nodded her approval as he lay on his stomach and handed her the towel.

Whether or not she used a drape depended upon the client; she generally preferred to work without one. She was able to use more full body strokes and create a better energy flow. She wanted no barriers between her and Garson. She had established the relationship she needed with him; it was time for a more progressive massage.

Outside, in the rain which had begun to fall harder, the watcher slunk deeper into his raincoat, cursing the foggy window of the room he was peering into. He pressed his face closer and strained to see in through the partially open blinds. He was looking into a bathroom.

The masseuse's table was directly across from the open door. Although the room was dim and shadowy, he could catch glimpses of her and the naked man. He felt that racing sensation inside, that ache of pleasure that was almost agonizing as it signaled the churning excitement that seemed to originate deep in his bowels. He liked the feeling.

But his pleasure was temporary. He wanted to see more. He wanted to be inside. As he stood outside in the dampness, chilled, the rain dripping off the brim of his hat, he caught the strains of some highbrow music. He stared harder into the softly lit room. Everything looked so damned cozy. For the man and the woman, but not for him.

He touched the glass of the window tentatively with his fingers. Then with his whole hand. Then with both balled-up fists, wiping furiously, trying to get a better view. His sexual excitement was turning into anger and frustration.

He tested to see how secure the individual glass panels were. Then he pressed with more force. He had an almost uncontrollable urge to break the glass into a thousand fragments. He wanted to hit something. He wanted to vent the hostility that was twisting and turning inside him.

He pressed his face nearer still, until his own breath steamed the panes and he could no longer see anything. He frantically wiped at the glass, but it did no good. He started to pant. He was getting that dizzy feeling. He had to do something to relieve the pressure. Automatically, he reached for the thin cord he carried with him constantly.

Garson's mind had begun to drift the moment he stretched out on the table. Despite an almost eerie sexual awareness of Mia, he was relaxing already. Intensely aware of the perfumed air and comforting atmosphere, he was drifting back to the time when he had wed Eileen, to the time when he had been much more of a man. He couldn't account for his train of thought, but it was sure and steady.

When Mia had warmed the oil in her hands, she turned back to Garson, to rhythmically massage his muscular back with a mix of vegetable oil and jasmine. She knew about his impotence; she used jasmine because of its rich floral scent and its powers as a euphoric and sensual stimulant.

Skilled in all methods of massage, she carefully and conscientiously matched her own version and combination of the massage to the client. For this man she had selected polarity, because of the block that kept him from being sexually active.

She worked leisurely and thoroughly, using her firm fingers to give warmth and stimulating sensations to counteract Garson's tension. She had no doubts about her ability or the end result. He would respond to her when the time was right. This evening was only the beginning.

Thirty minutes passed as Garson lay beneath Mia's skilled fingers. He was preoccupied with thoughts of his self-worth, his manhood. The very house seemed to radiate a sensuality that sent a spiral of memories of better times flooding through him. Times before Eileen had left him for a younger man after twenty-five years of marriage. Times when he had seen himself as an expert cocksman.

Superbly endowed, with a sex drive that few women could match, he had always reasoned that he had more than enough for one woman. Yes, he had had other women. After all, he had been a military man, a high-ranking officer at that; and there had never been a shortage of uniform-loving females. But it had *never* occurred to him that Eileen was cheating, and with that—that *boy!*

Mia felt Garson grow tense, his muscles tightening beneath her fingertips. When she noticed him clenching his fists, she couldn't help but wonder what was going through his mind. People came to her for all kinds of reasons; some talked about them, some didn't. Her job was to help them to the best of her ability, whether they discussed their personal lives or not.

Garson had told her he was impotent, and that the impotency was psychologically induced. Beyond that, he had offered no more information on the subject, which obviously embarrassed him greatly and hurt his ego.

"Relax," she murmured gently. "Relax. Take a deep breath and exhale slowly."

Garson seemed surprised to find himself on the masseuse's table, his stomach knotted up, his mind twisted with hurtful memories. This was the one place he had thought he was safe from his past.

"Sorry," he grunted. "The past is tracking me with old troubles." He managed a bitter laugh. "The present is presenting me with new ones. Women!" he muttered beneath his breath. "They'll cut your heart out."

Mia was thoughtful for a moment as she waited to see if he would open up and tell her more. When he didn't, she began to massage him again. She knew about old troubles and new ones. She had some of her own.

## ← CHAPTER 2 →

When Garson was instructed to turn over on his back, he did so, his eyes still closed. Mia continued to work her magic, her fingers deftly moving, ever in contact with him. The time with her always passed swiftly, for she neglected no area of his body. She lessened the tightness in his thighs with slow, deep movements, then used a gentle pelvic rock to ease lower back discomfort. To Garson, the rhythmic rocking motion seemed to echo the haunting ocean waves which caressed the shore far below the rear of the small house.

Perched on a cliff that dropped sharply and abruptly to the sea, the cottage seemed as much a part of the landscape as the trees and water. It seemed to breathe and move with the elements; in the distance he could hear nature's eternal cycle as the cries of seabirds and sluggish seals who sought the elusive sun on the mammoth rocks blended with the wind and lapping water.

Now that he had become used to the sounds, Garson couldn't imagine Mia living and working anywhere else. This area was so much like her, full of steady, soothing perpetual rhythms that seemed to be in harmony with the universe itself, so synchronized were they.

For most of the massage, Mia followed a standard routine

she had established, working steadily, nurturing the bond, the connection she had with her client. Tonight, however, she was expanding her treatment. Gradually, skillfully, she began to stimulate Garson's sexual organs by working with a pressure point an inch below his navel. Then her hands moved lower and lower still.

Unexpectedly, Garson felt a rush of warmth followed by shivers up and down his spine at a feathery touch on his penis. At least he thought that was what had caused the shivers. He came partially out of his languorous state as the provocative sensations increased. He imagined that he felt the tantalizing caress again, fleeting and teasing, awakening his dormant sensuality and his totally relaxed and vulnerable body.

He opened his eyes and gazed at Mia. Her dark lashes downcast, she continued to work easily and without inhibition. Garson sighed heavily and shut his eyes again. He must have been dreaming, drifting in and out of awareness. Of course Mia hadn't been responsible. It had surely been a fleeting erotic dream, brought on by thoughts of Eileen. *Something* had happened, for he still felt a stirring in his loins.

Mia smiled as she moved lower to work on Garson's legs. She had experienced no sensual response to the touch of her fingers on his genitals. But he had felt it. And that was what mattered. She was on her way to making him well.

The smile faded only slightly when she thought of her husband. If only she could make him well. If only she could find some magic potion to put him back together—to put *them* back together.

At first they both had thought he would get well; neither of them believed the doctor's prognosis that Troy would never walk again after the crash of his private jet, that he would be tied to that wheelchair for the rest of his life, paralyzed from the waist down.

Mia had tried to understand his bitterness, his inability to include her in the early stages of his rehabilitation. He was a proud man, and his condition both humiliated and infuriated him. He had turned away from her time and again, but she had never imagined that he would turn from her forever. They had loved each other deeply.

She had been too hurt to cope when he asked her to leave six months later. She hadn't believed he really wanted that; however, she knew that they needed some distance between them, time to get a different perspective, if anything was to be salvaged of their relationship.

She had started to travel alone then, not wanting to share her misery with anyone else. Her trips had taken her around the world, but her love for Troy had been strengthened in the time they were apart.

More than ever, she had realized what an extraordinary man he was. She had met Troy at a party when she was twenty-two and had just graduated from college. They had been attracted to each other instantly.

In spite of everyone's prediction that the age difference would kill their romance eventually, it had never happened. Until now.

Never had she imagined that their life wouldn't go on as it had. She still couldn't. She had made her odyssey and come home. Yet the one man she loved remained inaccessible to her.

When she returned, Troy had been more distant than ever. He had endured her herbs and oils and massages as the weeks stretched into months, but he had not improved. He had encouraged her to continue to build a life for herself, to share her skilled hands with other people in need, and she had done so.

Then he asked her to leave a second time, telling her that he couldn't bear to have her in the house. She had gone quietly, without the tears and tantrums of the first time. Although she had left her husband, she couldn't let him go. She was still Troy Jorgenson's wife.

Despite her mental conditioning, her control, her struggle to accept her and Troy's situation, sometimes she was overcome by her loss and the sadness that stalked her.

Generally she permitted herself to deal with it only in the dead of night, when shadows fell and memories called out until she, as restless as the wind, as relentless as the waves tugging at the shore, paced the rooms of her mind in search of elusive answers.

She pushed the thought far back into her mind, to the small section reserved for her husband. She had a client, and he was where she should be directing her thoughts.

When the massage was over, Garson quietly dressed while Mia washed her hands and busied herself at her supply cabinet.

"Will you be in town next week?" he asked, his voice thick and low. As he gazed down at her, asking a perfectly perfunctory question, he felt unexpectedly virile for the first time in months. He couldn't explain it, but he welcomed the feeling as if it were an old friend. The word *cocky* came to mind, and he almost smiled.

"Yes," she said, opening the door to the hall. "In fact, I think you should start coming twice a week now if you can. Is Tuesday free for you?"

"Any day you say. I'm ready when you are."

"Good. Tuesday, same time."

He pulled several bills from his wallet and dropped them in the jade Oriental vase on the supply cabinet. He would have paid any amount of money this woman requested.

When Mia led the way back to the living room, Garson walked with an unaccustomed jauntiness. He felt different, better. He knew that nothing out of the ordinary had happened, but he was filled with optimism.

He wanted to talk to Mia about it; however, it seemed ridiculous to discuss something so elusive as a momentary high—a resurrection—or should he say re-erection? Enjoying his double entendre, he smiled at her, then went to his truck.

From the window Mia saw Garson begin the circuitous road down. When he slowed to a crawl to let another car pass, Mia smiled to herself. Nora was on time. Unmindful of the shadowy figure watching her in the misty rain, Mia went to prepare for her next client.

Nora Simpson moved as far to one side of the narrow road as she dared to let the black truck pass. She had seen the driver for weeks now and knew he had the Thursday appointment before hers. She tried to be friendly, but this man had never responded to her smiles, never returned her waves, and she had finally given up.

Pity, too, for she found him attractive. She had seen him leave when she was early for an appointment. She had even purposely arrived ahead of time hoping to meet him, although she knew that Mia kept to a strict schedule. It had all been in vain.

She sighed at the thought. She had been lonely since George had died, but she didn't know what to do about it. There just didn't seem to be enough men to go around, not in this small Oregon community, especially for a woman on the verge of her fiftieth birthday. Sometimes she told herself that she should move away. But where?

The question always made her regret that she had never had children. As the years had flown by and her only relatives passed away, she realized more and more how few ties she had. However, she had had George. He was always there, cushioning life's blows, filling the voids, making her happy. She had never imagined that he would make her a widow so soon.

She looked into the face of the driver of the black truck as he passed inches from her window. He seemed to stop for the briefest of moments, and although it was difficult to be certain in the fading twilight, Nora thought he smiled at her. It made her feel better.

She smiled as she continued to the masseuse's house. The smile faded slightly when she thought she saw a movement in the woods beside Mia's cottage. She scanned the spot. When she didn't see anything else, she concluded that it must have been a wild animal. There were plenty of them in the area. Still, she was left feeling a little unsettled as she walked up to the door.

Mia quickly eased Nora's discomfort with a smile. "Good evening," she greeted.

Mia usually adjusted her conversation to the client. Because of massage's power to lower stress and inhibition levels, many people talked with Mia as freely as they might with a psychiatrist or trusted friend. Most of her clients were physician-referred; consequently, she knew something about them before she worked with them. She and Nora had established a good rapport.

"Oh, good evening, Mia," Nora returned cheerfully. "How are you tonight? Isn't it wonderful to be alive?"

Mia imperceptibly arched dark brows. What accounted for this upbeat mood? She had often watched the passing of the two vehicles and was aware of Nora's interest in Garson. Had he perhaps spoken on his way past? No, she didn't think so. Although he had paused, she didn't think he had said anything.

She thought somewhat wistfully that it would be nice if the two of them could get together. She knew about Nora's longing for love, and she knew Garson needed someone. However, her own personal code of ethics and patient confidentiality forbade the introduction of clients. She did, on occasion, arrange a social event to which select clients were invited. Perhaps it was time to plan such an evening.

"It *is* wonderful to be alive," Mia agreed. She smiled at Nora. "Are you ready for your body work?"

"Oh, yes, indeed, I am," Nora answered. "You have no idea how much I look forward to our sessions."

Mia nodded. She did have an idea.

A slight blush colored Nora's cheeks. "I get such a—a restless feeling inside since George died. A buildup of tension."

There was a brief pause. "Sexual tension," she added, taut-lipped with determination, her eyes meeting Mia's fleetingly before she looked down at her fingers clasped in front of her. The pink in her cheeks deepened until it was crimson.

"Sexual energy is natural and powerful," Mia reassured. "It's nothing to be embarrassed about."

"But at my age—and me a widow . . ." Nora murmured, her words trailing off, leaving only the implication of the point she wanted to make.

"Age and marital status have little to do with it," Mia noted. "It affects all living creatures."

Nora slowly shook her head. "You're young and beautiful and worldly, Mia. So tall and shapely and secure, with your lovely body and beautiful black hair. I feel like a small brown wren—an old wren—in your presence. I don't know why I'm going on about such a subject. I'm sure you don't know how it is being celibate."

Mia was not tall, not unusually shapely, and her hair wasn't black. She was five feet five inches; her hair was dark brown, and her eyes were blue-gray. However, she had grown used to her clients seeing her as they wanted to see her, according to their own need. She never bothered to dispute them, but a flood of tangled emotions rushed through her at the other woman's comment. She fought them back. This time was not for her. It was for Nora.

Their situations were very different. She was comfortable with her sexuality, her femininity, even her celibacy. It was, after all, a choice she had made. She elected to make celibacy work for her, to rise above the frustration, to direct that powerful energy into her work.

Her path wasn't always easy. Nor was it the one she

preferred. And it was not free of pitfalls. She had her highs and lows, but she tried to ensure that the highs overshadowed the lows.

"You, no doubt, simply live your life, no matter what," Nora continued, "but I can't bring myself to have a fleeting affair." She laughed nervously. "In all my life I've only known George, and I was shy even with him. I think he liked me that way, but perhaps some other man wouldn't understand. Funny," she said, "I never dwelled so deeply on sex in those days."

The laughter abruptly dried up. "No, it isn't funny," Nora contradicted herself. "It's like the old saying that you never miss the water until the well runs dry. I never knew what sexual frustration was. I'm not sure I ever knew what sexual satisfaction was, either, but I know I'm missing something now, and I don't know what to do about it. Even if I could have a casual fling, who would I have it with?"

She pressed her lips together and tried to compose herself, suddenly ashamed. "I'm sorry. I don't know what got me started on *that!*"

"You needed to talk about it," Mia said simply. "That's what got you started."

Nora managed a trembling smile. "You're so perceptive and nonjudgmental, Mia. I did need to talk, but I'm embarrassed." Her eyes met Mia's again before she looked away. "I know some women masturbate, but I can't bring myself to—to touch myself down there. I just can't," she said in a small voice.

Mia lifted the woman's lowered head, her gentle hands on each side of Nora's face. "You're not comfortable enough with your own body," she said, reaching down to unclasp Nora's white-knuckled fingers. "There's nothing wrong with self-love," she added evenly. "It's not as wonderful as having a partner, but it's not wrong."

Still holding one of the widow's hands, she smiled, then turned toward the hall. "Let's see what we can do about getting rid of that tension."

"Mia," Nora began tentatively, "who is the man whose appointment falls before mine?"

Looking back over her shoulder, Mia shook her head. "I'm sorry, but I can't discuss one client with another. Occasionally," she added casually, "I arrange a social event for those who wish to participate and meet each other." She smiled. "Or they meet on their own—en route to the house, or elsewhere."

Nora was sorry Mia wouldn't tell her about the man in the black truck. She was curious to learn if he was married. On the other hand, it was reassuring to know that Mia didn't discuss her with anyone else, either.

"I only wondered because I pass him often when I come," she said, "and tonight, for the first time, I think he actually smiled."

"Oh?" Mia murmured.

Despite her noncommittal comment, Mia was pleased. She knew that Garson's smile hadn't been necessarily directed toward Nora, but it was a start in the right direction for him. Maybe he didn't find the thought of women as painful as he'd indicated.

Feeling feverish, his emotions whirling violently, the watcher outside the cottage found himself wishing that he could somehow stop the river of anger running through him. Sometimes he imagined that he could control his rage if only he could reach inside and plug it up some way, if he could block it at its source. Maybe it would only take something like that tale about the kid sticking his finger in the dike to stop the whole flood.

But then if he did that, he was positive it would just bottle up inside him and he would go crazy. It would stay down in his privates and cause them to swell and swell until he would be poisoned and maybe even explode.

He got a buzz just thinking about it. Immediately his head began to swim as a roaring sound filled his ears. It scared him, but he wasn't sure he wanted to stop it. There was no other feeling that even came close. He both loved and hated what happened to him at a time like this.

Abruptly the woman he'd seen go into the masseuse's house stepped into the bathroom. He sucked in his breath. He could see her fairly well now that some of the steam and fog had cleared while he was in the woods. He was especially intrigued to see what the masseuse would do with a woman. He honestly hadn't considered that a woman might come here.

There was a source of light somewhere in the room, and even though it was dim, he could see most of what was happening. In fact, the dimness only enhanced the woman as she took off her clothes. His heart began to pound. She was old, but in the muted light she didn't look half-bad.

She methodically hung each garment on the back of the bathroom door. The man liked that. He admired neatness. When she wrapped herself in a towel, without turning around so he could see what she looked like from the front, it griped him. He pressed his face closer to the window and watched as the woman went into the massage room.

Then she shut the bathroom door completely. That pissed him off worse! It was almost as if the two women knew he was here watching, waiting, anticipating, and they'd deliberately thwarted him. He was so mad that he couldn't stay at the window any longer. Frustration making his head spin, he slipped back into the woods.

Mia had only one evening appointment left after she finished her work on Nora. The man was a new client, and she had purposely scheduled him well after the woman's departure.

She needed time to revive her own physical and mental energies, and she also wanted him to have no contact with her other clients. An ex-convict who had served time for rape, he had been referred to her by a private therapist interested in his welfare—and the public's. The man's probation officer had finally approved, believing that his charge would indeed benefit.

Mia, too, was interested in the public's welfare, as well as the man's. This wasn't the first case of this kind she had taken in the three years she had worked as a masseuse. Clientele included all kinds of people from all walks of life across the country; as her reputation had grown, she had been approached by counselors, psychiatrists, and others wanting her to put people in touch with themselves, thereby enabling them to live more compatibly with the rest of society.

At first she'd been reluctant, but she'd finally agreed because she felt strongly that something had to be done to help blend problem people into mainstream society. Obviously, the prison system didn't always work as a rehabilitation tool. She'd accepted the challenge when a sex therapist commented that Mia was hardly in more danger than any other professional in a similar field.

She'd had to agree. And, after all, she'd majored in psychology in college. She found that gave her an edge. Still, she was careful about accepting risky clients; she could usually tell over the phone or in the initial meeting if she should take them.

However, in this man's case, she was uncertain. She had expected his hostility, and even his suggestive tone, despite extensive counseling in which he was made to understand her role, but she'd sensed an underlying threat in his voice. She'd scheduled a trial appointment only.

She was well aware there were people who wouldn't respond to massage. In some rare cases it was too late. In others the person wasn't willing to cooperate. This ex-convict might be one of them.

She drew a steadying breath. Her success rate had been excellent, and she took pride in that. She'd worked with some people who couldn't bear to touch another human being, and who had rarely been touched. Mia found that kind of client the saddest of all. No one had loved them, and they had loved no one. She believed in unconditional love, the ultimate gift, the real meaning of living.

A sudden harsh rapping on the front door interrupted her reverie. She hadn't realized it was time for her client already. She hadn't heard a car come up the road. The man had come much too soon, too abruptly, and with too much force. She could feel herself being jarred internally by his fierce pounding. Soot, her cat, fled from the room on silent feet while Mia tried to repress her feelings of unease.

## ⟵ CHAPTER 3 ⟶

Donevan hesitated, frowning at the woman in the doorway. Although he had spent hours at the cottage, watching the masseuse ever since his parole officer mentioned her, he hadn't expected her youth or beauty. He hadn't been able to see her well as she stood at the window. When he watched through the bathroom blinds, he'd only gotten partial glimpses of her. He guessed her to be somewhere in her early thirties, although it was impossible to tell.

She could be as much as ten years younger or ten years older. Her hair was brownish, almost auburn, or was that only the way the light shone behind her? Her eyes, too, were an almost indescribable color—perhaps blue, maybe green. He hadn't expected her to be so small, either, small and single and staying here all alone.

She was an odd one, standing there in that foreign getup, her gaze steady. Her eyes were large. He suddenly wondered if that meant she could see more than other people. He didn't like that at all. It made him very nervous because he didn't want anybody to know his thoughts. They were his business and his alone. Somehow this woman unsettled him already. Worse than that, she threatened him.

"Donevan Raitt," he introduced.

"Hello," she said with forced cheerfulness. "Come on in." She opened the door farther. "Don't be uncomfortable."

"I'm not," he added too quickly.

He was, of course, terribly uncomfortable. Not only did he not like to be threatened, especially by women, he didn't like the fact that he had no choice in coming here.

He couldn't believe that damned probation officer and the therapist thought this was a good idea. A masseuse! All women wanted one thing from a man. Then they screamed that they *didn't* want it. His gaze roved insolently over the woman before him. Despite her appearance, she was no different from the rest. In fact, she was worse; he was sure of it.

He didn't know why he had agreed to come here. He didn't know why he had listened to all that bullshit about him needing to get in touch with his own body, to be comfortable with himself so that he could be accepting of himself, and, consequently, others.

He hadn't been sold on that crock of crap in the slightest, but he was nobody's fool. His probation officer and therapist had come up with the massage idea; they had acted like they were giving him a gift. Well, maybe they were. What the hell? It wouldn't cost him much. He'd check it out.

He had become smarter in the pen. He had learned things. He'd learned to play the game. He'd also learned something that wouldn't leave his mind: he'd heard that screwing was like a little death, but that screwing and a big death was supposed to be the greatest thrill of all. The thought sent a warm shudder up his spine.

He stared boldly into the face of the woman. He was on to her. Masseuse, hell! He knew what she was, and he knew what she wanted.

Mia found that Donevan looked ordinary enough, despite the unnecessary vigor with which he'd announced himself and the fact that he hesitated so long at the door. He certainly didn't have the appearance of a hardened criminal. Actually, he was rather attractive with compelling ice-blue eyes that seemed alert to every detail of his surroundings.

About five feet ten inches, he was lean and hard and honed to a muscular specimen of a man. He was dressed in blue jeans, a blue work shirt, a denim jacket, and black boots, a costume not at all unusual for rugged Oregon.

He ran a hand through neat brown hair and snickered a little. "Been to India?" he drawled, still openly accessing her.

"Yes, as a matter of fact, I have," she answered calmly, stepping back when she saw that he'd made up his mind to enter.

She rarely addressed clients by name; it identified them too closely with her, made them too familiar for her to be objective and do what was in their best interests. It also made the relationship too personal, and she dealt with too many people to develop personal relationships.

Anyway, there was Troy. Always Troy, in the back of her mind.

Donevan sauntered inside with an arrogant bravado Mia had seen before. Although she knew it was usually a facade to hide insecurities, she wondered if this man believed the image he had created.

An unexpected shiver went up her spine as she closed the door behind her. She felt as if she were losing her way and fought to find that place inside herself where she could escape this moment and draw strength to face the next. She would not allow fear to cause her to fail before she'd even had a chance to work with this man.

Donevan looked back over his shoulder, his mind filled with a thousand thoughts. He wondered what the masseuse would say if he reached for her; he wondered what she would do if he flung her to the floor and drove himself into her.

For a moment Mia clung to the doorknob, unable to face Donevan. She drew on her inner strength, warming herself with visual images of a hot and glowing flame of fire, willing spirals of warmth to emanate from the center until the heat spread throughout her, driving back the cold. When she felt calm and self-contained enough, she faced the man.

Suddenly Donevan felt a coil of cold grip his insides, instead of the usual feverish swell of power his thoughts created. The warnings of his therapist and probation officer whirled in his head, reminding him that this woman was supposedly a respected professional wielding a lot of influence with powerful people in the community.

But the two men were jerks! What did they know? This bitch was a masseuse. He knew about them.

"Are you one of them who likes it or hates it?" he asked. He had heard that all prostitutes felt one way or the other. None of them were normal.

"What?" Mia asked, determined to stay in control.

Many men had come to her with the wrong idea, yet no one had ever tried to force himself on her. She told herself that this one wouldn't, either, but she couldn't forget that he was a rapist. Something about him would not permit her to find that place of peace within herself that allowed her to work with the most base human misery. She had to keep reminding herself that he was here out of need.

"You know," Donevan prodded.

Mia glimpsed a hint of uncertainty in his blue, blue eyes. "No, I don't."

"You know you do," he whispered softly. "You want it, don't you?"

*"It?"* she repeated coolly, forcing him to discuss what was on his mind.

He ran a hand through his hair. He didn't like her jerking him around. She knew what he was talking about. He was getting angry.

"Sex," he said as calmly as he could, even though he felt like spewing the word from his lips as if it were incredibly dirty and contaminating.

Mia drew in a steadying breath. "The subject of sex was thoroughly discussed with you before you came here," she returned evenly. "Massage has nothing to do with sexual intercourse."

Donevan made himself grin. "Don't try to stand there and tell me that you don't know what goes on in massage parlors."

"I know what goes on in legitimate ones," she carefully replied. "And I know what goes on here. That's all we need to concern ourselves with, isn't it?"

She smelled raw fear in him, and she struggled not to get caught up in it, not to let it frighten her.

Donevan studied her for a moment. He didn't want to mess up here. She could get him in a lot of trouble. At the moment she was pulling the strings. But he would have his chance to change that.

"I'm just kidding," he finally said.

His upper lip began to twitch; he caught it between his teeth briefly, irritated by the gesture. "Jesus, I'm just so damned nervous about being here," he added with a sheepish expression that made him look almost boyishly young. "You aren't going to tell Mr. Hardin and Mr. Larch, are you?"

Mia hadn't missed the betraying twitch of his lip. He really was uneasy, she realized. That wasn't unusual with a first-time client. She allowed herself to exhale. They were both nervous, she admitted to herself. This was clearly very difficult for him; he felt trapped and insecure.

If she hadn't been focusing on her own problems, she would have been more sensitive to his feelings instead of reacting so defensively. This man was afraid, as an animal might be afraid. He was all raw nerve and primitive motivation. He needed her. She felt that she was up to the challenge.

Slowly she shook her head. "No, I won't tell Mr. Hardin and Mr. Larch, not as long as you're sure we understand each other."

A rush of bile so bitter that it almost choked him filled Donevan's throat. Prick tease! he thought to himself. They understood each other. She was playing a game with him. She wanted it, all right. *They* all wanted it!

His thin lips moved in a semblance of a smile. He was very good at this kind of game. He knew how to wait. Sometimes it seemed like that was all he had been doing in his life. He didn't make his move until he knew a woman's routine, and these days he had to be more careful than ever. When he decided to do it to the masseuse, it would be on *his* terms.

"Fair enough," he replied with another grin to let her know he was on to her.

Mia allowed herself to relax a little. She concentrated on the good that could come out of Donevan's treatment. If she could help him, she might also help some woman who could otherwise become his victim.

Despite her unease, she knew that this man needed her help, perhaps even more than the rest of her clients. Wasn't that why she had taken his case? He had been a model prisoner; the parole board believed that he had been locked up long enough. Shouldn't she share their confidence in him?

He had made a woman suffer, perhaps made a shambles of her life—Mia didn't know and she didn't want to know, unless the woman needed her—but the rapist had suffered, too, had he not? Somewhere along the way he had been damaged, and he hadn't had the resources within to cope. He had committed an act of violence on a stranger. Why?

Whatever the reason, she was convinced that if she could help Donevan Raitt understand himself, if he could learn to respect himself, love himself, then he could love someone else. Everyone would benefit.

"Are we doing it or not?" Donevan asked impatiently.

What kind of mind game was this bitch playing? He was in the house. What now?

Mia shook her head in apology. She had been so lost in her introspection that she had once again ignored Donevan. She wasn't making much of a first impression on the poor man.

"I'm sorry. I'm so distracted today. Please follow me. You must wonder what kind of professional I am."

Donevan resisted the urge to snicker. He *knew* what kind she was. She didn't need to lay it on the line like that. They *both* knew.

With an arrogant swagger he slowly followed the woman. He took his time, studying every corner of the cottage. He wanted to know what her house was like. He intended to come back without an appointment.

When they reached the massage room, he shoved his hands into his pockets. His fingers touched the thin cord; he closed his hand over it as he swiftly assessed the layout he had only seen parts of from the bathroom window.

The room must have been built as the master bedroom. It was large, with the bathroom off to one side. There was a good-sized walk-in closet with the door standing open to reveal stacks of towels, sheets, and pillowcases, all in various shades of green. Trays of incense and candles and all kinds of oils were lined up on shelves.

Donevan's gaze strayed back to the pillowcases. He was feeling real hyper and his mind tumbled with bizarre thoughts. Something he'd heard one of his cellmates talk about danced through his brain: He'd been told that a pillowcase was a good way to strangle somebody.

He reminded himself to pay attention to his surroundings. He wasn't here today to think about strangling anybody. His perceptive eyes continued to rake the room. The massage table was placed near a floor-to-ceiling fireplace, where a fire burned brightly. Green blinds were closed; the light came from two big oil lamps on the fireplace mantel.

The masseuse went into the walk-in closet and took a

towel from a shelf. When she handed it to Donevan, she indicated the bathroom.

"You may remove your clothes in there. You can hang them on the hooks on the back of the door."

"All of them? The first time I come here?"

His modesty neither amused nor annoyed Mia, but she made note of it for future reference. She met his blue gaze.

"Whatever you're comfortable with. All is usually customary."

Donevan knew the other man and the woman had taken their clothes off, but he didn't want to strip. He hated doing that in front of strangers, but the masseuse had him over a barrel because of Hardin and Larch. He just wished he'd been able to see more through the bathroom window so he would know just what she'd done to her other two customers.

Angry, he strode into the bathroom and slammed the door behind him. Bitch! Apparently she was going through with the pretense of a real massage. He reminded himself that he'd heard some women did that until they got to know the man.

And, after all, she had told Hardin and Larch that she was in a legit massage business. But he was pissed off all the same. He didn't like this setup. He didn't like some whore telling him to take his clothes off. It was supposed to be the other way around.

He stared at the window, studying the blinds. When he raised them to peek outside, he saw that the window wasn't locked. He dropped the blinds and turned the wand, closing the slats completely. He knew you could see in and he hated the idea of somebody watching him. He always had and prison had made it worse.

Sullenly he began to remove his clothes, carefully hanging them on the hooks. When he was down to his underwear, he wavered.

"Whore!" he muttered, finally stepping out of the white boxer shorts.

He felt exposed and vulnerable, but he didn't want the woman to think he was a pussy. When he had wrapped the towel around his waist, it suddenly occurred to him that she couldn't wait to see him naked. The thought made him only a little less furious as he stalked back into the room.

"Massage's main purpose is relaxation," Mia said, taking time to explain her techniques before she motioned for Donevan to get on the table, turning her back to ensure his privacy as he did so. She gave him a few minutes to settle down while she mixed her oils.

When she placed her hands on him, she was alarmed by the hostility pulsating like a heartbeat through his body as he lay tensely on the massage table. She had worked with reluctant clients before, but this one was like a finely wired time bomb. Her very touch seemed to repulse him.

Sticking strictly to the most basic of massages, she worked only on his back, feeling the resistant tight flesh beneath her skilled fingers, as unyielding as the man himself. Not a word passed between them after her initial attempts at conversation.

Lying on his stomach, his eyes wide open, Donevan flinched every time Mia stroked his flesh. He didn't like a woman touching him. If any touching was to be done, he did it himself.

He didn't like lying naked on her fucking table like a newborn baby, either. He felt unprotected and unguarded. He had never taken all his clothes off with a woman, not even for sex. When he wanted it, he just unzipped his fly, did it, and left. He didn't like any more body contact than he could avoid. And he didn't like this bitch smoothing her smelly oils into his skin as if he were some girl. He didn't like *her*.

"Relax," Mia urged softly, interrupting Donevan's thoughts. She needed to establish some kind of rapport with him, and it wasn't happening.

Instead of relaxing, he grew more and more tense. He felt repulsed. He told himself repeatedly that if she forced her fingers against his skin one more time, he would turn around and strangle the life out of her.

She might have fooled that idiot of a probation officer, but she wasn't fooling him. She was like all the other masseuses he had met. Only *they* didn't make any pretense of giving a hands-on massage—unless it was on a specific body part. And that was usually mouths-on.

He had never let them do that—take his dick in their mouths. It was bad enough putting it up inside them. He sometimes truly feared that he wouldn't get it back. That was why he had to be the one always in charge, working fast and furious, ramming his rod in again and again, getting it over as quick as he could.

Thinking about it excited him. He liked that feeling of powerfulness; he liked to be able to relieve himself in a woman. But what he really liked was the feeling of fear that flooded through him every time he did it. He got off on it. He got off again when he had zipped back up and left, his dick still intact and waiting to be cleansed and purified at the first opportunity.

He felt himself growing hard, and he shifted on the table, trying to make room for his erection without the bitch knowing about it. She wasn't going to get it. At least not now.

Sensitive to his mood, Mia gradually ended the massage, letting the firm strokes fade until she turned back to her supply cabinet, feeling oddly defeated, though she had known from the start that this client would be difficult. He hadn't relaxed at all under her ministrations; his tension filled the room. His sweat filled her nostrils.

"You can get dressed now."

Yeah, sure, Donevan thought to himself. He could get dressed now that he had a hard-on under the towel. He glanced obliquely over his shoulder at the masseuse. When he saw that she wasn't even looking at him, he frowned.

Wasn't she interested? Didn't she want to see what she

had done? Well, it didn't mean shit to him. With a careless shrug he slid off the table, quickly strode into the bathroom, and shut the door.

He stared down at his erection. He couldn't deny he loved it because of the string of sensations it set off inside him.

The raw throbbing, the accelerated tingling, the sense of losing control, were really exciting as he grew bigger and bigger and more powerful and masterful. In fact, he liked it tremendously when his dick got rigid and his balls got so tight they ached in a peculiar kind of good pain.

Grasping his penis in his hand, he made short work of his erection, ejaculating explosively, catching the semen on the soft green towel. In minutes he was dressed and back in control.

Grinning to himself, he went over to the blinds and opened them even wider than they had been when he stood outside the window. Then he sauntered back into the massage room.

"I want you to know how much I appreciate you giving me a second chance," he said, smiling slightly as he addressed Mia's back. "I feel a lot better. Not as uptight."

He did feel better. He always felt better once he got some of the poison out of his system, once he experienced the little death.

Mia turned around, mildly surprised by the agreeable tone of his voice. She hadn't expected it. His presence seemed stifling, and she had anticipated only further animosity from him. He had caught her off-guard, which was unusual. She considered herself experienced enough to handle these cases.

But was she? She didn't want to be naive; still, perhaps she had had more effect than she thought with this man. She hoped so. At any rate she took heart. She knew he needed help, needed it desperately.

"Same time next week?" he asked civilly.

Mia was aware that he had the potential ability to con her,

and she wondered if he was playing a game with her. She pondered whether or not she was wise to see him again without discussing it with Mr. Hardin. Yet she wanted to help if she could. And yes, she did believe she could.

"All right."

Donevan nodded. "Thanks."

For nothing, he added silently. After all, he had done it all himself. And he did it so well.

## ⬥ CHAPTER 4 ⬥

Mia didn't even bother to tidy up the massage room. Disturbed, she followed Donevan to the front door. When she had closed it behind him, she stood at the window for a moment, lost in her thoughts. She didn't quite trust him. But then, he didn't trust her, either.

And after all, it was too early for trust. In these cases trust had to be earned. God knew the man needed to begin somewhere, to trust someone. Why not take the risk? Maybe she could start the healing process.

The drizzle had ceased, and the stars had come out. Seeing the moon riding high in the sky, Mia added more logs to the dying fire, then made her way to the back of the house.

Although the night was chilly, she merely wrapped a shawl around her shoulders, slipped her feet into some sandals, and walked out on the sun deck. The moist air, filled with the smell of salt and sea, rushed against her cheeks. Far down below the waves pounded the sand and rocks, angrily churning and spewing.

The violence of the motion reminded her of Donevan

Raitt. She did not want to think about him right now. He had taxed her reserves of energy. She was weary and drained from her work. She wanted to renew herself.

Finding her way to the wooden steps in the moonlight, she went down to the sea. With each step she let herself absorb the sights and sounds and comforts of nature, of the elements. She forced herself to focus on the soothing repetitions of the water caressing the shore, the occasional call of a night bird, and the darkness. Soon she was aware of only the peaceful place inside her where she sought and found succor.

Under the dark cloak of night Donevan hid behind a huge tree, watching the masseuse walk beside the water. The stupid cunt was oblivious to the world around her, to the menace that was ever constant in life. She strolled along like she had some kind of magic protector looking out for her.

Well, she didn't. Nobody did. Nobody gave a damn what happened to somebody else. She would find that out soon enough. He stared after her until she had gone all the way down the steps to the shore. Then he sneaked around front, crept up on the porch, and eased open her unlocked door.

Soot, who had been waiting for his mistress to remember him so he could go out, emitted a shriek of fear and raced out the door past Donevan as the man slipped inside.

"Damn," Donevan swore. "A black cat. Bad luck!"

Mia strolled along the sand, feeling it resist her steps, her mind miles away. Deliberately turning her thoughts to something positive, she considered her work schedule for the next day.

Rand Mason was coming tomorrow. She experienced a rush of warmth at the thought of the movie star. He was the only one of her clients with whom she had to fight to keep from becoming personally involved.

He was one of the few movie people from the past she'd accepted as a client. She had known when she did it that she was testing herself. She was sure Rand didn't know who she was, but, years ago, he had attended a party Troy had given.

Though he was just one Hollywood hopeful out of many, he obviously was his own man. Mia had been introduced to him only once; their eyes had met only once; they hadn't even shaken hands, but he'd touched her all the same.

She'd never imagined in a million years that he would come into her life again. She hadn't wanted or needed him to be a part of her future. Troy was her life. Still, she realized that she'd never forgotten that single moment when she and Rand became something to each other, no matter how elusive and brief the connection.

Now each time she gave him a massage, she felt that she failed her own test a little more. And each time she promised herself this would be the time she would wipe her mind free of all temptation.

But she could no more do that than she could hold the wind in her hand. Besides, somewhere deep inside her, she knew she didn't want to. No matter what she did with the others, male or female, she knew in her heart that she was still faithful to Troy.

But with Rand, anything would amount to adultery. She knew it. She wanted him; she wanted him more than she had wanted a man in a long, long time. She had already made love to him in her mind: delicious, erotic, forbidden love that surpassed anything she'd ever known. Because that's how she suspected it would be with Rand.

Superstitious, Donevan cursed the black cat mightily while invading Mia's house. Funny, now it didn't have the warmth that it had when the woman had been in it. He stood brazenly in the living room, studying the contents, noticing the overstuffed couch in earth colors, the plants growing everywhere, and lastly the fireplace, which was filled with fresh logs. They snapped and crackled as the fire ate at them.

Turning away from the flames, he peered around in the

dim light. He wanted to see what else was there; he wanted to see what held the masseuse's interest besides the men she manipulated on the table in the other room. He carefully scrutinized everything, looking for possible hiding places in case the woman appeared suddenly.

When he spied the closed door of the room across the hall, he approached it cautiously. After he had eased it open, he stepped into a room that looked like a library.

For a moment he stood very still. Even though the room was ordinary, he felt strange in it. There was a stillness, a spookiness about it, almost like the masseuse was somewhere in there. Donevan's hair felt as if it were standing on end. He was eager to escape until he saw the bulletin board.

Intrigued, he checked it out, noting the schedule of clients. Each of the women's names caused his pulse to quicken.

"Frannie Welch," he said aloud unconsciously when he came to that one. "Frannie Welch. F.W. F.W."

He shook his head. Once he'd known a girl named Frances something or other; he couldn't remember what. The name teased him for a few minutes, but it wouldn't come to him.

He frowned. He probably didn't want to remember. That bitch had scared him shitless. He had never gotten over it. He owed her for that. She hadn't paid nearly enough that night, but he hadn't known it at the time. He'd just wanted to get the hell away from her.

Then. Now would be different. He wasn't a scared boy. He was a man. And nobody fucked him over without paying for it.

He looked for an address book or client file. He might check her out. Just in case. He felt a small shiver of satisfaction at the thought. But he couldn't find what he was looking for. Not in or on the desk. There was nothing like an address book on the shelves. Nowhere.

He went back to the bulletin board and made careful note of the names again. He wished he had something to write with. Scanning the room, he saw a vividly colored jar with pencils in it. But he didn't have any paper. His gaze fell on the many books on the shelves. He saw one with a nearly naked couple on the cover. The book was about erotic massage.

Donevan snickered as he pulled it from the shelf, closed the space with other books, and returned to the bulletin board. In very small, precise script, he wrote down the names of the clients as he mumbled them aloud.

"Garson Hundley. Nora Simpson. Donevan Raitt." He said his name twice, then wrote it down on the paper, too. "Rand Mason. Angie Esterbrook. Lane Ross. Brett Williams. Frank . . . no last name."

Donevan puzzled over this, wondering about the significance, then finished his list. He jotted down times, paying special attention to the number of women who had appointments. He became increasingly cold as he stood in the room. He didn't like the place. As soon as he'd finished his notes, he thrust the thin book inside his shirt and left.

He seemed naturally drawn to the massage room. When he saw the green towel still on the bathroom floor where he had dropped it, he scowled.

"Filthy pig," he muttered. He hated untidiness most of all. It was a sign of a messy mind, and he liked everything orderly. But then he expected no less from a woman; women were dirty animals with dark secret places that no man could really know.

Gingerly picking up the towel, he carried it out of the room, looking for a wash facility or a clothes hamper. He found a white wicker one in the bathroom across the hall. He turned on the light and searched the room with penetrating eyes.

It was filled with things associated with women: soaps, perfume bottles, powder, makeup, a pink shower cap. A couple of pairs of pantyhose were drying on the shower rod.

Donevan ran his hands over them. He had heard that a stocking was an excellent tool of strangulation. When his rough hands suddenly snagged one of the nylons, he shoved them aside, then bent down to look in the cabinet beneath the sink.

The first thing he saw was a box of sanitary napkins. "Dirty cunt," he muttered, slamming the cupboard door. He hated it when he caught a woman on the rag. He wasn't about to get that slimy red poison on him. He wasn't about to shove his dick up somewhere he knew was bleeding.

Irritated now, he left the bathroom and went down the hall. He saw an open kitchen–dining room combination on one side and a closed door on the other. When he opened it, he discovered Mia's bedroom. The sight pleased him.

Slowly turning around, he tried to decide where to look first. His eye was caught by a statue of a fertility goddess on the nightstand. He had seen one like it in the library. His lip curled in distaste as he studied the bulging stomach. He hated to see pregnant women. Bellies all swollen and distended, announcing to the whole fucking world what they'd been doing. They disgusted him.

His gaze settled on the mahogany bureau. In moments he was rifling through sheer panties and lacy bras.

Mia was surprised to hear Soot's strident mewing as she walked farther down the lonely beach, unaware of time or how far she had traveled.

"Here, kitty," she called. When she had scooped him up in her arms, she decided to return to the house. Cold all of a sudden, she savored the thought of warming herself in front of the fire she had built up before she left.

As she started toward the steps that led to her house, she saw a light shining in the bathroom. She paused, trying to remember if she had left it on.

She had been so unsettled by Donevan that she wasn't sure what she had done. That wasn't a good sign; she didn't like memory lapses, no matter what the cause. She glanced down at the cat in her arms. In truth, she didn't recall letting him out either.

Hurrying in the damp night air, she raced up the steps with Soot in her arms. It had been a long day. They both could use a good night's sleep. Anyway, she wanted to be fresh for Rand tomorrow. His face vividly etched in her mind, she climbed step after step until she reached the sun deck. Then she opened the back door and went inside.

Donevan heard the slam of the door signaling Mia's return. Furtively, cleverly, as if he knew every nook and cranny of the house already, he slipped into the small walk-in closet in her bedroom. Then he breathed deeply and evenly, listening to the sounds of the masseuse as she made her way down the hall.

For several minutes he stood in the darkened closet, waiting for the woman. Time ticked slowly by. He began to get restless. Then he began to get angry.

After a few more minutes he eased out of the closet and crept down the hall. A floorboard creaked, and he paused, his breathing labored.

In the bathroom Mia replaced her toothbrush in the holder and turned off the water. Then she removed every trace of makeup from her face. After she had smoothed lotion over her skin, she reached down into the cabinet for a sanitary napkin.

Donevan stepped up to the open bathroom door in time to see her take the napkin from the box. "Damned black cat," he muttered beneath his breath. "I knew he was bad luck. The bitch is on the rag." Instantly growing enraged because she had foiled him, he glared at the masseuse for a moment, then left the house by the same door he had entered.

When Mia slipped off her sari and opened the wicker hamper, she discovered the green towel. For a moment she stared blankly at it, unable to believe she had brought it in here. She never mixed the clients' towels with her own.

She felt a prickling sensation at the back of her neck; a

picture of Donevan flashed into her mind, but she quickly calmed herself. There was no justification for thinking the man had somehow returned and moved the towel, of all things, while she was gone.

If she was going to work with him, she had to banish such thoughts from her mind immediately. She couldn't accomplish anything if she began by thinking the worst. If she wanted him to trust her, she had to trust him.

She was simply on edge and not thinking clearly. Today hadn't been an ordinary day. Donevan hadn't been an ordinary client. Subconsciously she must have separated his towel from the others, bringing it to her bathroom instead of depositing it in the washroom. That would account for the light being on.

She attempted to dismiss the unease in her mind, but the nagging doubts hovered as she finished her nightly ritual, then went to the living room, where Soot was already curled up on the couch in front of the fire. She settled down by the cat, taking him on her lap.

The night seemed darker and colder than usual. She hoped she could sleep tonight. She was too weary to battle with the shadows that sometimes followed her long into the morning hours.

Restless, angry, feeling unsettled, Donevan shoved the book he'd stolen into the glove compartment of his truck and drove downtown to check out any action he might find. When he stopped at a red light, he scanned the side street across from him. There was a drug deal going down. Everybody seemed to be into drugs these days.

But not him. He wanted a clear head. He needed it. He had important plans. They required a smart mind and he had one.

His attention was riveted to a woman with long dark hair hanging down her back. She reminded him of the masseuse. His hands tightened on the steering wheel as he watched her.

Dressed in tight jeans and a snug blue sweater, she was

nervously twisting gold chains around her fingers as she waited for the dealer to get to her.

"Jesus, there's a fucking line of customers," Donevan muttered aloud. "A fucking line of people right on the fucking street buying dope."

The light changed and he drove on, but the picture of the dark-haired woman lingered in his mind. He wanted to see what her face looked like. He went around the block. When he got to the side street again, the light was green. He slowed down anyway. The woman was ready to make her buy.

Suddenly the dealer glanced in Donevan's direction, spun on his heel, and disappeared. The woman, looking anguished and angry, turned around to glare at Donevan. She gestured to him with her middle index finger.

"Cunt!" he spat. Someone behind him blew the horn. He glared belligerently into his rearview mirror. He couldn't afford any blatant trouble. He was on probation.

Shoving the truck into gear, he started to circle the block again. He was halfway around when he saw the woman with the dark hair walking toward him. He slowed down. She looked young and small as she passed under the street lamp, unusually fresh-scrubbed and clean. When she spotted Donevan, she threw up her finger again.

The gesture had angered him the first time. Now it enraged him. Frantically he searched for a place to park on the residential street lined with cars. Making an abrupt move, he whipped into a driveway with a "Tenants Only" sign and braked to a halt. The girl saw him stop, and she started running, her hair flying like a dark banner behind her.

In excellent physical condition from his prison regimen, Donevan jumped out of the truck and rapidly gained on her. When he had almost reached her, she suddenly turned around and smiled coyly at him.

"You're a whole lot of man, aren't you?" she asked in a little-girl voice made breathless by the exertion of the run.

"Man, you can really run! Do you have that much energy in bed?"

Donevan glowered at her. He wasn't fooled by the bitch in the slightest, but as he watched her, his gaze was drawn to the rise and fall of the long gold chains she wore. They rested on her chest, and he liked the way they were illuminated in the faint light of the street lamp as her breasts heaved while she tried to catch her breath.

When the girl saw where Donevan was staring, she boldly outlined her bosom with her hands, then toyed with the chains, running one finger along the length of them, pausing right above her nipples, which instantly became erect from her touch. While she played with the chains, twirling them and teasing with them, she traced her mouth with her tongue, making a provocative circle.

Donevan felt that spinning inside him again. His heart-beat accelerated. The chains seemed to beckon to him in the scant light. He wanted them. He didn't give a fuck about the bitch now that she'd pissed him off, but he really did want those chains—one in particular which glistened brighter than the others. His mouth grew dry as he contemplated how they would feel in his own hands.

Abruptly the girl disappeared down the steps of an apartment building. Although Donevan dashed after her, he reached the small cement porch just in time to have her gesture with her middle finger a third time, then slam the door in his face.

Rabid with anger, Donevan raised his fist to beat on the door. It was all he could do to control the compulsion to knock the door down and beat the hell out of the girl.

His lip began to twitch, and he drew in a shuddering breath. He wasn't that stupid. Or that obvious. Control, he reminded himself. Control. They'd talked a lot about that in prison.

He would take care of the bitch. And have the chains. But now wasn't the time.

When he had regained some small measure of calm, he

went up the steps and crossed the street. But he made careful note of the area. He wondered how that fucking bitch would like to feel those chains pressing into her flesh as he choked the life out of her. The sudden thought consoled him as he returned to his truck.

In fact, the idea was tremendously appealing. She hadn't outsmarted him; she'd given him time to plan.

He quickly drove away in case the girl decided to tell someone he'd chased her. When he was out of the neighborhood, he pulled the massage book from the glove compartment. For a few minutes he was distracted by the pictures of a man and a woman demonstrating massage techniques, but he soon got back to his original objective in taking the book.

He wanted to check out the masseuse's client list in the phone book. He could look at the couple massaging each other in the privacy of his rooms. There were lots of things he wanted to think about: the masseuse, the girl, the client list.

This whole situation was getting more and more exciting. He was considering things he had never dreamed of. He had to do some serious thinking. Trembling slightly, he automatically fondled the cord in his pocket.

## ⮞ CHAPTER 5 ⮜

Randolph Mason felt a heightened sense of anticipation as he smoothly maneuvered the long winding road. All morning he had been filled with thoughts of Mia. Now the time had finally come after the tiring plane trip up from California.

He had known her for years, and the thrill never ceased at the thought of her. Of course, she didn't know that he knew who she was. Mia Jorgenson: Troy Jorgenson's exquisite wife.

What man could forget her? Rand remembered the very first time he had seen her that night five years ago; she had been beautiful with a distinctly heart-shaped face, ivory skin, expressive blue eyes, and the body of a goddess.

He had been an extra in the movies then, and he realized that Mia didn't recall ever meeting him. For that he was glad. He had been told that of the people with whom she had former connections, she worked on a select few. Not that he could remotely call himself a former connection, he noted.

When he had met her that night at a big bash in her Beverly Hills home, she had clearly been interested only in her husband, a successful producer. Rand had been told that the love he had seen on her face for the older man was genuine, that no other man had any hope of winning her.

He hadn't tried. He *had* dreamed enough about her, though, when he happened to see her in the jet-set crowd as she and Troy made the rounds from L.A. to New York. He had savored the sight of her, but he had been busy with his career, working his way up from a scrappy extra to a current box-office hit. The road had been rough, and he'd compromised himself more than he'd ever thought he'd have to, but he'd settled with himself on the price.

In the meantime, Rand had lost track of the couple, although rumors abounded. There was talk that Troy, injured in the crash of his private jet, was wheelchair-bound, a bitter shell of a man who stayed locked behind the gates of his Palm Springs home. There was talk that Mia had gone to China and India on some soul-searching mission. They had both dropped out of the social scene.

Rand frowned. He believed there was truth to the rumors. He believed that Mia had found some answers in her quest.

She had changed in subtle ways from the lovely lady he had met all those years ago. She had let her hair grow long, wore very little makeup, and she dressed differently.

But the changes weren't all physical. She was a devoted masseuse; she had a talent, a gift she wanted to share. He felt privileged that she had consented to see him, and he was grateful that a colleague had finally managed to arrange an appointment.

At first she had flown to him, making a block of appointments with other prominent people in L.A. when she was in town. But finally she had invited him to the secluded cottage in Oregon. He was eager to see her home. He wanted to learn more about her, to see her material surroundings, how she lived and what she valued in life. She was an enigma to him, a mystery.

If he understood her better, if he could know the woman behind the haunting smile and healing hands, he would feel more confident about his chances with her. He suspected that he was already a little in love with her. Maybe he had been playing hero roles too long, chasing after his dream girl too often. He wanted to see Mia look at him as she had looked at Troy that night five years ago.

He had seen the invitation to her home as a good sign. But he was probably being overly optimistic.

Mia fluttered about the house like a young girl, making sure everything was right for Rand Mason's appointment at three. She knew she should be ashamed of the excitement she felt at the thought of his arrival. Still, she couldn't seem to stem the ebullience that billowed within her. Savoring her time with Rand was one small luxury she allowed herself.

After all, the mind needed succor, too, and she only dreamed about the pleasures that might be hers with him. She could never act on them, presuming Rand was willing, as long as she remained married to Troy. But the dreams made her feel alive again. She opened the door to the smiling man before he could knock.

"Good afternoon," he murmured, his voice filled with warmth. He enjoyed her beauty and never permitted himself to be rushed when he saw her.

Today she wore a pearl-gray sari which enhanced the gray in her eyes and set off her lovely skin to perfection. Her lustrous dark hair was woven into a single braid that hung down the middle of her back. He had seen many lovely women in his line of work, but this one had a beauty that he couldn't define. It seemed to come from the very depth of her.

Mia was well used to his perusal, and she couldn't deny that it pleased her to have him look at her with such frank admiration.

"How was your trip?" she asked.

"Tiring," he answered honestly. "But seeing you makes it all worthwhile."

"I'm glad."

She didn't add that seeing him brightened her life. He lessened the agony of those long nights and gray days when even her work couldn't hold back her unhappiness. She loved to caress his skin, to feel his warm, vibrant body beneath her fingertips. She loved to give him joy. But she kept all those things to herself.

"Did you have any difficulty finding the house?" she asked, seeking a neutral topic.

He grinned and looked around the living room as he thought of a reply. He wasn't surprised to find simplicity and warmth here.

"A little, but I had more difficulty renting the car. The girl behind the desk wanted to go with it. She tried to give me a special deal."

Seeing the teasing twinkle in his eyes, Mia laughed gently. He had a sense of humor about his fame; she liked that. He was very natural and unpretentious. She liked that, too. She realized that there wasn't very much about him she didn't like.

"I'm ready if you are," she said, leading the way toward the massage room without further ado.

"It was, too, him, Buck!" Emma declared, whipping off her glasses to wipe them on her apron. "I saw him just last month in that movie playing at the theater on First Street. As I live and breathe, that was Randolph Mason that went up the hill!"

"You been too many hours at the window, woman," Buck muttered. "What would a famous movie star be going up the hill for?"

"Hmph. For the same thing as the rest of them. What do you think?"

Buck kept rocking for a moment without replying. He stared at the TV set, blind to the soap opera that mimicked life on the small screen. Then he frowned, his bushy brows merging over deep-set eyes. "Beats me. It really does."

What would a famous star go there for? What was it that the mystery woman on the hill *did* do? He was getting as curious as his wife.

Mia's hands trembled slightly as she listened to Rand settling down on the massage table. She tried to concentrate on her task, but it was difficult with such a compelling man.

All at once she realized that she had made a mistake in having him come here. He had persuaded her that he had to have a massage before he could go on the set of his next film, and she had relented.

But she hadn't given in because he needed her. It had been because she wanted to see him.

"Mia."

The gentle way he said her name caused her to turn and face him, her eyes questioning. Involuntarily her gaze traveled over his handsome face.

"I want to thank you for seeing me today." He laughed. "I'd psyched myself up to believe that I couldn't go on that set until you rid me of some of the stress left over from the last film." He shook his head. "Ahh, fame. Being in the limelight has its price."

Her smile was faintly melancholy. "Yes, it does. But you must think it's worth it."

He nodded and answered truthfully. "I do. Being a box-office draw isn't heaven, but it isn't hell, either."

Mia looked away for a moment. Troy had loved the movie-star crowd. He had savored the glamour and the excitement. Sometimes she had half believed that he imagined himself a famous star with a worshiping public at his feet. He certainly had been handsome enough, and he had had his share of adoration.

She returned to the oils, forcing herself to focus on the cedarwood mixture she had chosen for Rand. Cedarwood helped to balance the energies, and that was what she felt he needed.


Donevan stabbed a piece of litter with unnecessary force as he cleaned up the trash lying around the grounds of the fast-food restaurant where he worked. He hated cleaning up other people's filth. Damned bunch of pigs. But he had needed a job before he could be paroled, and the do-gooder who ran the restaurant was a real patsy for ex-cons.

Donevan would have preferred almost anything to doing this kind of work. He hated the toilets most of all, especially the women's. Those foul sluts! Wads of paper towels and bloody napkins littered the floors around the trash cans where they had carelessly tossed them at the containers instead of bothering to put them in. Rubbish was even lying about in the stalls.

It beat the hell out of him why women couldn't seem to hit the pot when they peed. He'd heard they straddled it, rather than sit on it, for fear of getting somebody else's germs. Shit! He didn't know why they were worried about somebody else's uncleanliness when they were all alike anyway.

A picture of the masseuse's bathroom, with its perfume

bottles and soaps, filled his mind. At least it had been clean. The house had appeared clean, too. Except for that towel in the massage room. Why had she left it lying there where he had dropped it? Had she found it in her hamper yet?

He smirked a little. There was one way to find out. He would go see for himself. Maybe today, when he finished here.

He looked up when one of the young girls who worked the counter called his name.

"Donevan!"

"Yeah?"

"Both the women's toilets are stopped up. Somebody must have thought they were funny and dropped rolls of toilet tissue in them. Mark wants you to come in right now and unstop them."

Donevan nodded. Then he watched the girl walk away, her hips moving from side to side in the too-tight black uniform she wore. She reminded him of the first girl he had ever done it to. Like all the others, she had acted like she wanted it, then said she didn't.

She had bled, and when he first pulled his bloody dick back, he'd been terrified that she'd cut him somehow. He'd beat the hell out of the bitch. It wasn't until later that he realized she'd never done it before. But he didn't forget the fear he'd felt when he first saw his dick. He didn't want that to ever happen again. Ever.

He had a sudden vision of the whore who had sent him to prison. She had wanted it, all right. He'd seen the way she looked at him when he made deliveries to her office. Her eyes would dart around, from him to the door and back again. He was sure she wanted him to close it. And she kept talking constantly, like she wanted to keep him there.

She did that on the day he'd decided to do it to her. She'd kept talking even after he'd locked the door. He'd known she wanted it, even though she kept saying she didn't. It was only because a pair of delivery men arrived earlier than they usually did and forced themselves into the office while he had her down on the floor that she yelled rape. She'd even told the judge that she had tried to stall him by keeping him talking. Lying bitch!

When the door closed behind the counter girl with a thud, Donevan viciously shoved the sharp-pointed tool he was using into the ground. He'd like to find the little twit who stopped up the toilets. He'd ram this pick right through her!

## ➤ CHAPTER 6 ➤

Beginning at the base of Rand's spine, Mia started to slide her lightly oiled hands up the length of his muscled back to his neck. The moment she touched him, she was aware of an incredible energy. She had never felt anything quite like it before; everything else paled in its wake. She felt as though she had connected with a field of electricity, and for a moment she couldn't go on. Her concentration was completely shattered.

She had to remove her hands from Rand's back, something she never liked to do, for it broke the connection she wished to establish with the client. She had been aware of Rand's power to disturb her when she worked on him before, but this surprised her. Shaken, she fought to steady herself so she could go on.

Rand looked back over his shoulder. "Mia, is something wrong?"

She moistened her lips with her tongue. Wrong? Just a small thing like wanting to make love to him so badly that she couldn't think straight. Just a little disturbance inside her that cried out to have him in her, holding her, moving with her.

She cleared her throat. "No. I'm sorry. I lost my concentration."

He laughed. "Now, that's something I can relate to. I have no concentration when you touch me. I have to really get inside myself to relax."

He didn't add that he wanted to get inside her desperately, to know how his body would feel joined with hers, to know the sweetness and fullness of her touch, her wonder, her magic, because he truly believed she was special.

Attempting to regain her professional demeanor, Mia murmured, "Let's both concentrate. You're tense."

He chuckled. She'd be tense, too, if she wanted him as badly as he wanted her.

"Fine."

Mia made herself resume her work. The positive charge was there, but this time she was prepared for it; she succeeded in making it work for her as she swept her hands across his broad shoulders, getting in touch with the force instead of fighting it.

She drew on the natural affinity she felt with this man as she massaged the defined muscles of his magnificent body. She began to feel in harmony with him. She savored the touch of his skin beneath her sensitive fingertips.

Compelling herself to focus on her work, she moved down the outside of Rand's strong back to his narrow waist and then swept out over slim hips and muscled buttocks, stroking slowly and rhythmically, using firm pressure on the upward stroke, light on the downward. Then she moved up to his shoulders. She began to make circular movements, repeating them three times in succession.

"Lord, that feels good," Rand murmured.

Mia didn't say anything. If she broke the bond this time, she was lost and she knew it.

With her right hand she squeezed slowly up his neck to his hairline. She hesitated slightly, resisting the urge to fan her fingers through his black hair. She made herself turn her mind away from her own desires.

Firmly pressing Rand's occipital bone with her thumb and fingers, she worked from his hairline to the base of his neck and back again twice. Finally she found the natural rhythm of her work, and at last she was able to lose herself in the continuous swirls and patterns of her fingers and hands on the man before her.

After she had completed the back area, she moved down to his buttocks, her hands cupped as she worked vigorously. When she finished there, she utilized the knuckles of her index and middle fingers to work his spine again, sliding up each side to the top of Rand's neck.

She covered him while she poured a little more oil in her hands. Then she began to massage his feet and legs. Next she used the knuckles of both hands to move up the back of the knee, repeating her movements three times smoothly and slowly, progressing to the thigh, then working the whole leg. She completed the leg and foot massage with sweeping, stroking movements up and down the entire limb, ministering thoroughly before she repeated the process on the other leg.

Then she was ready for Rand to turn over. She shook her head. In truth, she wasn't ready at all. She clearly hadn't prepared herself well enough. She knew that when he turned over he would follow her with his eyes. No matter how often she had told him to close his eyes, he insisted on keeping them open.

"Please turn over now, keeping your eyes closed," she instructed, trying to sound firm.

The handsome man on the table rolled over and grinned at her, his eyes open. "Sorry, I can't resist looking at you. I refuse to miss a chance," he said, his voice thick.

"I can't work well when you watch me," she insisted, although it didn't bother her with other clients. "And *you* can't relax," she added, trying the same inducements she always used. It had almost become a game with them.

"I know," he all but whispered. "But not relaxing this way is so nice."

Mia knew she should tell him that she wouldn't continue to work if he didn't close his eyes. She should. But she never did. She took secret pleasure from knowing that he studied her every move, that he responded more intensely because of it.

"Shh, you're destroying the rhythm," she said, hoping that he couldn't detect the slight quiver in her voice.

Easily moving his six-foot frame, Rand settled back more comfortably on the table. His dark eyes were glazed and the expression on his face was that of a man sated.

"You do know you're wonderful," he murmured, his voice husky as he gazed at her. When Mia worked with him, he felt almost as satisfied as if he had been making love. Almost.

Her face flushed, Mia looked away as she poured more oil into her hands. "Thank you."

Her blue-gray eyes met his again when she faced him. "Have you any particular aches and pains? Any places you want me to work on specifically?"

Rand was tempted to tell her that there was a particular ache she could work with, a place that troubled him—but only when he thought of her. He wanted to make love to her so badly that he would trade almost anything for the experience.

Always, when she initially touched him, he seemed to be on fire with the need for her, filled with a raw and burning energy. Today had been worse than usual. Fortunately, she had cooled the flames with her soothing strokes and caresses as she worked. She had cooled them, but she hadn't smothered them. The embers lay smoldering deep inside, waiting only for her touch to cause them to leap to new life. His thoughts read like a movie script, and he smiled a little.

When Mia saw the glow in his eyes, she couldn't help smiling in response. "What's going on in your mind?"

"Would you believe it if I told you I'm thinking about you?"

She shook her head. "I'd have my serious doubts."

"Don't you believe that I was thinking about you?" he murmured, testing the water slightly as Mia began to stroke his right arm.

Mia didn't reply to his last question. She required all her resources and attention to work on him. When she gazed down at his body, she wanted to stroke the skin with abandon, without the pressure and pace that a massage demanded, without the rhythms and patterns that were now automatically integrated into her work.

"Mia," Rand murmured, "I was wondering whether or not you would have dinner with me tonight." His breath hung in his throat, and he was surprised by his increased heartbeat. He was afraid she could feel his anxiety, sense his excitement. Her answer was very important to him.

Mia paused only briefly, her eyes meeting his. The fantasy was safe and stirring. The reality could be dangerous and damaging. And there was Troy.

She smiled faintly. "I don't think that's a good idea."

He wanted to plead and protest. He wanted to say that he had come all the way from California and that one meal together wouldn't breach her rules. He wanted to tell her that she had hurt his pride. He wanted to offer her the moon.

He made a wry face instead. "That's too bad. I thought you might have pity on a stranger in a strange land."

She laughed lightly, hoping to diffuse some of the tension. "You're not a stranger anywhere. Just walk out on the streets. Any woman would share a meal with you."

He made himself smile. His voice was remarkably free of the driving desire he felt. "But not you? You aren't the slightest bit interested in sharing a meal with a famous ol' movie star, are you?"

"Rand, I—"

She met his gaze. Time stopped. Without conscious

thought, he reached out and caught Mia's hands in his to pull her down to him. He had wanted her so very long. He ran his fingers through her hair, dislodging the band that confined the long braid.

Her hands on his chest, her heart beating madly, Mia tried to fight through her heated awareness of the man. When he drew her face to his and hungrily caressed her mouth, she trembled. There was a current between them so powerful that she couldn't break the connection for several minutes in which Rand teased her body and mind as no man had done in a long, long time.

His experienced tongue circled hers, tantalizing and enticing, and Mia joined in the sensual dance. She couldn't get enough of the taste of him. Her mouth, tongue, and teeth nibbled and sampled, taking love bites, exchanging hot kiss for hot kiss.

She wanted him so much that she throbbed with the ache of desire. She was already wet, her vaginal muscles contracting at the mere thought of taking him inside her. The months of abstinence, the mental conditioning that had allowed her to direct her sexual energies into her work, vanished in that single moment when Rand touched her.

She felt the hot rush of passion surge through her as her taut nipples pressed against his naked chest. She had never wanted to reach out and hold a man as much as she did now, to take him in her hand and body and explode with ecstasy.

She never knew where she got the strength to draw away. She was trembling visibly. "Rand, I'm married."

He looked at her as if he didn't understand. He knew she was married. He had heard from people who knew the couple that they had never divorced. But they didn't live together. At least not in the same house all the time.

"I know, but I thought—" He didn't know what else to say. "I'm sorry if I was out of line." His voice was low and thick. He wasn't going to promise that it wouldn't happen again. Although he was shaken by the fire that had burned between them, he found the strength to smile.

Mia turned away from him. "I think we need to stop for today."

Without another word he got up and went to the bathroom to get dressed. Mia clutched at the edges of the cabinet with unsteady hands and inhaled deeply until she could restore some sanity. She knew she should tell him not to return tomorrow. But she also knew she couldn't.

Donevan went into the supply room for some rubber gloves. He wasn't about to work on the stopped-up toilets without some protection from the filth and germs. His rage was at the boiling point as he shoved open the door to the bathroom. A frightened customer gave a startled protest when she saw him as she washed her hands at the sink.

"What are you doing in here?" she cried.

"Didn't you see that the toilets are stopped up?" Donevan demanded. "Did you use one anyway?" He wanted to call her a stupid bitch, but he needed the job too much.

Her eyes wide, her face red, the woman fled. Donevan slapped the "Closed" sign on the bathroom door, then went into the first stall, plunger in hand.

"Jesus!" he muttered.

As he'd been told, there was a whole roll of toilet paper shoved down in the bowl. The pot reeked of urine and waste that had accumulated when the toilet wouldn't flush.

"Jesus!" Donevan muttered again, his disgust as tangible as the stench in the room.

Even with gloves on, he wasn't about to reach down into the bowl. He returned to get his pick, then viciously jabbed at the mess, managing to lift it mostly intact and dump it in a trash can. Then he rammed the plunger into the toilet over and over with unnecessary force.

He began to breathe harder as he worked. Suddenly he heard the counter girl call out.

"Haven't you got those toilets clean yet? Customers want to use them!"

"Fuck the customers," he muttered to himself. "Yeah,

almost," he called to her. Then he pulled the handle on the toilet, watching as the water rose to the top, then gurgled noisily as it finally flushed.

Donevan's breathing eased somewhat as he went to the second toilet and repeated the procedure. When he'd finished, he called out to the counter girl. She could clean the damned things. It was part of her job, not his.

He went to the men's rest room and started to strip off the gloves. Then he stopped and walked to the sink and began to wash his gloved hands. He looked up at his face in the mirror as he soaped the rubber thoroughly.

As he washed his hands, he became mesmerized by the gloves. They felt nice and snug. They were just the thing he needed. No fingerprints.

He studied his reflection; his lips turned up at the corners. He was feeling good as his mind began to spin with thoughts that made him both nervous and excited.

He wondered how that druggie bitch would feel if he was tightening those chains around her neck. He wondered if she would cry and beg. He wondered how long it would take to stifle the breath out of her, to squeeze and squeeze and squeeze.

His heart began to beat fast at the thought. His breathing became labored. He felt a tightening in his groin area. He turned the hot water faucet on harder and made sure the gloves were thoroughly cleansed. They felt soft and slightly spongy. He liked the feeling.

When he had carefully dried them, he went into a stall and locked the door. Then he unzipped his fly and took his penis in one gloved hand. He liked the feel of the rubber real well. He closed his eyes and thought of squeezing the girl's neck. Harder and harder. He stroked faster and faster until he finally climaxed.

Mia was troubled by Rand's kiss because she had wanted it so much. She knew the bond she felt with him was too strong to be encouraged. After he had gone, she sat down on the couch with Soot and tried to compose herself, but there seemed to be no reconciliation between her emotions and her mind.

Restless, she began to putter about the house, trying to exorcise her troubled thoughts, but they only increased with the additional energy. Without realizing it, she began to pace, unconsciously trying to outrun her turmoil. At last she could stand it no longer. She reached for the phone and dialed Troy's number in Palm Springs. Daniel, the live-in male nurse, answered.

"Yes?"

"This is Mrs. Jorgenson. I'd like to speak with my husband, please."

There was a lengthy pause on the other end of the line. When Daniel finally spoke, his naturally gruff voice was vaguely sympathetic, but firm. "He's resting, Mrs. Jorgenson. I don't think we should disturb him."

"Daniel—" She fought to control her emotions. Both she and Troy had chosen the burly nurse over other applicants because of his excellent credentials, his familiarity with paraplegics, and his physical strength. Now she was beginning to see him as a barricade between her and her husband.

"Is he asleep? I need to speak with him," she said more firmly.

There was another pause. "Yes, he's sleeping. He's had a bad day. Another time would be better."

She drew in a steadying breath. "Another time" seemed to be the answer she increasingly received. She hadn't spoken to Troy in two weeks. She hadn't seen him in three months.

"All right, Daniel. Please tell him I'll be coming to California later this month."

There was the expected pause, as though Daniel had something he wanted to say, yet was resisting. "Yes," he said at last. Then he severed the connection.

Mia's thoughts were turbulent as she replaced the phone. The distance between her and Troy was growing, no matter how hard she fought to keep the connection, to nurture the fragile bond that was all that had been left after his accident.

An overwhelming anxiety swept through her. She felt the hopelessness, the futility of the love she harbored for Troy. She began to despair that he would ever find a place for her in his life. In her thin-soled shoes, still dressed as she had been for Rand's massage, she fled to the beach.

Emma stood at the window, watching the movie star's car as it slowly wound its way out of sight.

"Darn it," she muttered aloud.

Buck had missed him. She'd told him to stay at the window until the white car came back down the hill, but he had tired of watching. Wouldn't you know he would be out back getting wood at just the moment the man finally passed? Now he would never believe her.

Her fingers tightened on the curtain as a black truck began climbing past her house. Today was Friday. She hadn't expected anybody else to go to the masseuse's cottage today, especially not the man in the black truck. As she gazed out the window, she realized that this man wasn't the regular one. This was a new one. *Another* one!

"Buck!" she called. "Buck!"

## ⇌ CHAPTER 7 ⇌

Donevan shut off the engine before he got to the top of the hill. Pulling off on a dirt road he had found on his previous visit, he stopped in some trees where his truck couldn't be seen from the masseuse's house. In fact, it was fairly well hidden from almost all except the most discerning eyes. He was afraid to drive too far into the trees for fear of getting stuck in the soft, muddy soil. Anyway, he didn't want his black truck messed up. That and his white car were the only decent things he owned. He had bought them before he got arrested.

After easing the door closed, he quietly and quickly made his way around the back, through the trees toward the cottage. He'd felt a compelling urge to come to the masseuse's house. He couldn't seem to stop thinking about her.

He paused, listening. All he heard was the wind in the trees and the crashing of the waves on the shore. The angry roar of the ocean attracted him, and he edged toward the turbulent water. Lured by the violence, he stood high up on the cliff watching the water below crash against the jagged rocks.

The wind whipped his sandy hair, and he automatically, repeatedly, smoothed it back. He didn't really like heights, but he got off on the feeling. Sometimes he would stand on a bridge, watching the river, until he was dizzy with the motion. The dizziness in his head caused a rush that made him tremble and throb inside.

He moved a little closer to the edge of the cliff. If he stepped too close, there was the danger that he might fall to his death far below. He teased himself with the fear for a moment, then eased back, his heart pounding. He had a sudden vision of hurling a woman's body down into the turbulent ocean water.

Occupied with his thoughts, he didn't see Mia running along the beach in the cool air. As he watched the tumbling body in his mind, the size and shape changed and changed and changed, flipping and whirling and spinning like the fury that was always building and lessening inside him. He began to breathe harder and harder until he was panting.

He could get rid of all the women, he realized, by flinging one of them off the cliff, by heaving her so hard that she could never come back. Unconsciously he reached down to his crotch as he followed the progress of the body in his head, waiting to see it dash itself to pieces on the rocks in the foamy surf that resembled masses of dirty semen.

His breath came faster and faster; the body spun wilder and wilder. Suddenly he saw it hit the rocks and explode. When it turned over, limp and spent, it was his mother.

"Whore!" he mouthed bitterly, letting the wind carry the word away as he turned toward the house.

When he had slipped around front, he stealthily made his way to the door. He had a plastic credit card ready, sure that was all it would take to get inside. The masseuse was too stupid to know about dead bolts. When he tried the handle, he discovered he didn't even need the card. The door was unlocked! The dumb bitch was really asking for it!

He eased into the living room, eyes alert, searching everywhere in the shadows. The day was a dismal one, as were many of Oregon's days, and the house was naturally dark, shaded by trees, the windows covered by partially open blinds.

A fire was barely alive in the fireplace, and the house was distinctly chilly. Donevan had felt that chill the last time, when the woman wasn't home. He was going to be very angry if she wasn't home today, after he'd come all the way up here.

He could have spent this time studying the druggie girl's routine or doing more investigating of the masseuse's client list. He hadn't found a phone number or an address for the woman he was most interested in. Frannie Welch wasn't in the phone book, and he wasn't about to go asking around town, but it irritated him because she was the only one he couldn't locate. Did she really think she could hide from him in this town?

The black cat suddenly reared up on the couch, his back arched, hissing in fright. Donevan's heart pounded at the unexpected movement. He hadn't seen the animal, and it took him a moment to get over the scare. When he waved his arms menacingly, the cat leapt from the couch and vanished.

Donevan paused for a moment, listening, his ears straining to catch every additional sound. He heard nothing. He'd like to kill that damned cat, but because it was black and belonged to the masseuse, he fought the desire.

He moved quietly down the hall, taking care to avoid the squeaky floorboard in front of the bathroom. Barely breathing, he flattened himself against the pale green wall and listened for some sign of the woman. When he didn't hear anything, he pushed gingerly on the bedroom door. The room was empty.

Disappointed, Donevan combed every inch of the house. The masseuse was nowhere to be found. He went into her bedroom closet to wait.

Mia grew chilly out on the beach. Realizing she might catch a cold if she didn't go back to the cottage, she hurriedly retraced her steps, tears falling from her eyes.

She thought she had stopped crying over Troy; she thought she had made peace with herself. She had vowed she would be patient for however long it took.

Her session with Rand this afternoon had made her see that she didn't have the control she hoped she would have. She drew in several deep breaths, trying to fill herself with the sea air until she was calm again. The tears still fell; it was as if she had an ocean of them backed up inside her. She hadn't known that until today.

The return trip up the steps seemed to take forever, and she was thoroughly chilled when she finally reached the house. After she had brushed the sand off her damp shoes with cold hands, she hurried to the fire in the front room and quickly piled more wood on it.

The house seemed colder than she could ever remember it. She felt the cold right to the center of her being. When she had stirred the fire to new life with a poker, flames of red and blue danced before her. The sight helped offset the chill.

She wrapped herself in a shawl and pulled up a footstool. Huddled in front of the fire, she slipped off her shoes and held her feet out to the heat.

Gradually she began to thaw. At least outside. Inside, the cold emotional storm was still brewing. Finally she gave in to the futility of fighting her tears. Telling herself that she was long overdue for a good cleansing cry, she retreated to the couch and began to sob.

Donevan had heard the woman return and impatiently waited for her to come to the bedroom. The minutes had ticked by, and he had grown more irritable. He didn't know why nothing went his way. Didn't the bitch ever come into this room?

Then he heard her crying. The sound scraped across his nerves. He hated to hear anybody cry. Especially a woman. It filled him with rage.

A vision of his mother flashed into his mind. He had seen her cry twice. Once when his father left, then again when she left. And he'd been blamed both times.

She was another stupid bitch. She had lived her life blaming him for what happened to her, blaming him for being born, blaming him for his father walking out. As he stood there, lost in his past, the fury began to rise inside him.

After his father left, there had been just him and his mother and the welfare checks. That's what his life had been made up of.

Her life had been made up of saying, "Donevan, don't do that; Donevan, wash your hands; Donevan, don't touch yourself there, *ever;* Donevan, sex is dirty; Donevan, decent people don't"—don't *everything* it had seemed to him. It had become a fucking crusade with her after she caught him playing with himself in the bathroom that one time.

But when he had found her in bed with that bastard, it had suddenly been, "Donevan, sex is all right between a man and a woman; Donevan, you're nearly sixteen, almost grown, you have all your life ahead of you; Donevan, I'm moving back to California with him. *Donevan, you can't come.*"

The bastard hadn't wanted him. His father hadn't wanted him. His mother hadn't wanted him. Well, screw them all!

Her bout of sobbing subsiding, Mia sat up on the couch and brushed at her tears. It wasn't like her to sit around and feel sorry for herself. Life was too important.

What she needed, she decided, was to get out of the cottage and mingle with the townfolk for a little while. She knew a very good small restaurant where the clientele was pleasant.

Suddenly the phone rang. Startled, Mia reached for it on the first ring.

"Hello."

"Hello," Rand drawled.

Mia's heart started to pound. She had already forgotten her bout of crying. All she could think of was Rand and how she must not let him tempt her. As if that were possible.

"I just wondered if you'd changed your mind about dinner," he said. "I swear I'm like a lost soul here in this town. I don't know where to go to eat."

Mia laughed. "You're incorrigible, Rand Mason."

"That may very well be," he agreed amicably, "but will you have pity on me, just this once?"

"No," she said quickly, before she could relent. She was going out, and she would like nothing better than to go with him. That's why she had to refuse.

"Well, don't say I didn't try," he joked with more merriment than he was feeling. He really was hoping she'd change her mind.

"I will suggest a couple of places that you might like," she said.

"Fine." He listened and jotted down directions, then asked, "Are these places where you eat?"

She smiled to herself. "Rarely. I like little out-of-the-way places."

"Me, too. Give me a few more suggestions. Better yet, just show me the way. Then you might find it in your heart to share dinner with a stranger."

A stranger, Mia thought. That was the last thing this man was. She felt like she knew him extremely well, even more so after that potent kiss.

"Sorry," she repeated against her will. She did mention a few small local spots, but not the one where she was going. She didn't want to see him there.

"Thanks," he said agreeably enough. But when he had hung up, he couldn't deny that he was unreasonably disappointed.

Donevan stiffened when the masseuse abruptly walked into the bedroom. He had been so absorbed in his thoughts that he hadn't heard her coming. That happened sometimes when he let himself think about his mother. He seemed to have gaps in time that he couldn't account for. He hadn't even realized that he was gripping his thin cord in both hands.

When the closet door opened suddenly, sending in faint light from the bedroom, Donevan eased back behind some clothes and stood statue still. He felt his heart beat like it would erupt inside his chest.

Everything in him seemed to speed up, racing around and around at a breakneck pace, rushing and rushing and rushing. The feeling he loved and hated. The chance that he might be discovered at any time caused an incredible high of combined thrill and fright.

It always reminded him of jerking off and half expecting his mother to walk into the cubbyhole he had called his room. He knew full well how she would freak if she caught him playing with his prick, but the fear had become part of the pleasure over the years. He had worked faster and faster when he thought his mother might plunge into the room and shriek at him about how filthy and disgusting it was to touch his *privates*.

His attention was drawn back to the masseuse when she shut the closet door. Then he heard muffled sounds as she opened and closed drawers. She began to hum. As Donevan listened, straining to determine the tune, his heartbeat slowed.

Hardly daring to breathe, he sneaked over to the door. With a shaking hand, he reached for the knob, and slowly, very slowly, turned it. Then he opened the door the tiniest crack and gazed out with one eye, but he didn't see anything. When he heard a floorboard creak, he knew the woman had gone down the hall.

In the bathroom Mia reached for her pantyhose. "Darn it!" she cried aloud. One pair was snagged, and she had only recently bought them. She must have done it when she washed them. Shaking her head in annoyance, she slipped off her sari and placed it in the hamper. Then she returned to the bedroom.

Nude, she sat on her dressing-table stool and began to slide the other pair of silky nylons up her legs, one at a time. She had taken her hair down and now it fell across her shoulders, draping her body like a dark, glossy curtain.

From the closet Donevan watched Mia's reflection in the mirror, his field of vision limited. He had never seen a naked woman as pretty as this one. Not that he had seen that many, he reminded himself. He hadn't quite been the lover-boy kind in high school, and when he'd dropped out to fend for himself, he hadn't exactly had women falling all over him. But then, he hadn't wanted them, he assured himself bitterly.

Studying the masseuse, he was fascinated by her hair. He imagined winding it around his fingers, over his hand, around her neck.

A frown creased his face as he watched Mia slip on a red bra. Red reminded him of the box in the bathroom. He tried to see if the masseuse was still on the rag, but he couldn't tell.

She put on a blouse and buttoned it, then stepped into a

skirt, looking in the mirror, making sure that the garment was straight. She picked up a hairbrush and thoroughly brushed her hair. Then, taking a brightly colored scarf in hand, she tied it around her head like a headband, leaving the ends trailing down along the left side of her face. When she had slipped on a pair of orchid boots, she walked back to the closet.

Donevan swiftly blended back into the clothes, his pulse racing, his throat tight. Again Mia reached into the closet without turning on the light; when she had taken a purple jacket from a hanger, she closed the door again.

Donevan stood there for a moment, thinking how cleverly he had hidden himself. The slut had never even suspected he was there. She had come to the closet twice and taken out clothes, and she hadn't even known that he was part of them.

But then, he himself had been so distracted by thoughts of his mother that he hadn't even known what the masseuse took out. Although she'd obviously picked the first outfit on the rod, he should have been paying more attention. He wondered where she'd got the scarf from.

A vision of it around her head rose into his mind. He felt himself growing excited. Carefully making his way out of the bedroom, he eased down the hall in search of the masseuse.

His search proved futile. She was gone.

# ⚔ CHAPTER 8 ⚔

Buck sat in his rocking chair reading a pornographic magazine he had hidden between the pages of a much larger sports magazine. He knew Emma would throw a fit if she ever caught him reading such stuff, but what Emma didn't know wouldn't hurt her.

Chances of her picking up the sports magazine and finding the other one were slim to nothing. She just read those trashy movie magazines. Besides, as long as she was rattling pots and pans as she got ready to cook dinner, he knew he was safe.

When he heard the sound of car tires crunching gravel, he made his way over to the window to see who was passing by this time. His house was the last one on the road before the mystery lady's, so he knew it had to be someone coming from her place. Either that, or somebody who had taken a wrong turn.

To his surprise, he saw the woman herself driving by. Although she seldom ventured out of the cottage, he'd recognize her a mile away. Her long dark hair was hanging down around her shoulders and she had some kind of scarf tied in it. He could see that she was all gussied up, and he wondered where she was going. Damn, she was a beautiful woman!

He thought about the men who came and went from her house, and admitted to himself that he wanted to know just what she did with them. And the women. Was she a hooker? As pretty as she was, did she really sell herself to men?

He found the idea very naughty—and more than a little exciting. After all, he still had those things on his mind, no matter how many times Emma told him he was too old to be so horny.

As he gazed after the woman's car, seeing it wind out of sight, he was reminded of his younger days, days when he was still sowing his wild oats with the pretty girls. Then he had married Emma.

It wasn't that he didn't love her. They'd been married for nearly forty years, and she was like half of him. But he was still a man with a man's needs. Although Emma never turned him down, she never welcomed him, either.

He had to wonder if the mystery lady was as man-crazy as folks said. He just might wander up there and poke around to see the setup. No one would be the wiser. She wasn't home. And he could simply tell his wife that he was taking a little stroll before dinner.

He rolled up both magazines, then took the wide rubber band off his wrist where he kept it readily at hand. When he had secured them, he went to the room he used as a kind of den. After he stuffed the magazines in a box, he went to tell Emma about his walk.

Mia felt better as she opened the door to the small restaurant and stepped inside. She saw people she knew and liked, as well as a couple of strangers hidden away in a booth in the back. She grinned and waved to a man in the first booth, then glanced at the strangers, seeing that they were both men; the one facing her was young, and she couldn't tell much about the other man, whose back was to her.

She smiled. Although the restaurant was more than adequately heated in part by a wood stove at the back, the man was dressed in a topcoat and hat. He was probably up from California and thought he would freeze to death before he ever adjusted to the Oregon weather.

"Hello, Mia."

She turned to smile at the proprietor. He was one of only a

handful of the businesspeople in the clannish community who seemed to genuinely like her. She was aware that she was a constant target of gossip, but she didn't dignify the rumors by acknowledging them. She hoped that eventually she would earn the respect of the townspeople.

"Hello, Mike. How are you?"

"Making a living," he said, his tone light. "What can I get you?"

She climbed up on one of the tall stools at the counter. "The usual. A vegetable club sandwich on whole wheat pita bread, and white wine."

He grinned. "A girl after my own heart."

While he made the sandwich, Mia turned to a man in the first booth, who was strumming a banjo.

"How are you tonight, Frank?"

He smiled warmly and answered her in a distinct New England accent. "I'm doing okay for a displaced boy."

"You're about as much of a boy as I am," she teased.

He laughed. "You don't look like a boy at all, Mia, displaced or not. In fact, you're looking exceptionally pretty tonight."

"Why, thank you, Frank."

Sitting in the back booth, Rand couldn't keep himself from looking at Mia. He couldn't believe she was here. The hotel owner had suggested this place when Rand asked about small local hangouts, but Mia hadn't mentioned it at all.

She was more beautiful than ever. It was almost a shock to see her in something besides a sari. He was tempted to take off his movie-star disguise and join her, but he knew she wouldn't welcome him. She'd already turned down his dinner invitation and cut short his massage after that torrid kiss. He dared not press his luck further. But when he saw Mia place her hand on the arm of the man she was talking to, he felt a ridiculous flash of jealousy.

"Play something I can sing to, Frank," she urged. "Something sparkling and lively."

With a wry grin the man obliged. Rand watched curiously as Frank plucked the strings with amazing agility. His lean body bent low over the instrument, the auburn-haired man's eyes brightened as he played with obvious relish. He struck Rand as one of those antiestablishment types. That wasn't at all unusual in Oregon, nor was the gold hoop earring he wore. Still, there was something about the man that stated "rebel" as if he were wearing a badge.

Offering encouragement, Mia clapped her hands. Her laughter mingled with the upbeat notes of the song. Soon she began to sing in a beautiful, pure voice.

Mesmerized, Rand watched the interplay between the two. He was impressed by the sound they were creating. Mia sang better than many professionals he had heard, and Frank had skilled fingers.

"Why do I think you came to this isolated burg for more than a massage?" the pilot with Rand murmured.

Rand tried to smile, but he found it impossible at the moment. He *had* come here for more than a massage, much more, and he didn't like being held in limbo when he wanted the woman so much that the pain was palpable. That kiss had left him aching with longing.

He shrugged, trying to appear nonchalant. "I haven't the slightest idea."

"I don't want to point this out, but you got it bad for her," the pilot said.

Rand shoved his fingers through his hair in frustration. "You're absolutely right," he murmured.

As he picked up his hamburger, his total focus was on the woman at the front of the restaurant. He had another session with her tomorrow. He couldn't get the thought out of his mind.

The banjo player had taken off his baseball cap. His hair was short and curly. When he closed his eyes, a dreamy expression altered his very ordinary features.

Rand wondered if Mia was responsible for that enchanted

look. She was sitting very near the man now, her hand resting on his blue-jeaned leg as she sang a soft ballad in her crystal-clear voice. Another couple had joined them in the booth, and they were watching her with rapt attention.

When the cook brought Mia's meal, Rand was ridiculously relieved. He didn't like her shared intimacy with the banjo player, but he realized it was none of his business. He had no hold on the woman, none whatsoever. He made himself stop watching. He could hear their voices as they talked, but he couldn't distinguish the words.

Mia didn't stay long; as she left, she called out to Frank, "See you tomorrow."

Rand wanted to know if he was one of her clients. Or was he something more?

Buck was breathing hard when he reached the top of the hill. He hadn't realized what an undertaking he had attempted. The road was about a mile up from his house to the mystery lady's, but he couldn't have very well told Emma that he was driving up here to satisfy his curiosity.

He walked up on the porch and peered into one of the front windows. The blinds were partially drawn, and he couldn't see much. When he stepped back to cross the porch so he could look into the other window, he bumped into a wicker chair. It made a grating noise on the wooden floorboards as it moved. Buck stood still, holding his breath. Even though he knew the woman wasn't home, he felt strange snooping around up here.

Inside the house Donevan heard the noise. He had been waiting in the bedroom for the masseuse's return, checking out her jewelry box, alert to every sound. He paused, totally immobile, his fingers gripping a necklace, as he strained to hear further sounds.

He told himself that it must have been the cat, because he hadn't heard the woman's car come back up the hill. He had been listening very, very carefully. He had real good hearing. He wouldn't have missed the whine of a car engine or the sound of tires biting into gravel.

Still, it paid to be sure. What if it was somebody else? He couldn't be caught up here. He wasn't going back to prison. When he made his move on the masseuse, he was either going to have one hell of an alibi, or he was going to be long gone to California before anyone knew what had happened.

He dropped the knotted rope necklace in his pants pocket and shut the jewelry box. Then, moving so silently that he could hardly hear himself, he worked his way to the front room to sneak a look out one of the windows. He tilted the blind ever so slightly, then stared out.

Son of a bitch! There was some old bastard out on the front porch! He let the blind go, then jumped back into the shadows.

Outside, Buck sucked in his breath and gazed at the blind, which was swaying slightly. Somebody was home! He was sure he had seen a face on the other side of the window. He glanced back down the hill. He was almost positive the woman hadn't returned, but maybe she hadn't gone anywhere. Maybe she had changed her mind, turned around and come back before he began his walk. Her car could be parked beneath the trees at the side of the house.

Durn! He didn't know what to do now. He reckoned since he was here, he would make the most of it. After all, he could say he was just being neighborly. He and Emma hadn't met the woman yet.

He knocked on the door. "Hello!" he called out.

Inside, Donevan cursed his bad luck. He was sure now that the old man had seen him. But how much of him had he seen? And what should he do about it?

Jesus! This was the last thing he had expected; he should have been smarter. The masseuse probably knew a whole lot of people, just like the therapist and the probation officer had said. He would have to be more careful in the future, but what should he do right now?

"Hello," Buck called again.

Donevan pressed himself against the wall. He decided to wait and see what the man would do. *He* wouldn't do anything unless he was forced to. He could feel his lip twitch and he caught it between his teeth.

Out on the porch Buck frowned. Maybe he was so nervous that he was imagining things. Suddenly the sound of a car coming up the road caused him to start. He glanced over his shoulder.

The mystery lady! He could still slip away before she saw him. He didn't want to take the chance that Emma would find out he had been up here. If he spoke to the woman, there was always the possibility that she would see him somewhere in town while he was with Emma and talk to him.

Mia's state of mind was tremendously improved as she drove back up the hill. She had enjoyed the outing; she was still softly singing the last song she and Frank had done. She felt more relaxed. She was sure she would sleep well tonight. A smile on her face, she parked in the carport and got out of the car.

Buck slipped into the shadows at the side of the house and waited, breathless, feeling like a naughty boy. He hadn't satisfied his curiosity in the least, but now wasn't the time. He just wanted to get back down that hill.

Inside, Donevan made his way to the back of the house. He couldn't take a chance on the old man coming in with the woman. He was sure to tell her that he had seen someone inside.

Hell! The law could be up here before he knew what had happened. He had to get away.

Slipping out the back door, he moved across the sun deck and ran down the steps two at a time.

## ⟨ CHAPTER 9 ⟩

Determined not to fall prey to her earlier mood, Mia entered the house singing. She stopped just inside the door, the song fading from her lips. There was an unnatural stillness in the room. The house had that coldness she'd felt when she returned from the beach, despite the fire that still burned.

She closed her eyes for a few moments, trying to reclaim the warmth in herself. Apparently she had left the bleakness here behind her when she went to the restaurant. She would not indulge it again.

When she opened her eyes, she realized that Soot wasn't in his usual place on the couch. That might account for some of the lack of life she experienced.

"Here, kitty," she called. "Here, kitty, kitty."

He soon came racing down the hall. Mia lifted him in her arms and nuzzled his face. Troy had given her the cat seven years ago. She loved him as if he were a child.

While she stroked his silky black fur, she walked over to the front window and looked out. A storm was coming. Soot hated them and had, no doubt, been hiding under the bed in her room while she was gone.

She scratched his head and placed him on his favorite cushion on the couch. Then she filled the fireplace with fresh wood before going to her bedroom to take off her clothes. After she had hung them in the closet, she took a flannel nightgown from her bureau and went down the hall to the bathroom.

She poured in scented bath oil as the tub filled with warm water. Sighing in anticipation, she settled down for a nice, long soak. She intended to sleep well tonight.

Donevan was actually shaking when he got back to the run-down house where he rented two upstairs rooms. He had stayed on the beach a long time to make sure that the old man had gone. He had been sorry there was only one road to the masseuse's house, but he told himself that so many cars came and went from there, he wouldn't be noticed.

Still, he would have to be more careful the next time. He had been pretty fucking scared. He smiled a little, thinking of the rush he felt when the fear gripped him, and how wonderful it felt when it was all over.

He parked in the garage he shared with the old woman who owned the house. Rain was pouring down as he blended into the dark shadows of two tall trees while he climbed up the steps leading to the back entrance, where his rooms were.

He wanted to take his time, but he didn't dare. He really liked the rain; it cleaned things—people, places, the air. The whole world was so dirty. He stood by the door a minute before opening it, watching the rain fall.

But tonight he found that he was not calmed by the storm. The rain seemed to strike him deliberately, even though he was under the cover of the entrance to his rooms. He didn't need to be washed. He was *always* clean!

"Fuck you, rain," he said aloud, feeling oddly as if it, too, had turned on him. He entered his rooms.

He had a living room–kitchenette, a cramped bedroom without a closet, and his own bath. He insisted on his own bath. It was one of the few appealing things about this dump. Most of the houses he'd looked at hadn't had two baths, and he wasn't about to share one. Not ever again.

He glanced around the front room, checking the place

out, making sure nothing was awry. He always made a routine search when he came home, including looking behind the sagging brown couch. Except for a few items, the sparse furniture belonged to the landlady. He owned the weight bench and an old leather trunk. A special leather trunk with a small hidden compartment that no one knew about. No one except him.

In the bedroom he bent to look under the bed, then sat down and took off his shoes. When he had systematically lined them up with the others, he hung up his clothes and put his socks in the plastic trash can he used as a clothes hamper.

He had use of the laundry room downstairs, but he preferred to wash his clothes in his own sink. He didn't think the old bag who owned the house was very clean, and he didn't want his clothes put in her washing machine.

Donevan pulled on a faded terry robe, then reached into his pants pocket and removed the rope necklace. He ran his fingers over it for a moment before shoving it into his robe pocket. He smiled as he went to the kitchen.

When he opened the old refrigerator and discovered a tray of food there, he gritted his teeth. He'd told that dumb bitch not to bring him anything. He didn't want to eat her food. That's why he rented a room with a kitchen. He liked to cook for himself. And he didn't like her invading his place. He couldn't trust anybody!

Suddenly furious, he swept the tray out of the refrigerator. He watched as a bowl of homemade soup, a pink-colored beef patty, and a single slice of bread crashed to the floor. He didn't even like vegetables. And he liked his meat well done. For a moment he stared down at the mess, his anger deepening. Then he started to clean it up.

A knock on the door made him tense. Still shaking with anger, he strode to the door and pulled it open. His landlady was standing in the hall.

"Are you all right?" she asked, wrinkled brow furrowed. "I heard a loud noise."

Donevan flexed his fingers and wondered how the old broad would like to never hear anything else in her life. If she didn't mind her own damned business, he'd choke her senseless.

He liked the thought of the old woman lying helpless at his feet. It excited him. He felt that tingling beginning down in his privates.

"Mr. Raitt?"

His name drew his wandering thoughts together. He had to stop thinking so wild. It might make him do something stupid. He'd almost made one mistake today. He wouldn't make another.

He smiled his imitation smile, trying to make the nosy hag think he was glad to see her. You never knew when her good opinion might come in handy.

"I'm starving. I was in such a hurry to eat that food you fixed me that I dropped the tray," he said, impressed by his ingenuity. He gestured behind him and did his best to look apologetic. "I'm afraid the dishes broke and the food spilled everywhere, Mrs. Smith."

As the woman peered around him at the strewn food and utensils, her weathered face creased more deeply. "Oh, Mr. Raitt," she said in a sympathetic tone, "I'm so sorry. And I don't have anything else to give you. It's a pity you dropped them."

"It really is," Donevan said, his mind whirling. He had to get out of here before he went nuts. "Listen, I think I'll go to the store and get a steak."

"I'll cook it for you," she offered.

"No, I couldn't ask you to do that."

She beamed at him. "I insist. I want to."

Donevan didn't want to encourage her to start coming around his rooms any more than she was already doing, but he just had to get the hell out of here!

"Do you want me to get you one?" he asked.

She shook her head. "You're such a dear to offer, but really, I've already eaten."

"There's nothing like a woman's cooking, and I sure was in the mood for it," he added hastily, barely able to keep the sarcasm out of his voice. "That prison food—well, you know . . ." he said, letting the words trail off. When he rented this place, he'd had to tell her he'd been in prison.

The landlady gave him a motherly smile. "I'll be more than happy to cook your steak, Mr. Raitt. I have sons, and they always did say the same thing—nothing like a woman's home cooking."

"I won't be gone long." Donevan then closed the door and hurriedly pulled on street clothes. He was glad it was still raining. He would wear the green raincoat and hat. He liked them. Tossing a scarf around his neck, he raced out the back entrance.

He was proud he'd rushed away before he'd said something he might regret. He hated that mother-son shit! He didn't think he could have talked to the old lady another minute.

He didn't really know where he was headed, but he got in the truck and drove off. Soon he realized he'd started in the direction of the druggie girl's house. It was what he'd wanted all along, and he knew it.

Sure, he'd buy a damned steak and come back for the old lady to cook it, but first he was going to the girl's place. She had been on his mind too much. Besides, he was angry about the old woman snooping in his rooms. Somebody had to pay for his anger. It always produced poison, and that had to be released.

Adrenaline surged through him, heightening all his senses as he stomped the pedal and roared out the driveway. He could shave five minutes off his time if he sped just a little going and coming. He recalled seeing a market on the way. He would hurry in the market.

And then he'd pay that druggie bitch a little visit. But this time she wouldn't slam the door in his face. He wouldn't give her the chance.

# ⟳ CHAPTER 10 ⟳

The excitement was building in Donevan. He could feel that rush going through him; he was getting a hard-on. He wished he had time to do something about it, but he didn't. There would be time later, when he rethought about it.

After he had parked in the supermarket lot, he walked very quickly into the store. An employee was stocking shelves. Distracted, in a hurry, Donevan bumped into the display, causing a pyramid of grapefruit juice cans to crash to the floor.

"Jesus," he muttered. This was the last thing he needed. Then he suddenly grinned to himself. What the fuck? It would work fine—make one hell of an alibi if he needed one.

"Shit! I'm sorry," he exclaimed loudly, calling more attention to himself. He was tempted to touch the man to make more of an impression, but he couldn't bring himself to put a hand on the stranger. Instead, he bent down and began to gather up the scattered cans.

"I'll do it," the employee said in a disgruntled voice.

"Thanks," Donevan said, looking at his watch. "I've got a dinner date. Listen, man, I'm really sorry. I'll pay for the damage."

"That won't be necessary," the employee muttered.

"You're sure?"

"Yes."

The man's expression said that he'd remember Donevan

for a long, long time, and all he wanted at the moment was for him to get the hell out of there.

Donevan nodded and did just that. He grabbed up the first two steaks he saw and impulsively took a loaf of bread and an apple pie on the way out. He might really be hungry when he got back to his place.

He found himself in a dilemma when he reached the girl's apartment. Shit! He really hadn't had time to think this out carefully. Where was he going to park? And what about a disguise?

Jesus! What was he doing here anyway? But he knew the answer to that. He'd had to come. Hell, she'd practically invited him. The dumb bitch just didn't know that he never forgot that kind of invitation. Or forgave it, either.

He was getting nervous. He took comfort in the familiar panicky feeling. He savored it. It only added to his pleasure.

He glanced at the apartment where the girl had vanished. When he didn't see a light, he cursed bitterly beneath his breath.

"Fucking son of a bitch!" Maybe she wasn't home.

He drove around the block to the busy street and boldly parked in the long line of vehicles. Then he glanced around, slid away from the truck, slipping on the gloves he had taken from work, and used the side street where the drug dealer had been selling to cross over to the girl's street.

Sneaking around to the back entrance of the apartment, Donevan felt his head throbbing. He had that feeling that he liked best of all: that mix of fear and excitement. His heartbeat seemed to echo in his ears, booming louder and louder. His palms were so sweaty that he could hardly get out the credit card.

He was in luck. The door didn't have a dead bolt. The ignorance of women always amazed him, though he didn't know why it should. Holding his breath, he eased open the door. It didn't make a sound. He was inside.

His gaze darting everywhere as he tried to adjust to the

darkness, he quietly shut the door, making sure it was unlocked in case he had to make a hasty escape. He was in agony and ecstasy as he made his way stealthily through the seamy apartment.

The curtains at the windows had been made from old bed sheets, so there was some light filtering in from the street lamps. He was disappointed by the shabbiness and disarray. He'd thought the girl looked especially clean. He'd been wrong, obviously. Still, that did little to dampen the thrill for him.

He sucked in his breath when he reached the bedroom. A little teddy bear–shaped night light cast a faint glow over the crummy mattress and box springs on the floor. The dark-haired girl was home! She was asleep right there in front of him!

Excitement sped through Donevan. He couldn't believe his luck! He acted without thought. Ripping the scarf from around his neck, he rapidly crossed the threadbare rug and grasped the girl's arm to pull her into a sitting position.

He'd never strangled anyone, and this girl was perfect. She was young and fragile-looking. Smaller than the masseuse.

She didn't cry out. She seemed to be in a sleep- or drug-induced stupor as Donevan, his heart hammering wildly, his mind spinning with the mix of madness and fear, wrapped the scarf around his hands and looped it around the girl's neck.

"Wayne!" she gasped, startled into a state of semiconsciousness. There was almost no struggle as she groaned and grimaced while she tried to get her fingers into the scarf cutting off her air supply. She jerked a little as Donevan tightened the material. He was breathing harder and harder himself. He felt a little dizzy. His mind spun wildly.

The power and the thrill he felt were almost excruciating in intensity. He climaxed without fully realizing it as the girl went limp beneath his stranglehold.

It had been so easy! He let her fall back on the mattress as he yanked his scarf away and stuffed it into his coat pocket. Her head jerked with the movement, then tilted to one side.

Donevan watched in fascination for a moment. He hadn't noticed until then that the girl was naked beneath the worn coverlet. His breathing was so ragged that it sounded like he was in the room with something wild. He was sweating profusely.

The thin gold chain around her neck seemed to glow eerily in the darkness. It had twisted to one side, pointing to her left breast. Donevan had forgotten all about the chains. He reached, then remembered there had been more than one chain.

"Shit!" he said aloud. What had happened to the other two? He didn't want their absence to ruin his fun, but he was pissed.

Hypnotically he ran his gloved fingers along the single strand of gold. He felt a tightening deep inside as he impulsively yanked the chain off, causing her head to loll.

Even in the scant light, he saw that somebody had beaten the bitch up. She had big bruises on her body. Donevan looked around, wondering where she might have hidden the other two chains. There was nothing else in the room. Hell, somebody else had probably beaten him to the gold, or she had sold it for a fix. He hit the girl's head with the back of his fist, causing it to roll in the other direction.

"Cunt!" he muttered, then jerked the cover over her face. What the hell? He'd done what he set out to do.

In fact, he felt wonderful! He had pulled it off! He was so high that he just wanted to get away and think about it all in his rooms. The thrill had been beyond compare. He felt such a release, such overwhelming freedom. He liked killing even better than rape. And it was cleaner.

But he still wanted to know what the big death and little death felt like coupled. With the masseuse.

It wasn't until he was back in the truck that he realized he had to hurry so the landlady could cook his steak. He looked at his watch. The old bitch probably hadn't paid any attention to the time.

Anyway, he didn't care. Suddenly he was exhausted. All he really wanted to do was think and then go to sleep.

Mia welcomed the morning when she got up the next day. She had slept unusually well, and she thought about the day ahead of her while she sipped herbal tea and enjoyed fresh fruit and toast and butter.

She glanced at her watch. Frank was on her appointment list today. After she gave him a massage, he was going to do some work around the house—the usual routine for Saturday. He oversaw the house and Soot when she was out of town.

Mia noted that Angie Esterbrook and Frannie Welch were also coming today. She finished her toast, poured herself another cup of tea, and went to her study. She stared at the bulletin board pensively. Rand was coming today, too. But then, she had known that before she checked the board. She was looking forward to it more than she should. At least he was the last appointment; she could give her attention totally to the others before she lost herself in Rand.

She pondered her choice of words as she recalled Rand's kiss. It would be so easy to lose herself in him, so very, very easy.

Mia knew Frank was at the door by his lazy knock. He was perhaps the most laid-back person she had ever met. He was five minutes late, but then, she had come to expect that from Frank, too. He never hurried. And apparently he rarely worried.

She went to the door, eager to see his slow smile. "Good afternoon, Frank. How are you?"

He shrugged. "Same as always."

"Yes, I'll bet you are," she agreed with a laugh. "Do you want a cup of tea before your massage?"

He shook his head. "No, thanks. The massage will put me

to sleep. I don't want to have anything else going on in my body when you work on me."

Knowing that he wasn't joking, she smiled. He had fallen asleep on her table plenty of times, but he wasn't the only one. Some people relaxed so totally that she had to rouse them to get them to turn over or go home.

"Come on back," she said, leading the way.

"Looks like I'll be doing some fertilizing today after I prune," he commented. "Spring is well under way. It's a mighty fine day out."

"Yes, it seems to be," she agreed. "The rain has stopped for a while. I think I actually saw sunshine when I looked out."

"Yep."

The day was still chilly, and Mia had a fire going in the massage room. Frank, completely comfortable in the nude, stripped off his clothes and walked to the bathroom to hang them up on the door. Mia welcomed his nonchalant attitude. She herself often went nude when she was alone in the house so that her skin could breathe.

She recalled how fortunate she was to have found Frank. When he applied for the handyman job, she had been reluctant to hire him. He was an educated man, and she couldn't help but question why he wanted menial work. He had offered only the sketchiest of explanations.

Mia was thankful she'd taken a chance on him, despite his antisociety attitude and colorful earring. As they grew to trust each other, he hinted at a skirmish with the law which had involved cocaine. Apparently he had barely escaped serving time; when he had the opportunity, he had left town. He had envisioned Oregon as the last frontier, and he had not been disappointed. Extremely intelligent, with a music degree, he chose to make his living at odd jobs and teaching an occasional pupil to play stringed instruments.

"I wrote another song for you last night," Frank said, getting on the table and casually stretching out.

"Did you?" Mia was excited. She loved his songs and was always pleased when he said one was especially for her.

"Yep."

"Sing it to me before we start," she eagerly requested.

She leaned against the cupboard and listened as he sang the words in his precise, accented voice. When he had finished, she clapped her hands.

"It's wonderful. Why don't you try to sell it?"

"Money doesn't matter to me, Mia. You know that. I write for the pleasure of writing."

"Doesn't everyone want to be rich and famous?" she teased.

Frank frowned. "Rich doesn't interest me, and fame is definitely not for me," he said succinctly.

"But, Frank," she reasoned, "why deprive the world of such a lovely song?"

He shrugged and closed his eyes.

Mia dropped the subject, turned back to her oil, and got ready to work. In minutes Frank was sleeping soundly.

Angie parked her Mercedes in the drive and idly tapped her artificial nails on the padded steering wheel. She was early, and she knew that Mia kept strictly to her schedule, no matter *who* the client was. That fact had annoyed her terribly when she discovered that she was expected to wait out in the driveway like everyone else.

But what could she do? The masseuse didn't seem to care in the least if she was upset about it. Mia had calmly suggested that Angie clock the distance to the house and allow only enough time to drive here.

When Angie attempted to secure better treatment by hinting that she could triple Mia's business if she chose to tell the right people, the masseuse had politely responded that she had only limited openings and more clients than she could accept.

Angie leaned back against the plush seat. She supposed

she should be grateful *she* received an appointment. Even at that, she suspected it was only because Dr. Housen had asked Mia to see her.

She pulled down the sun visor and stared at her reflection in the long, narrow mirror. She generally got what she wanted. If her husband, James, couldn't buy it for her, he could spend enough money to influence someone to get it. The best of everything: that was what she wanted, and that was what she got.

With one exception, she reminded herself bitterly. Sex. James doled it out in stingy amounts once every three months.

She toyed with a short dyed black curl as she studied her features. James should be eager to go to bed with her. She really looked terrific at fifty-four, even if she did have to work at it. The face-lift had helped, but she only had that done because Retta Block kept bragging about getting hers done by an incredible doctor in Tahiti. That's where she had gone, too.

She raised the visor and glanced down at her watch. She still had five minutes to wait. She was tempted to go to the door and rap until Mia answered, but she didn't have the nerve. She laughed to herself. Imagine a little masseuse intimidating *her!*

But she didn't want to anger Mia. The massages were miracles. The headaches had lessened considerably in the past five months. She didn't want them to return to their original full horror.

She recalled reading somewhere that some president had said if he didn't have sex every night, he got a headache. Sometimes she seriously wondered if that wasn't her problem.

When she saw movement in the yard, she gazed out at the gardener. He wasn't bad-looking; however, he certainly wasn't good-looking. The man was really rather ordinary, about five feet ten inches, lean, with reddish hair.

Angie wondered what Mia saw in him. She was so

exceptional. She was sleeping with him, of course. Everybody in town knew that. Angie's gaze flickered over him again. Perhaps he was an extraordinary lover, a real stud. There had to be some reason for Mia keeping him around. She would give her eyeeteeth to know what it was. It would make delicious gossip at her next party.

She wished Mia would come to one of her parties, but so far she had been elusive. Wouldn't that be a zinger if she could get the masseuse to attend? The woman would be gossip fodder for weeks. She was going to have to try some other way of persuading Mia—discreetly, of course.

When she glanced at the front door, she saw the masseuse standing there. She slid out of the car and made her way to the front porch without bothering to speak to Frank. After all, he was only the gardener.

"Mia, sweetheart, how are you today?" she asked, sweeping into the house. "I've been waiting for ever so long. Are you running late?"

Undaunted, Mia shook her head. "Perhaps you're early."

Angie pretended to study her watch. "Oh, I hope this isn't on the fritz! James paid two thousand dollars for it. He'll be so upset."

"Shall we get started?" Mia asked, leading the way to the massage room.

"By all means," Angie said, following closely behind. "By the way, dear, have you heard that the little writer who has the appointment after mine is in serious financial trouble? They say she's almost broke! Can you imagine? After she earned all that money on that book! I wonder if it's true."

Mia drew in a calming breath. "I wouldn't know. I hope it isn't."

"Oh?" Angie pursed her lips. "I think it would serve her right. Who is she, anyway? Strutting around, expecting everybody to fawn over her. Ridiculous!" She smiled smugly. "Whether or not you have a social life in this town depends upon whether or not Angie Esterbrook includes you on her guest list. I invited her to only one of my parties.

I'm told she was a little nothing before the book. Now she will be again."

When Mia didn't comment, Angie waved a ringed hand in dismissal. She could never seem to interest the masseuse in her gossip, and it irritated her. "I'll just go and change."

Mia watched as the other woman went to the bathroom, and she wondered how she was going to reach her. Should she continue to try? Even though she worked at not making a difference in her clients and fully realized that Angie had very real problems, including crippling migraine headaches, the woman tested her patience. She seemed to live her life to be a thorn in everyone else's side.

Mia saw her behavior as the bid for attention that it was, but she found it difficult to cope with the woman's intentional malice. She had to be in a generous state of mind to work with someone who wreaked havoc on other people's lives with no regard to the damage she did with her sharp tongue, with no thought to the inevitable results of her anger, envy, and careless use of money. There were other people who seemed in much more desperate need.

Distracted while she worked, Mia barely listened to Angie's pointed chatter. Most of it wasn't worth listening to anyway. She was glad when the massage was over and was tempted to tell Angie she wouldn't work on her again.

Yet to do so went against Mia's nature. She knew, despite Angie's vindictive streak and cruel tongue, that the woman benefited from her massages. It wasn't in Mia to deprive Angie of that.

As Mia watched Angie put her jewelry on, she imagined how much it must have cost. She wondered if the woman valued it at all.

Mia's own favorite piece of jewelry was a hemp necklace an old woman had made especially for her when she was in India on her travels. She didn't recall seeing it in her jewelry box the last time she looked. Although it was worthless to anyone but her, she would be very disappointed if she'd lost it.

When Angie left, Mia went in search of her necklace. It wasn't in her jewelry box. She had a sinking feeling inside. Even though she knew better than to become attached to material things, she loved the necklace dearly. She couldn't imagine what she'd done with it.

She wondered if someone had stolen it, then quickly brushed the thought aside. As long as she had worked out of the cottage, no one had ever taken anything. There was no reason to believe the hemp necklace, of all things, would be stolen. Who would have possibly taken it?

## ━ CHAPTER 11 ━

Frank was working in the yard when Frannie Welch arrived. Mia watched from the window as the young woman parked her car and climbed out on impossibly tall heels. She always had a smile on her face, no matter how strained.

Mia sometimes thought her brittle cheerfulness would break and fall about the woman in a hundred pieces, but it never did. Frannie waved to Frank. He waved back, then continued to work.

Her smile intact, Frannie tossed back her long, frizzy blond hair as she paraded up the walk. She paused for a moment, glancing back over her shoulder at the man. Then she stepped up on the front porch. The split in the front of her skirt revealed more than a little of her leg, and she glanced back once more to see if the gardener was watching.

"Hi there," she cooed as seductively as she could. "How are you today?"

Frank grinned at her. "I'm just fine. And you?"

She winked. "I'm always fine."

"You're sure looking good, I'll have to say that."

Frannie smiled broadly. She wondered if the man knew her; if he had read her book. It was a small town and she was a big deal. At least, she had been.

It was the local-girl-makes-good story, and it had been played to the hilt. She had hit the fiction best-seller list with her first book; she had been interviewed by every newspaper, radio program, and television talk show from here to Los Angeles, earning a quarter of a million dollars.

But that had been five years ago, and she hadn't written a decent word since. Every day when she sat at her expensive computer, all she could bring to her mind was increasing terror.

She wasn't a *real* writer. And she certainly wasn't an overnight success. She wasn't a glamorous darling of the publishing world. She wasn't even Frannie Welch.

She was Frances Wachasky. She had grown up thirty miles down the road with parents who could barely speak English. As an only child who had inherited the worst of both parents' features, she had been teased and tormented and talked about until she had retreated behind her big nose, her big breasts, and her library books.

Her sensational best-seller had taken seven years to write. Seven long years of pouring out her heart and her soul and her gut-deep despair. While she lived at home, afraid to step out into the world and make her own way. While she worked alongside her mother, making crafts that her father sold in a little roadside shop.

She had written about her dreams and her hopes and her real-life failures, camouflaging it all by setting the story in an earlier century. And she had kept rewriting the story until the heroine succeeded. She was twenty-five years old when she finally found an agent, and still she had to keep reshaping the book to please the agent and the editors when they were finally interested.

Then she had waited that agonizing year for it to be published. To see if she had failed once more. In the interim she took a healthy portion of the advance and reshaped herself. She took a bus to another city and had both her nose and her breasts reduced. She also had her hair lightened and permed.

When the book started to do well, the savvy agent took Frances under her wing and coached her in the ways of the publishing world. They created a bio, complete with an aristocratic European ancestor and a lover who was the model for the hero in the book.

The ancestor hadn't made any difference to Frances, but the lover had. At the time the book was published, she had slept with only two men—actually one boy and one man. The boy had been a blue-eyed nightmare who lived still in her mind in the middle of the night, a nightmare that so shamed and frightened her she'd never told another soul. She still bore the scars. Mentally and physically.

Her mind began to drift to that awful, awful time.

She had been such a lonely teenager, so lonely and so innocent. She had seen the blue-eyed boy many times in class or hanging around the schoolyard. He, like she, was always alone. She'd tried repeatedly to get up the nerve to speak to him, but, though he stared at her sometimes, he never responded to her trembling smile.

Until the day of the Sadie Hawkins dance. Heart hammering, knees shaking, she'd waited for the blue-eyed boy after school. She had asked him to go to the dance, and he had agreed.

To this day she recalled every word of the limited conversation and the events that followed. She just blurted out the question the moment she caught up with him.

"Will you go to the dance with me?" she'd stammered, sweating and hoping and praying she wouldn't be rejected.

He'd looked startled, as though he didn't know if she was talking to him or not. His eyes narrowed as he looked around, then right at her. He paused for a bit, then grinned oddly.

"I'll meet you behind the gym at nine o'clock."

The dance began at seven. Why was he waiting until nine to meet with her? She tried not to let her disappointment show. At least he'd said yes to her invitation.

"Nine o'clock," she affirmed.

After he left she hurried home to tell her mother the news. She was so excited! She had a date! There was no time to spare. Even though dress for the dance was costume, hillbilly outfits, she wanted hers to be special. After all, this was her very first date, no matter how she got it.

Together she and her mother worked on cutting off a pair of jeans for her, patching them with colorful swaths of cloth, and making a matching top and matching ribbons for her hair, which she would wear in braids. She had doubted that her date could have afforded to attend a dance that required a suit, but this should be easy for him. She imagined him trying on boots and old clothes for his costume.

The week seemed to drag by endlessly, and then finally the night of the dance arrived.

No matter how many times she tried to forget, she remembered the occasion in horrid detail. He had been waiting for her behind the gym at nine as he'd said, but he was dressed in ordinary clothes—slacks, a shirt, and loafers.

Frances wondered if he knew what a Sadie Hawkins dance was, but she'd tried not to show her dismay. He seemed reluctant enough as it was. He nervously smoked a cigarette as she arrived, all aflutter, her heart dancing before her feet ever had the chance.

"I'm a little uptight," he announced abruptly.

Although Frances's heart was beginning to slow down and she was starting to think that she didn't have a date after all, she tried to make things all right. She told herself he was really just nervous, and so was she.

"We'll be all right once we get inside," she said in a voice too high to sound reassuring. "I've never gone to a dance, either."

His blue eyes narrowed. "Listen, let's just walk around the grounds a little first, okay. You know, kind of get our nerve up." He looked her up and down in the scant light of the naked bulb over the gym's back door. "The truth is," he confessed, "I've never had a date before."

Frances smiled. "Me, neither," she admitted.

They started walking down the hill toward some bushes, and Frances braved attempting to take his hand; however, he shoved both of them in his pockets. Feeling hurt, she went along behind him, hoping this night wasn't going to be a complete disaster.

When they reached the bushes, he suddenly tossed his cigarette to the ground, deliberately and slowly crushed it with his shoe heel, then grabbed Frances and threw her to the ground, too. She was so caught by surprise that she didn't even have time to cry out. Before she could decide what was going on, he put his hand over her mouth.

"Don't make a sound or I'll mess you up bad," he muttered.

She didn't think she could make a sound if she had to. This was supposed to be the fulfillment of her dream, her first date. She'd been so elated to finally find a boy who wanted to go out with her that she couldn't believe this devastating situation was actually happening.

She looked up at the sky and fought the tears that rushed to her eyes. A three-quarter moon seemed to mock her as she lay beneath this boy who was treating her so cruelly. His hands hurt on her body, and she was more scared than she'd ever been in her life.

She kept asking herself over and over why nothing went right for her. Why couldn't she be an average teenager like the other girls? Why didn't people like her? Why did everybody mistreat her? Why would this boy agree to go out with her, then do this?

Suddenly he removed his hand to unzip his pants, and Frances wanted to scream with every ounce of strength in her. But she found that she had none. She was crushed just as surely as the cigarette had been.

He roughly tugged at her jeans and panties, uncaring that

she was lying on hard, uneven stony earth. It actually hadn't dawned on her that he intended to rape her until he tossed her clothing aside and tried to shove his rigid penis up inside her.

It hurt so bad that she gasped in surprise.

"Don't!" she whispered weakly. "Please don't do this."

She was startled into submission when he struck her across the face, but that pain was nothing compared to the pain in her vagina. It was almost unbearable. She was a virgin, and it felt as if he were literally trying to rip her apart as he rammed and rammed himself at her. He was having an awful time penetrating, and she could tell that he was getting angrier by the minute.

"What the hell's going on, bitch?" he demanded. "What are you doing? What's wrong with you?" He held on to his penis, trying to help himself force his way in. His hand added to the pain Frances felt.

"I don't know what's wrong." She sobbed. "I've never . . . "

He struck her again. "I know you're not a virgin, bitch, so don't try that shit on me. Whatever you're doing to block my dick, you'd better stop, and I'm not kidding!"

"I—I'm not doing anything," she said, tears falling. "I—"

"Shut up that fucking crying!" he hissed. "You stupid cunt, do something to make this work before I hurt you bad. This is your fault!"

Frances writhed in agony. It hurt so bad now that she could hardly stand it, but he kept hammering away until finally he seemed to physically tear into her, shoving himself up inside her with such force that she thought she might throw up from fear and pain.

Suddenly he withdrew his penis and stared down at it.

"I'm bleeding, you fucking cunt! What the hell? You *cut* me with something! You sick bitch! What have you done to my dick? Jesus, I hate blood," he groaned.

"I . . . " Frances moaned.

"Shut the fuck up!" he growled furiously. "I've heard of bitches who put things up in their snatches to hurt a man, but, Jesus, I can't believe it! I'm bleeding," he repeated, clearly shocked.

Frances tried again to tell him that she was a virgin, but he began to hit her. Then, spying a jagged rock close by, he picked it up and slammed it down on her forehead.

Frances groaned and lay quiet and still, hoping the boy would kill her and get it over with or leave her alone.

He was trying to look at his penis. Abruptly, he shoved it back in his pants, zipped up, and ran off.

Frances didn't know how long she lay on the ground, wounded and petrified. The sounds of laughter and music reached her when someone opened the back door to the gym. She struggled to get up, even though she didn't want anyone to see her. She knew that she was hidden in the bushes, but she had to get home. Her head pounded like the wrath of God, and she ached to sit in a tub of water and wash herself clean of the filth spilling from her.

She was bleeding from down there and from her head wound. She didn't know what he had struck her with, but her forehead felt like it had been split open. She struggled to sit up and find her clothes. At least he was gone.

When the noise at the back of the gym quieted down, she stiffly, slowly made her way back up the hill. There was a water fountain outside the door, and she knew she had to wash up before she went home. She couldn't possibly tell her parents what had happened. She was too hurt and humiliated. She would never tell anyone.

Donevan lay on his small cot flipping through the pages of the book he'd stolen from the masseuse. Some of the pictures were very sexy, but he wasn't all that interested. What really interested him was the client list he'd written in front of the paperback.

Frannie Welch's name taunted him. Today was her appointment day. Donevan had wanted to go to the masseuse's house and see what this Frannie looked like. Apparently she was unlisted or lived with somebody else. She was probably married.

He'd found the addresses of the others and had even driven by their houses. But he really wanted to know about this woman. The fact that he couldn't find her griped him real bad. It was almost like she thought she could outsmart him.

However, he'd just been too drained to drive to the cottage. He'd had to put up with the ruse of dinner with his landlady after he'd returned last night, then he couldn't get to sleep. He'd spent all night reliving the events of the day, especially the strangling.

He began to get excited all over again as he thought of tightening the scarf around the girl's neck. Jesus! What a high! What power!

He strained to hear the news as it came on his small portable radio. He didn't hear anything about the murder. Just as he'd suspected. Nobody gave a shit about a dead druggie bitch. He was a little disappointed. Somewhere inside he wanted the whole world to know what he'd done. On the other hand that would be real stupid.

He knew that what he really wanted to do was go back over to the girl's apartment and look at her again. Now that it was all over, it seemed kind of like a dream. It had happened too fast.

But he was too smart to return. He'd just stay right here for now. He reached for the chain he'd ripped from the girl's neck. He'd washed it in bleach and discovered that it was a piece of shit. It had turned green. He fondled it a few minutes anyway, then laid it aside in favor of the rope necklace he'd taken from the masseuse's jewelry box.

It was three strands of hemp woven together. At least a foot long, the necklace had been knotted at three intervals. A little silver cross hung at the bottom. Donevan kept fingering the knots, then jerking the rope between his hands, making the cross dance.

He wondered where the masseuse had gotten the strange piece of jewelry. He wondered if she wore it often. He swung it around his fingers and tugged on the strands, testing the strength of the rope. It appeared to be very strong. When he slipped it over his head and felt it around his own neck, he expected it to itch, but it didn't. He pulled it tight and held it with his hand.

He liked the feel of it, and he teased himself with it for a few seconds, twisting it a little more and still a little more. Then he had a better idea. He took it off and made a slipknot. He eased the necklace back over his head and gradually began to move the knot closer to his Adam's apple.

His heart started pounding. He felt his pulse race. The excitement was building deep down in his genitals. He was burning and quivering. He thought about the powerful feeling he'd had when he strangled the girl.

Suddenly there was a knock at his door.

"Shit!" Donevan muttered, the word raspy, his breathing harsh. "Who the hell?"

"Mr. Raitt?"


While she waited for the masseuse to come to the door, Frannie absently fingered the necklace around her throat and tried to stop thinking about the boy who had changed her life. A man had changed it, too. He had been nine years older with a wife and five children.

The liaison had created tremendous guilt in her, and fear that she would be found out. She had finally had the courage to end it after five years, although she had loved the man deeply. He had been good for her, even if she had been a dirty little secret he didn't want the world to know about.

"Penny for your thoughts," Frank said, breaking into her painful reverie.

Frannie started. She had forgotten the man was standing

there! "They aren't worth a penny," she replied, thinking how ironic it was that men now found her attractive. She had slept with a few, but it hadn't amounted to anything. None of them had talked marriage. Not even when they thought she was wealthy, she reminded herself bitterly.

She knew why. They had all read her book. And she couldn't live up to the character she had created. Beneath all the obvious changes, she was still Frances Wachasky, wallflower.

It was just as well. Her money had gone almost as fast as her fame. It was only here, in town, that people stopped her every day and asked how the new book was going. She always smiled and said fine. What else could she say?

Then she went home and got down on her knees and prayed that the book would finally be fine, that she could come up with something, some idea that would work. Yet she knew that she had written it all when she wrote the first book. She knew that, but she couldn't stop trying.

She had exhausted all her other resources. Her editor had gotten tired of waiting for a proposal for a second book. Her agent had finally given up, too. Even her parents had deserted her, dying in an automobile accident last year. Frances had only herself to rely on.

"Good afternoon. Come on in."

Frannie whirled around, her long blond hair bouncing with the movement. She hadn't realized Mia had opened the door.

"Hello, Mia," she said with exaggerated warmth. "How are you today?"

"I'm fine. And you?"

"Fine! I'm always fine. It's the creative energy, you know. It keeps me so up, so high. It's wonderful to sit in my office and create marvelous characters who do the most incredible things all day long. I never know what they'll do, but that's part of the joy, the excitement. They're just like real people to me, like my friends. I wrote fifteen pages today, and I could sense that they were very good," she said passionately, breathlessly, her words chasing after each other. She smiled. "It's because I love my work so much."

She didn't know why she kept up the lies, the pretense. The illusion of the famous romance writer living the good life was so ingrained in her that she responded automatically with pat answers. The interviews had trained her to have a stream of ready replies, and now she couldn't seem to stop using them.

"I'm glad," Mia said, even though she suspected that Frannie was lying to both of them. As she had before, Mia heard the desperation beneath the boast. She heard the plea for reassurance. When she was in California, she had often seen the mating of ego and insecurity; she was familiar with the neuroses intimately connected with artistic temperament. But she believed that this author was in deeper emotional trouble than the usual ups and downs of the career.

She had heard the woman's tales, and she had heard the town's tales. There was talk that Frannie shut herself up in her office for days and had crying fits. While Mia didn't generally give gossip the dignity of belief, she suspected that there was more truth to the tales than even the townspeople knew. Five years was a long time to work on any novel, particularly without tangible results.

"I've been trying to understand God and His will for us better," Frannie said brightly, keeping up a stream of chatter as she went to the bathroom and undressed. "I believe He means for us to live a full life. He doesn't want us to labor without reward."

Mia thought about what Angie Esterbrook had said about Frannie being broke, and she wondered if the other woman had learned it from her bank president husband.

"I love writing," Frannie continued, climbing up on the massage table, "but surely God wants us to stay sound in body and mind. I can come for massages for the body; still, they do cost money."

As Mia began to work, she listened to Frannie discuss

God and work and money. She felt sad because the woman didn't know that in fighting herself so hard, she was denying God. She wondered what the writer would say if she told her. She reminded herself that she couldn't make people see anything they weren't ready to see.

Frannie was on a crusade of cheerfulness, her mask firmly in place. Mia couldn't change that. She could only hope that she could somehow put the woman in touch with herself and her potential. Frannie had written a best-seller; she had given Mia a copy. She did have a real God-given talent. She needed someone who cared to help her see it.

Mia made herself concentrate on the woman's chatter about her fan mail. "Isn't it incredible that it's still coming after all this time? The book isn't even on the shelves anymore. They really, really loved me," Frannie said with a forced smile.

"I'm sure they did. They still do. You wrote a wonderful, compelling book."

"Do you really think so?" Frannie asked, glancing over her shoulder.

"Yes, I do," Mia said, motioning for the woman to turn over. "I want to work primarily in the head area today to free your creative juices."

Unexpectedly, before she even smoothed back the bleached, curly hair, Mia recalled the jagged scar she had seen previously beneath Frannie's fluffy bangs right at the hairline. She was reminded that Frannie had suffered a brutal blow at some point.

"That's why I come," Frannie said brightly.

When Mia had finished the massage and sent Frannie on her way, she watched from the open doorway as the woman spoke to Frank again, her voice artificially high and bright.

"Good-bye."

Frank turned around and smiled at her as he leaned lazily on his shovel. "Bye."

Frannie spun on her heel and headed for her car. She looked back over her shoulder once more to see if Frank was watching. When she saw that he was, she made a production out of getting into the car, then smiled again and drove off.

Sadly shaking her head, Mia returned to the massage room to ready both it and herself for Rand's appointment.

## ← CHAPTER 12 →

When Rand arrived, Mia tried her best to treat him as any other client, but that proved impossible. The moment she saw him, her heart began its crazy rhythm.

"Hello, pretty lady," he murmured in that sexy voice of his.

"Hello, Rand." Mia frantically searched her mind for casual conversation. "Did you find some place to eat last night, or have you arrived on my doorstep starving?"

He laughed. He wanted to tell her that he was indeed starving and what for, but he just nodded.

"I found a place."

"Well, let's get busy then," she said nervously.

As he followed her down the hall, she kept recalling his kiss. It was only natural to think that he would try to kiss her again. Or did she think that because she wanted it so much?

When he returned from the bathroom, dressed in a towel, she could hardly catch her breath. She kept her back to him while he got on the table, but she couldn't seem to shake the sexual attraction to this man, raging full blown inside her. Her control and concentration were minimal, at best. This time she couldn't tune into the power she needed to work. She had to stop halfway through the massage again.

This was really impossible with her hands trembling and

her breathing labored. When she resumed stroking Rand's skin, she considered telling him that this would be the last massage she could give him. While she was thinking of how to say it, Rand began to talk.

"Are you coming to California soon? Isn't it time for your regular trek to the land down under?"

Mia struggled with a smile. "I thought that was Australia."

"In this case it's California," he said with a grin as he shifted on his pillow and looked back at her.

"I'll be there at the end of the month."

"Then I'll see you before I go to Australia?"

"So that's why you're thinking of the land down under."

"I'll be gone for several weeks working on my new film. I don't suppose I could talk you into coming?"

That was the last thing Mia needed, to be off with Rand in a foreign country. She tried to sound carefree in her refusal. "No, I don't suppose you could, but it is a wonderful thought."

Rand rolled over on his side and looked at her, his dark eyes serious. "People over there need massages, too, especially actors with hectic schedules."

She lowered her eyes and tried her best to continue to work. Did he have any idea how hard he was making this for her? "You're breaking the natural rhythm. Please lie back down."

"Sorry," he murmured, disappointed again. He hadn't really thought that she would come to the South Pacific, but once he mentioned it, he realized that it was the best idea he had had in months.

"I have clients booked weeks in advance," she said at last, knowing that she was tempted by his suggestion. She wouldn't allow herself to seriously consider it, of course, but she was suddenly coming up with all kinds of logic that might justify such a trip. She told herself that she really did need a break in her routine. Perhaps if she did go away somewhere again, she would be renewed as she had been in India and China.

She worked on Rand's back longer than was warranted, not wanting to face him. It took her some time to get a semblance of the flow of her work, and then she achieved it only at a cost to her inner stability. She understood that she wasn't fully in control when Rand turned over and she began to massage his chest; she was acutely aware that he was studying her. Her fingers moved through the dark hair too quickly, her rhythm ruined.

When she met his gaze, Rand said earnestly, "I'll pay you whatever you want for your time if you'll come with me, Mia."

"It's not just the money, Rand," she said with equal earnestness. "My clients need me."

Suddenly Rand sat up on the table and swung his legs over the side, the towel dropping down with the motion. "God, Mia," he said thickly, "I need you, too. You have no idea how much."

He pulled her in between his legs and caressed her mouth hungrily. Mia sucked in her breath as a tremor of intense desire shot through her. Rand was already aroused, his rigid penis pressing against her body. This time there was no denying the temptation he presented. It was too late to think about what she should or shouldn't do. Mia wanted this man as only a woman who's wanted too long can. She needed him.

She parted her lips, allowing Rand to stroke her tongue with his, plundering the sweet recesses of her mouth again and again to twine with his own. His hands roved searchingly over her face and neck, and soon he had found the single pin that held her sari up. He unclasped it and let the material fall away from her shoulder.

He drew in a shuddering breath as he gazed at her soft beauty. His fingers stroked down across the crest of her bosom reverently, lovingly, and Mia's nipples hardened at the gentle contact. It had been so very long since she'd been loved by a man, so very long since she'd let her body feel all these wondrous sensations. She ached deep inside with the quickening of desire and the flood of moist warmth.

She stepped back so that Rand could slide off the table, then she closed her eyes and held her breath as he removed her sari. She wanted to be everything he wanted her to be.

"God, you're gorgeous," he whispered huskily.

Mia could feel her mouth trembling. She opened her eyes, knowing that they were glazed by hunger. She allowed herself to look at Rand. She already knew how attractive he was.

"You are, too," she murmured. "So masculine and beautifully defined. I've always thought you looked like you were created by a sculptor."

Rand held one hand over hers, guiding her, encouraging her to stroke him while he caressed her breasts with the other hand.

"I've wanted you for so long," he said hoarsely. "So long."

When Mia quivered, he claimed her mouth again with his, drawing her fully up against his body. She felt the heat race through her as he gathered her tightly to him. His kisses were everywhere, at the corners of her mouth, across her nose, down her throat.

She moaned when he bent down to taste her aching nipple, his lips sucking gently, his tongue flickering back and forth across the sensitive skin.

"Rand, oh, Rand," she half sobbed.

She didn't think she could stand much more foreplay. She was throbbing with need. Her passion was a raging fire that roared inside her.

Rand traced the curves of her body with his hands, then stroked the soft inside of her thighs. Mia gasped when he slowly slid a finger inside her to test her readiness for him. The sensation was so erotic that she was afraid she would embarrass herself. She could feel her muscles contracting tightly as he moved his finger a little deeper inside her, then eased it in and out with long, slow, sensuous movements.

"You're so tight," he said huskily.

She tried to make a small joke, but she was shivering and quaking too badly to carry it off. "I'm a reborn virgin," she said.

"God, you feel like it," he whispered. "A virgin made for a man to love. Made for me to love."

He picked the towel up off the massage table, then guided Mia to the rug in front of the fireplace. When he had spread the towel out, he lay down on his back and held his arms out to her.

"Shit," Donevan muttered again. It was the old hag from downstairs. Who else had he expected? The police? His parole officer? His mother?

His lips turned up in an imitation smile at the absurdity of the last question. Then a vision of his mother filled his mind. He began to breathe harder as he felt his engorged flesh.

"Donevan," the old woman called in a softer, motherly voice. "Are you in there, son?"

Pretending that the landlady was his mother, ready to plunge into the room at any second, Donevan moved the knot up a tiny bit farther.

Sweat formed on his brow. The pressure of the rope bound his neck. He felt a little nausea and had to fight the urge to gag. The knots on the necklace bit into his skin. He wondered if this was what the girl had felt when he had tightened the scarf around her neck.

The fear began to swell inside him, riding the crest of the excitement, mingling and surging with each small tightening of the rope. Suddenly he ripped the cross off the end of the necklace, causing his head to jerk forward violently with the motion. Then he reached down and unzipped his pants.

With the hand that held the cross, he clasped his penis,

feeling the metal dig into the tender swollen skin. Then he masturbated with frenzied intensity, his hand moving faster and faster and faster. The rope around his neck seemed to get tighter and tighter.

Visions of the dead girl flashed through his mind with vivid clarity. They mingled with images of Mia. And of his mother. Donevan thought he would die from the thrill and the fear.

## ➤ CHAPTER 13 ➤

Donevan stood under the warm shower water, letting it pour down over his body. He still felt a little dizzy, but he didn't think about it as he gently washed his penis, giving all his attention to the angry red marks where the small cross had pressed into the skin. There were welts on his neck, but he would attend to them later. He still wore the necklace. As he leaned over, ministering to himself, the necklace swung away from his hairless chest. Donevan decided that he liked the feel of the rope. He liked it a lot.

He finished cleansing his penis, then cautiously touched his neck. It felt raw and sore, but the skin wasn't broken. He wouldn't have been happy if it was. He didn't want to feel any blood.

When he had completed his shower, he hung the necklace up to dry on the clothesline, next to the washed scarf he'd used to strangle the girl. He returned to the bathroom and put some ointment on his neck, smoothing it in until every trace of it was gone. Then he dressed in clean clothes and went to look out the window.

He couldn't seem to get the masseuse out of his thoughts. He considered going up to her house. The idea sent a shiver over his skin. He'd almost got caught the last time. Maybe it was too soon to go again. Especially after the strangling last night.

But that was what was so thrilling about it. There was a chance that he would get caught next time. But only a chance. He was too smart to have the odds against him.

Still, it had been so recent. Someone might have noticed his truck even though he had waited a very long time to go home. It really was too bad that only one road went to and from the house. Too bad, and very exciting.

Anyway, the next time he went when he wasn't scheduled for a massage, he was going to drive his car. And take the necklace. He couldn't do that now. It was wet.

He fingered the cord in his pants pocket. He really did want to go to the cottage today. The masseuse was staying on his mind more and more.

Mia was a bundle of nerves after Rand left. She had never intended to make love with him. He was forbidden to her, and she had only made the torture worse by loving him. It had been more fulfilling than she could have ever dreamed. But she wasn't prepared to become involved with Rand. Now she only wanted him more.

And she couldn't have him.

She had to work through her life with Troy until she was sure there was no hope for them. She believed in her vows; she believed in Troy. Most of all, she believed in the power of love to heal.

She was riddled with guilt. She truly felt her betrayal, her adultery. The fact that she had savored Rand with such complete abandon made it worse.

Although she had promised that she would see him when she went to California, she knew that this was one promise she would have to break.

How could she possibly give him a massage? How could

she even look at him and not burn with hunger, knowing as she did how exquisite, how explosive, his lovemaking was? No, she couldn't see him again. Of that she was positive.

She attempted every relaxation method she had ever studied, but she couldn't get control of herself. She stood staring out the window, watching the white car grow smaller and smaller in the distance, her troubles looming larger and larger as he vanished. A sudden knock on the door startled her.

"Mia."

She exhaled wearily. Frank. She had forgotten that Frank was still here. She honestly didn't know how she could deal with him at the moment. She forced a smile to her lips and went to answer.

"Come on in, Frank."

He held up two dead-bolt locks. "I want to install these. I'll do the front door today and the back next week. Vandalism has increased since the mill laid off so many people, and I don't want your house robbed while you're away."

"Oh, Frank, I don't really think that's necessary," she insisted. "I'm surprised you do."

He smiled. "I wouldn't for myself. I rarely lock my door. But then I'm not a gorgeous woman who has strangers in and out of the house constantly. Those same strangers will know that you're away when they can't schedule massages while you're gone."

"The house is so isolated. There's only the one road in and out of here."

"It only takes one," he said, arching red eyebrows. "One road, or the steps leading up from the beach."

"You're the caretaker," she said. "If you'll feel better about it, go right ahead."

"Good. I will."

"How long will it take? Would you like some dinner?"

"I wouldn't mind a bite," he said.

Mia went to the kitchen and scouted her refrigerator for something to prepare. She settled on yogurt with sliced fresh bananas, a garden salad, and hot whole wheat bread.

"I'm ready when you are," she called out to Frank as she placed the food on the table in front of windows which overlooked the ocean.

Seconds later he strolled into the room. "Nobody has to call me twice to dinner," he said with a grin. "I'll just wash up a little and be right back."

"You can use the bath in the massage room or the one down the hall."

By the time he returned, she had everything ready.

"This looks fine, especially if you're a bunny rabbit," Frank said as he seated himself. His laughing blue eyes met Mia's. "No wonder you never gain weight."

She smiled. "It's all very nutritious and filling, as I think you'll see."

They ate in silence for a few minutes, then Frank looked over at her.

"What's the story on Frannie Welch?"

"Now, Frank, you know I can't talk about one client to another," she said gently.

"Come on, Mia. I'm your friend, not just a client."

She shook her head. "It's a cardinal rule of mine, Frank." Still, she couldn't help but be curious about Frank's interest in Frannie.

He laughed. "You and your cardinal rules! Do you like the woman?"

"I like all my clients." She felt a blush steal over her skin. She wondered just what Frank would think about her cardinal rules if he had any idea that she had made love with Rand.

"If I don't," she continued quickly, trying not to recall how exquisite it had felt to be in Rand's arms, "I can't work with them."

A picture of Donevan Raitt rushed to mind, but Mia

suppressed it. She was sure he had his redeeming qualities, as did everyone. After all, she'd only had one session with the man.

"I read Frannie's book," Frank said. "I wonder if she's as hot as her writing suggests. She sure lives the life. Fancy house. Fancy car. Fancy clothes."

Mia smiled and shook her head. "I suspect not, Frank. After all, she's a writer doing a job. She creates fantasy."

"You don't think she lives all that stuff she writes about?" Frank looked disappointed, and Mia was both a little amused and surprised.

"Do you live your songs?" she asked.

He was thoughtful for a moment. "A lot of them."

Mia nodded. "You might, at that. Maybe songwriting and book writing aren't the best comparison, but they're both about emotions and feelings. I think a writer doing a four-hundred-page book has to rely heavily on imagination, don't you?"

He shrugged. "I suppose so, but did you see the way she looked at me?"

"Why, Frank, you're flattered by her interest," Mia teased lightly.

He laughed. "I'm thirty-four years old, and I've never been married. I'm weathered and worn and redheaded. I make my living doing odd jobs. I'm flattered by any woman's interest. And she *is* a successful writer. At least she was," he added thoughtfully. "I think five years is a couple of years too long to be on a second book. It sounds like to me she's resting on her laurels."

Mia nodded. "Maybe."

"Still, she's quite a combination—brains and beauty," Frank said as he went back to his salad. "She's accomplished more than most of us."

Mia reached out to touch his free hand. "Frank, you're more valuable and appealing than you know. You have healing properties. You're great with growing things, and you're very sensitive. You and I both know you do odd jobs because that's all you want to do. You have a real talent as a musician and a songwriter."

Frank was pensive for a moment, then he laughed aloud. "Now, why wasn't it you who looked at me that way instead of Frannie?" he joked.

Mia smiled to herself as she lifted a spoonful of yogurt to her mouth. She really cared for Frank. She'd love to see him happy. She'd love to see Frannie happy. The world was full of so many lonely, troubled people.

Lost in his thoughts, Donevan couldn't believe the landlady was at his door again, calling his name. He had important things on his mind. The last person in the world he wanted to be bothered with was that old bitch.

"Donevan," she called again. "I have a home-cooked meal for you, son."

He reached down and held his pecker in his hand. "And I've got something for you, too, you stupid old bitch," he muttered. Jesus, why couldn't she leave him alone?

He quickly left by the back way. She could shove her home-cooked meal up her ass. He headed directly to the masseuse's house and found himself getting real angry. If that nosy hag hadn't pushed him, he would have stayed right there in his rooms, which was the smart thing to do.

But, no, she had to come snooping and prying. He reached the top of the hill faster than he'd realized and carefully parked in the woods. Then he crept toward the cottage.

To his surprise, the masseuse was eating at the kitchen table with the redheaded queer gardener. He knew she gave Frank massages, and he'd followed the man home once to find out what he could about him. He'd been sure the weirdo was a queer just by the way he looked. He should know. He'd seen enough of the fucking mothers in prison.

His face warped with rage. He didn't want to think about prison and what happened there. It was sick, vile, and putrid. He fastened his gaze on the fag's gold hoop earring.

He was fascinated by the way the earring bounced as the fruit moved. Suddenly an idea occurred to him. He would pierce his own ear. He'd learned all kinds of things in prison. You just held two pieces of ice on the earlobe until it was numb, then jammed a hot needle through it. Even the biggest crybabies said it didn't hurt. It might come in handy to look like the homo.

It just might.

## ➤ CHAPTER 14 ➤

Sunday was Mia's day of rest. Often she spent her mornings lounging around the house with Soot, and her afternoons walking in the woods or strolling down the beach, looking for shells and sea urchins. She tried to keep her mind free of any troubling thoughts. She loved to commune with nature, and she never tired of the beauty around her. She had chosen Oregon for many reasons, but chief among them was the land. The state was still wide open and sparsely populated. She savored that after her years in California.

When Monday came, she was always rested and refreshed and ready to start a new week. She found that she especially needed her day of renewal after the week she had just gone through.

Rand played on her mind, persistent, despite her efforts to clear her thoughts of him. Donevan Raitt was almost as relentless. Mia wasn't going to see Donevan until Thursday; she needed to find some way to reach him before then, some way to unlock his emotions and defenses. She wasn't sure yet what it would be. She had to devise a technique that would allow her the freedom to work with a man who was clearly resistant to massage.

Sunday passed very rapidly, and Monday arrived almost before Mia realized it. She checked her schedule. Her first appointment was in the afternoon with Lane Ross.

Lane Ross sighed tiredly as he tried to placate the old woman on the phone. "Yes, Mrs. Ginnby, I understand. Of course I do, and I sympathize, but I only learned of your plight this morning. I'll have more property to show you tomorrow. We'll find something soon enough. Try to calm down."

She didn't sound really reassured, but she did hang up. Lane replaced the phone and hurried out of his office to his car. As he climbed into his navy Cadillac, he glanced down at his expensive watch. Three minutes late.

He didn't really have time for a massage. He still had two closings to do; he had a late appointment to show a house to a couple from out of state, he was behind in his bookwork, and the seminar he had attended last week had thrown him off schedule.

Then there had been the appearance of that frantic woman wanting to sell her apartment house because one of her tenants had been found murdered in the building. She had been nearly hysterical, saying that she herself lived there and wanted to sell as soon as possible no matter what it took. Lane shook his head. He wouldn't get out of the office until ten tonight.

But he needed a massage. He had met Mia when he had sold her the house on the hill, a choice piece of real estate that had netted him a handsome fee and seemed to suit Mia. Lane was glad. He had known when he listed the house that it would take a select client, and no one had been more surprised than he when a masseuse bought it. Mia had to have financial backing from somewhere; either that, or she was independently wealthy.

He exhaled raggedly. He didn't know why he was wasting his time thinking about the masseuse when he had so much else on his mind. Some days he didn't even know why he got up. He didn't know how or why he carried on.

He earned a six-figure income, had a loving wife to whom he had been married for twenty years and three wonderful daughters who showered him with attention, treating him like he was a king in his castle. He was healthy and attractive; he was active in the community and well-respected. Yet he didn't care if he lived or died.

Mia watched as the flashy Cadillac stopped far up in the driveway beneath the trees. If only, she told herself, Lane Ross was as vital and powerful as his car, if only he could stop gathering material possessions and community accolades and certificates and help himself. If only he would listen to his heart and body and mind. He was a seriously troubled man. She knew it. And he must know it.

She felt an urgency as she went to the door, and she forced herself to calm down. She was not in charge of this man's destiny, but she did have an opportunity to influence it.

As Lane climbed out of his car, he quickly removed his jacket. When he opened the door to put the coat on the backseat, he saw a fancy black silk scarf with the initials S.G. lying on the floor. Mrs. Ginnby's, the woman who owned the apartment where the girl had been found strangled. He recalled her twisting it around and around her hands in a compulsively nervous gesture. He would have to remember to call and tell her he had the scarf. But right now he was late.

From his position behind a thick, climbing bush in full bloom at the side of the house, Donevan watched the expensively dressed man leave the Cadillac. He didn't like the man's looks. He despised rich people on general principles, and this jerk was rich. No doubt about it. He looked like money. Donevan almost thought he could smell money in the air. He had discovered that this man, this Lane Ross, was a big-deal realtor.

"Lane, how good to see you," he heard Mia say in a voice he found irritatingly syrupy. "I was afraid you weren't coming."

Donevan couldn't help but notice how warm and welcoming she was. She didn't speak to this man like she did to him. He felt the anger build in the pit of his stomach. Who did that bitch think she was, anyway?

When the door closed behind them, Donevan tried to rein in his hostility. He would wait until the masseuse had had time to begin the massage—or whatever she did with the rich man—then he would sneak out of his hiding place. Lane Ross had done him a favor by parking in the trees. Donevan, too, had parked in the trees, but down the road at his same spot. This time he had driven his white car.

He glanced all around, then furtively stole out to the Cadillac, bent down, and peered inside. The interior was as sleek as the exterior. Donevan scanned the inside, not looking for anything in particular. He was just curious, just checking things out. He suspected Ross would be in the house a long time; he might as well kill a few minutes.

Donevan had seen the man take off his coat, and he studied the suit jacket for a brief time. It was good-looking. Donevan didn't have anything nearly that nice; he believed it might fit okay. But it went with the man's pants. He was sure to raise a stink if he found it missing.

Suddenly he saw the scarf lying in the backseat, a very expensive-looking scarf. The mere sight caused shivers up and down his spine. He opened the door and pulled the thin piece of sheer silk out, lovingly holding it in his hands.

It probably belonged to some whore the man had been pumping in the backseat. She probably had no idea where she had left it. Donevan would be doing him a favor if there was a wife involved. His heart pounding, he crammed the scarf into his jeans-jacket pocket.

* * *

"How are you today?" Mia asked Lane.

"Busy, per usual," he replied. He shook his head. "I really don't have time for a massage. I can't begin to tell you how swamped I am. I don't know why I'm here. I honestly don't understand why I keep making appointments with you." His laughter was husky and awkward. "It must be because I'm afraid I'll miss something if I don't come."

Mia's voice was reassuring. "I'm glad you did."

"I really don't have time," Lane repeated, even as he followed the masseuse down the hall.

It took all his willpower to pace himself to the slow, unhurried steps of the woman. He wished he could give her a little push, urge her to walk a little faster. Mia might have all the time in the world, but he didn't.

"Business is good?" Mia asked, knowing that business was one of the few subjects that Lane Ross would indulge, and suspecting that it was at the root of his trouble.

"Good? It's incredible! Sometimes I think all of Southern California is coming here to live. My god! I have so many clients that I can't keep up with them. My wife's father would turn over in his grave if he could see how good business is. He started Oreco Real Estate, and I want to tell you he barely eked out a living in those days. He simply wouldn't believe business today. It's almost more than I can handle."

"But you have a number of people working for you now, don't you?"

"Yes, I have good personnel, but I seem to be spending more time at the office instead of less. I guess that's how it is when you own the business. We're getting computers now, and at this stage it's only complicating matters until we get a system worked out. It's just one more thing to deal with."

Mia stepped aside so Lane could enter the massage room. "Why don't you take a vacation? I think you could use one."

"My god, woman!" Lane exclaimed. "I can't take a vacation. I don't have time."

Mia smiled and asked in a very soft voice, "What good is good business if you don't have time to enjoy the profits?"

Lane paused for a moment. Clearly Mia had never been poor; there was no point in trying to describe the humiliation, the desperation, the sheer panic of day-to-day survival. He had been just as poor as his wife, Davida, when he was growing up, wearing hand-me-downs and having people look down their noses as if they were seeing trash.

But with success and prosperity came a new fear: What if he should fall on his face at this stage of the game? What if times got bad and he lost everything? What if he simply couldn't keep doing it?

He smiled. "I enjoy the profits. Believe me, I do enjoy the profits."

"Do you?"

Mia's gentle question wasn't mocking in tone, and yet as Lane hurried to the bathroom to undress, he found those two words reverberating in his head.

He glanced in the mirror and absently smoothed a stray strand of wavy brown hair off his forehead. He went to the barber so regularly that his hair always looked like it had just been cut. There was only the barest minimum of gray, and that made him look distinguished.

His rugged face was almost as unlined as it had been when he had turned thirty. His dark brown eyes with their thick lashes were still his most appealing feature. Twice-weekly handball at the gym kept his six-foot body toned and trim, and looking much younger than that of a man who had turned forty.

Image was important in his business; he had to sell himself first, then the product. But he had never found that a problem. He could smile at some women, and they were willing to buy and sell even more than their homes and property. He wasn't interested. He loved Davida and his daughters.

Still, he knew all the little ways to please his clients, and he was just as able to work with the men as the women. He was scrupulously honest. He really believed that his name was his word, and his word was good.

No, business wasn't a problem. He didn't know what the problem was. He stuck to his routine without really knowing why. Without really caring.

Did he enjoy the profits? If he did, why was he so crushingly unhappy? Why did he wake up at four A.M. with his heart thudding and his pulse racing? Why did he wake up again at six, before the alarm went off, with an overwhelming sense of pointlessness?

Why couldn't he reach over and take Davida in his arms and tell her that he was standing in greased slippers on the edge of a very black, very deep pit? Why couldn't he tell her about the tranquilizers? Why couldn't he talk to her about Dr. Green's suggestions that he see a psychiatrist for the depression? Why did he keep sliding so far down in the pit that it seemed every time that it was harder and harder to climb out?

Why did he keep trying? Good god! Why did he keep on with it? Why didn't he just give up?

At least when he left the masseuse's house, he felt energized. He felt revitalized. Even if it was only briefly. Oddly, he also felt sated, as if he had taken one of the tranquilizers the doctor had given him.

Only better. Kind of mesmerized. Or something. Massage didn't merely mask the depression as the tranquilizers did. He didn't know how to explain it. But it never lasted long enough.

Suddenly he thought of Mrs. Ginnby's frantic calls. He wondered how badly the strangled girl had wanted to live. It seemed to him the ultimate irony of life that people were dying and no doubt didn't want to, and here he was hoping that he simply wouldn't wake up one morning.

# ~ CHAPTER 15 ~

Donevan stared through the blinds at the poised man looking at himself in the mirror. "Do you like what you see, you rich bastard?" he muttered aloud. "Fucking ass, standing there staring at yourself."

He pulled the sleek black scarf from his pocket and began to wind it around his hands. Jesus, he hated the son of a bitch. In fact, just watching the asshole admire himself, naked as a jaybird, anybody would know he had money. He had that groomed, pampered look.

Donevan tied a knot in the silk scarf and jerked it hard. He admired neatness, cleanness above just about anything, but this bastard griped him. This asshole went beyond being manly; every hair was in place, his body was toned and defined and tanned.

Donevan suddenly snickered. They'd love him in prison. The thought made his stomach turn sour, and he became lost in his own thoughts as Lane Ross left the bathroom.

When Mia had finished Lane's massage, she felt drained and depressed. He had lost himself in his own world while he was on the table; she had been able to reach him only with her hands, not her love or her mind. His tension was so severe that it was almost as bad as Donevan's, although Lane didn't consciously resist her efforts to help him relax.

He was somewhere inside himself, somewhere black and brooding, somewhere untouchable to her. She knew that she had accomplished the outward effect of relaxation, for his muscles had lost much of their rigidity and his breathing had become steady and regular.

She wanted to stay in the study and ponder Lane's situation, but she owed it to Brett Williams, her next appointment, to do her best by him. Not that he needed any mental help, she thought, smiling to herself. He was one of her most thoroughly enjoyable clients because his problem was physical. He was well adjusted and full of mischief. She pictured him in her mind and began to relax.

As Brett Williams raced up the winding road in his silver Corvette, he grinned. He loved going up the hill to Mia's house. The woman was full of warmth and beauty, and she was a hell of a good sport to boot. He got a real charge out of teasing her, and he was especially pleased with himself when he could get her to blush.

He was going to be one sorry son of a bitch when she told him he didn't need any more therapy for his leg. Damn! He'd almost be tempted to break something else just to keep on her schedule. He laughed out loud at the thought.

Mia would get a kick out of it when he told her. All the way to her house he thought of ways to tease her, which was really quite easy because she was such a classy lady. He was ready for her when she answered the door.

"Hey, baby, how you doing?" he asked in a low voice. "I'm ready today, honey. This is the day we're going to get it on, isn't it? The day we're going to do that erotic stuff."

He wagged a thick finger at her before she could speak. "Don't feed me that old line about you not being in *that* business, not being *that* kind of masseuse." He leaned down and whispered near her ear, "I've seen those *dirty* movies."

Mia met his twinkling green eyes, then tossed her head back and laughed. "You're in rare form today, aren't you?"

He moved closer to her. "Noticed, did you? That's a good sign. How about it? Can we get away from the therapy stuff and get to the *hot* stuff? You don't know how hard up an aging athlete can get." He laughed at his unconscious play on words. "Hard up? Get it?"

"I don't want to. Come on back and let's work some of that mischief out of you."

"Hey! A woman after my own body," he said, lumbering along behind her. "What do you think I was talking about?"

Mia looked back at the six-foot-four-inch man with shaggy blond hair. He reminded her of a big overgrown boy. "My, my, you're in a mood today."

His laughter was loud and booming. "I'm always in the mood. What the hell good is life if not for living? It's a game, and you either go for it or you don't. When are you going to let me show you what I mean?" He wiggled his hips suggestively.

Mia's mind suddenly filled with memories of Rand's lovemaking. If only, she told herself, she'd been as oblivious to his sexuality as she was to Brett's.

"Never. I'm never going to let you show me. When are you going to stop asking?"

"Are you kidding? Never! *Never!*" He preceded her into the massage room. His eyes met hers as he took off his clothes without bothering to go into the bathroom.

At thirty-six his nude body was more bulk than muscle, his stomach a testimony to too much beer, and his limbs a network of surgical scars. He raised and lowered heavy brows in a villainous parody.

"You could take a man to heaven with those magic hands of yours. Take me, Mia. I want to go!"

She couldn't help laughing. "You'd better hush before I send you somewhere else. I can't concentrate on my work when you misbehave."

Suddenly he wrapped his arms around her, crushing her against him. "Send me, oh, send me, baby! You do me and I'll do you."

"Will you get on the table before you smother the life out of me, you crazy man?" she said, barely able to contain more laughter. "This is serious business."

He stepped back and groaned. "I'm talking romance and you're talking business. There's no hope. I guess this means you won't go with me to California to film a new commercial."

"It does mean that," she replied, "but tell me about the commercial. Did you really get it?"

"You betcha!" he bragged, struggling up on the table with exaggerated moans and groans. "Couldn't you get a softer table? You know my knees are gone, my legs are shot, and my shoulder is made of spare parts."

"That's the penalty of getting rich on the football field," she said dryly. "Everything comes at a price."

He looked back over his shoulder. "How much are you? I might have enough left in my savings after being off the team for ten years to afford you."

Mia smiled. "I'm the same fee you pay every time you come, and for that you get the same treatment."

"Son of a bitch, you're a hard woman to do business with," he said with a grin. "I wish you'd been the one managing my investments instead of my accountant and my two ex-wives. What I really need is a rich widow. Are you rich?"

Pressing down vigorously on his back as she began to work, Mia said, "I'm neither rich nor a widow."

"Ouch!" he yelled. "All right. I get the point. You're rougher than a linebacker today. I'll shut up before you torture me to death."

"By the way, I'll be going to California myself at the end of the month. I'll be gone for two weeks."

"You're putting me on," Brett said. "You're not going to leave me, are you?"

Mia laughed at him. "You're leaving me to do the commercial."

"Yeah, but I wanted to make sure you'd be here to get me in working order before you left."

"When do you go?"

"The last part of the month. Hey," he said, brightening, "let's have a rendezvous there. What do you say?"

"I say no, you silly man."

"You're a cold woman, Mia. I guess I won't complain though, as long as you keep on doing me when you get back. You do me so good. I told myself on the way up here that I might have to break another leg just so I can keep coming."

"You're crazy. You really are." But Mia wouldn't have it any other way. Brett Williams was such a joy, such a contrast to most of her clients.


"Buck! Buck!" Emma called frantically. "Buck, you come here right now and listen to this!"

Buck hurried out of his shop wondering what Emma was up to now. He hadn't heard so much excitement in her voice since she thought she saw the movie star going up to the masseuse's house.

"What is it?" he asked. "What's got you in such a dither?"

"Shut up and listen," she said, pointing to the television.

Buck had been enjoying an especially risqué story in one of his magazines. He didn't appreciate Emma's interruption.

"It's started," she whispered, wide-eyed behind her glasses.

Sensing her genuine alarm, Buck sat down in his rocking chair and watched the newscaster give the details of the strangling of a young girl. The police were asking for the public's help in identifying her. Apparently she was a runaway using an assumed name. She had also been involved with drugs.

"I'll bet Frank did it," Emma said in a low, harsh voice. "Him or one of them people going up to that woman's house on the hill." She got up off the couch. "I'm going to call the police."

"Emma, for crying out loud!" Buck shouted. "It's just another drug murder. Don't you be going around pointing the finger at people."

Emma put her hands on her hips. "It's folks just like you, Buck Carson, who let this kind of thing go on till more and more innocent people get hurt. I'm going to call the police."

"You're not," Buck ordered, his voice growing rough. "It ain't your business."

Emma glared at him for a minute. "Go on back and read your filthy old magazine, Buck," she said, her voice filled with self-righteousness. "Don't think I don't know what you've been doing. I looked when you went for your walk."

His face red, Buck stared at his wife. For a minute he couldn't think of anything to say.

"Don't you be prying and snooping in my things, *old woman,*" he said, giving her the supreme insult. She hated being reminded that she was old.

"I'll do what I think is right," she said, her chin held high. "Don't think I won't. There's sin and shame and wrong all around me, and I couldn't sleep at night if I didn't do what I could to change it."

Buck shook his head. She was stubborn. He probably couldn't stop her, and he didn't want to argue with her anymore. What he really wanted to do was burn those dad-burned magazines before she found the rest of them.

## ✦ CHAPTER 16 ✦

On Tuesday Mia meditated in her study. Her mind was uneasy today, troubled by the problems of her clients, as well as her own. She couldn't seem to find in herself what was needed to help them. Then, too, she had heard from Frank about the strangling in town.

She saw a swirl of faces, including her own and Troy's. She would be glad when the trip to California was behind her. She had to sort out her life so she could be free to devote her time to the people on her bulletin board.

Donevan's face surged into prominence, blotting out the others. She knew he was a disturbing force in her search for inner peace. He hovered at the back of her mind as his appointment time grew nearer. She would be happy when she saw some improvement in the man.

She didn't know how long she concentrated, but when she heard the faint purr of an automobile engine, she went to the living room. Looking out, she saw no one.

She glanced at the clock and frowned. She must have imagined she heard a vehicle. Garson wouldn't arrive for twenty more minutes, and he was usually punctual. She stood at the window for a moment, listening to the classical music play, then went back to her study. The ringing of the phone caught her attention.

"Hello," she said.

"Mia, it's Lane Ross," the caller announced, sounding rushed. "Listen, you didn't happen to find a black silk scarf with the initials S.G. anywhere at your place, did you?"

"I haven't. But then, I wasn't looking for a black silk scarf."

Her heartbeat suddenly increased. The girl who had been murdered had been strangled with a scarf.

Surely— Her imagination was running wild today! She had to get a grip on herself.

Lane sighed. "I don't even want to bother with this, Mia, but old Mrs. Ginnby—she's the one who lost the scarf— owns the building where that girl was murdered. In fact, she lives there."

He sighed. "Things are getting so crazy around here. I could swear that I saw the scarf in the back of my car when I took off my jacket before my massage. I remember thinking I'd have to call Mrs. Ginnby and tell her." He sighed again. "Maybe I dragged it out of the car with my jacket, or maybe someone stole it. I don't know what the world's coming to. Thanks anyway."

"Lane—"

Mia stopped when she heard the buzz. Lane had already hung up. Unexpectedly, she felt a chill up her spine. She didn't know what to think about any of this.

Donevan looked all around as he parked in the same spot he had used before in the trees. For a little while he sat in his car, playing with the rope necklace in his pants pocket. He didn't see anyone, so he slipped from the car and crept into the woods. The sun was going down and the sky was a red-orange.

It reminded him of fire. He wondered if the masseuse had a fire burning. The day was growing cooler as dusk fell. The thought of a fire warmed him as he sneaked through the trees.

He wondered if she had a client in the house now. According to the bulletin board schedule he had seen, she had a man coming in fifteen minutes.

His pulse raced as he approached the back of the house. He didn't want to cut his time too short, but the mere thought caused the thrill and the fear to mingle inside him. He knew he could get into the house, even if the door was locked, and he suspected it wasn't, but he didn't know where the masseuse was.

He could handle her, of course, if she appeared suddenly, but he didn't want that. He wasn't ready yet. There was plenty of time. The thrill only grew with anticipation.

Sweat broke out on his forehead and palms, despite the coolness of the evening. The chance of being caught sent surges of adrenaline swelling up through him like the changing tides. The roaring in his ears was so exaggerated that it echoed like the rumble of thunder; it shook him deep inside as he hid behind the big tree and searched the area around the house. He made himself remain still, watching, waiting. He didn't see anyone.

Silently, swiftly, he slipped up on the sun deck and crept toward the back door. He quietly turned the knob. Shit! She had locked the door! Reaching into his pants pocket, he pulled out a credit card and eased it along the door frame. The flimsy lock slid back. He quickly opened the door and went into the house.

Immobile, barely daring to breathe, he tried to decide which way to go. The house was warm and quiet. He wondered if the masseuse was even home. Perhaps the schedule he had seen had been for last week only. He hoped not. He would be terribly disappointed if she was gone.

With skill he had honed over the years, he stole through the kitchen and down the hall. He paused by the massage room. The door was open. He moved close enough to look inside. No one was there.

He stopped by the closed door across the hall, recognizing it as the room where he'd seen the client list. His hand unsteady, he slowly grasped the doorknob and barely turned it. His heart pounded as he peeked through the small crack he'd made.

The masseuse was inside, her back to him. She was probably checking her schedule, seeing which client was coming. His blood pounding against his temples, Donevan quietly closed the door and slipped into the massage room to conceal himself.

Mia thought she heard a soft noise behind her and whirled around. The door was shut, just as it always was when she prepared for a client, but still a shiver swept over her. The chill was so intense that she lost her concentration. She couldn't explain it. Suddenly she was even more unsettled than she'd been by Lane's phone call.

Feeling foolish, thinking she was fighting shadows, she opened the door and scanned the hall. Nothing had been disturbed. Nothing was out of the ordinary. She wondered if Soot had made the noise. Had she even heard a noise? She was so easily spooked these days that her imagination seemed to be running away with her.

Despite her reasoning she didn't draw a steady breath until Garson's black truck came into view. She didn't know what was wrong with her tonight. She couldn't seem to get a grip on herself.

Donevan was beside himself with excitement. He had heard the truck stop, but he didn't dare try to see who was in it. Anyway, the window in the massage bathroom faced some trees. He held his position behind the dark green shower curtain in the dimly lit room. He had made the decision to hide in there rather than the walk-in closet. He was too afraid Mia would need supplies and discover him. He felt a quickening deep inside at the thought.

As he listened to the distant sound of voices down the hall, he imagined the man and Mia together. Their voices grew nearer and he stood very still, although he was trembling inside with that familiar mixture of fear and anticipation. The sensations made him dizzy. He tried to steady himself against the cool tile behind him.

The voices grew closer and Donevan's heart beat louder. Pounding echoed in his head and he wished it wasn't so noisy. He heard footsteps in the hall and held his breath, waiting. His heart thundered when the man walked into the bathroom and stripped. With great difficulty, Donevan altered his breathing, making it shallow and quiet so he wouldn't be heard.

With fingers gripping the rope necklace, he waited tensely, peeking out the tiny gap he'd left between the shower curtain and the end of the tub. Donevan breathed a little easier as he watched the naked man hang up his clothes and go back into the massage room without shutting the bathroom door.

Donevan smiled. He wanted to see everything the masseuse did.

"I'm having a little get-together a week from Friday," Mia told Garson as he stretched out on the table. "Just a few of my clients for a very informal dinner. I'd love to have you come. I'll be leaving the following weekend for two weeks in California."

"Leaving?" Garson repeated, more disappointed than he could believe. He hadn't considered the possibility that she might leave Oregon for any reason. It was stupid, of course, but the idea had just never occurred to him.

"I have a number of clients there," she explained. And a husband, she could have added, although there was no point.

Garson laughed a little nervously. "I've never thought of you anywhere else but right in this cottage on this hill."

Mia smiled as she started working with him, grateful to be doing something physical. She still hadn't completely lost her feelings of unease. "Hmm. What does that mean? Am I that uninteresting?"

"Not at all," Garson said, leaning on his elbows so he could look back at her. Nothing could be further from the truth. "I guess what I meant is that I count on you so much."

Mia smiled. "I'll be back soon. You won't even miss me."

"The hell I won't," Garson retorted. "I don't think you realize what a release this is for me, what a lifesaver, a safety valve. I was a man with a rope around his neck before you started treating me. Now I think I really might be all right."

Mia felt herself tense and fought it. She was behaving neurotically. Garson's dramatic statement reminded her of the strangled girl and Lane and the scarf. She drew in a steadying breath and changed the subject.

"Do you think you might come to dinner?" she asked again.

Garson lay down and closed his eyes. He hadn't gone to a dinner party in months. Eileen used to give them. She had been a wonderful hostess. She had been a wonderful wife, he realized in retrospect. Except when she took that young lover. Even at that, the marriage might have survived an extramarital affair on her part—might have—but she'd gone and married the little bastard.

Mia felt the tension begin to build in Garson's body. "If

you decide to come," she murmured, "I think you'll have an enjoyable evening."

He seemed so agitated that Mia was almost sorry she'd spoken. She wished she knew what was troubling Garson at this very moment. His words played back through her mind. Massage was a release, a safety valve for him. She pushed aside her thoughts when he spoke again.

"I'll think about it," he said gruffly.

Mia didn't know what else to say. Her intuition seemed to be shot, right along with everything else these days. Her personal problems with Troy—and Rand—were definitely getting in the way of her professional life.

Garson settled down again as Mia massaged his back. His mind began to drift to his earlier days with Eileen. When he relaxed, he couldn't seem to get her out of his thoughts. She was unfinished business with him, an element in his life that had changed abruptly and against his deepest wishes.

"Eileen used to give dinner parties," he said aloud.

"Your wife?"

"Yes. She was a very good hostess. In fact, she was very good at everything she did. Even taking a lover when we were married," he bitterly added. "The boy she married is half her age."

"I'm sure that was painful for you," Mia gently said. "Cheating partners almost always hurt deeply, whether they mean to or not."

"Painful?" Garson repeated harshly. "I wanted to kill the little bastard—and Eileen, too. With my own two hands." He wasn't kidding. He remembered the feeling so well. It had come the moment he heard that Eileen was going to marry the guy.

It *had* hurt. Deeply. Although he had cheated on Eileen, none of the women he had slept with had meant anything to him. Eileen had been his wife, the only woman he had ever loved.

When had she found out he was cheating? Was it long before she had taken the young lover? Funny, he hadn't thought much about her getting hurt. He guessed he just figured she wouldn't find out.

Even if she did, he hadn't thought she would leave him, much less get a lover and a divorce. He sighed tiredly. He would give anything if he could go back and do it all over again. But, really, he knew that was only because he had ruined everything at the end.

"I always thought men needed sex more than women. I always thought it was their right to have it if a wife wasn't interested enough."

Mia was at a loss for words. She was tempted to simply end the massage, but that wouldn't accomplish anything. She was still fighting shadows. Garson was opening up to her, and all she could think of was a murdered girl she knew few details about. She didn't think Garson had anything to do with the case—his bitterness was clearly directed at his wife and her lover. Still, his words had startled her and her concentration was scattered.

"Let's get some work done," she said, talking to herself as much as to him.

Determined to focus, Mia worked until she felt the tension begin to ebb in Garson's body. She knew that, painful though it was, he had to face the reason he was impotent before he could be cured. She firmly believed the reason was his ex-wife.

They were making excellent progress; she knew it would be foolish for her to end the massage when she was making headway. When he turned over, she employed the same techniques she had used Thursday, gradually moving down until she lightly stroked his penis.

A tremor went through Garson as he lay beneath Mia's stimulating fingers. Once more he thought that she had touched his genitals, but he had to be wrong.

It had something to do with his concentration on Eileen while Mia was working with him; he wasn't sure what. His mind seemed to be clearer when he was on the table. He seemed able to think more rationally and objectively. He felt more like his old self again. He had never imagined massage could be so therapeutic. The results were incredible.

Gazing through the gap he had created, Donevan watched, mesmerized as the masseuse let her fingers trail across the man's balls and dick. He had hit the jackpot! He was seeing what he had come to see. The bitch couldn't tell him that she didn't do it. He was seeing it with his own eyes.

His fingers tightened around the edge of the shower curtain, and he pulled it back a little farther. He could hardly wait until Thursday, his next appointment, when his turn would come. Wouldn't old Hardin and Larch be shocked if they could see this?

He was never wrong about women. He could have told the probation officer and the psychiatrist that, but he doubted if they would even believe this.

He slid the shower curtain closed. He was getting too excited. He didn't want to get himself so worked up that he lost control. Reaching into his pocket, he clasped the necklace and concentrated on it as he waited for the man to dress and leave.

It was only moments after Garson had gone that a woman arrived. Donevan eased the curtain open a little to see what she looked like. She was an old broad, not bad looking, but nothing that interested him. She was chatting away, and when the masseuse invited her to dinner, as she had the man, the woman accepted.

Donevan eased back against the cool tile, wondering if the masseuse was going to invite him. He decided that he wouldn't come, but he would be very angry if she didn't ask. He didn't like the way she treated him. If she was smart, she'd ask him just like she did the others.

He peered through the opening, glancing at the two women as Mia worked. He wished another man had come. That would have been much more exciting. Leaning back against the tile again, he became lost in his thoughts, wondering who else the masseuse would ask to her party.

Nora relaxed as she listened to Mia talking about what a wondrous piece of work the human body was.

"Too many women are ignorant of their bodies, uncomfortable with them, or ashamed," Mia continued. "They leave the responsibility of their pleasure and the blame for their pain to men."

Nora mentally agreed on all points. Her mind began to wander as though Mia had sent her off on some long-ago path. She had been taught that she must never touch herself "down there," must keep her legs crossed, must always be a lady, must wait for men to initiate *everything*.

She had been too early for the sexual revolution, and it was just as well. She *was* ashamed of her body. She always had been. She was sure when people made jokes about small breasts they were talking about hers, or when men talked about women who had as much sex appeal in bed as a board, they meant women like her.

She was nudged to awareness when Mia asked her to lie on her back. But reality was only fleeting. She drifted off again in a dreamlike state as Mia's words and hands caressed her. Gradually she began to experience the most exquisite tinglings, the most delicious shivers, as the masseuse's fingers skimmed over her with butterfly strokes.

Before she realized what had taken place, Mia had guided Nora's own fingertips to her nipples. For an appalling second, an alarm sounded deep inside Nora, but pleasure soon overshadowed it. As her fingers circled her throbbing breasts, sensations she had never experienced surfaced. It seemed so strange to trace the shape of her body, which was so familiar to her, yet so unknown.

Mia guided Nora's hands down the smooth skin of her stomach, to circle her navel, glide over the slight curve of her abdomen, then lightly linger on the lips of her vagina.

Nora's deepest instincts told her to wrench her fingers free of that place, and yet a new sensuality had been awakened in her. She could not pull back. It seemed so right, so natural to explore her own body, to follow Mia's expert guidance on the unknown journey as she coaxed a delicate caress, a gentle circling of a fingertip in just the right spot.

Inside Nora the most marvelous sensual responses began to build and build and build, rising and swirling and spinning until she thought she might explode from the delicious pressure. She could hear herself moaning, but it didn't really sound like her at all. Suddenly she gasped and cried out softly.

Then she lay there, letting herself sink into the erotic aftermath that left her tingling, throbbing, and satisfied. She had heard about orgasms, but she had never known just what it all meant.

Nora had experienced her first climax. It had been so incredible that she didn't think she ever wanted to move again. She just wanted to lie there and savor the experience, the warmth and the contentment she felt.

When Donevan heard the throaty moaning, he was distracted from his thoughts. He sneaked a look and what he saw made his heart beat fast. The damn bitch swung both ways. She was AC/DC.

He stared, entranced, and all he could think of was Thursday. He was dying to know what the masseuse would do with him. This was better than he had thought. He wouldn't have missed tonight for anything!

He let the curtain go and pressed himself back against the tile when the woman came into the bathroom to put her clothes on. She seemed to be in a daze, her movements slow and careless while everything in Donevan was speeded up.

He could hardly wait to get out of there. He left by the back door while the woman went out the front. He had seen enough tonight. He wanted to go home and think about it.

Suddenly he had come up with an idea for the black scarf he had stolen.

"Buck! Now! Come on or you'll miss him," Emma called. "The movie star. His white car is coming down the hill right now. Hurry!"

She looked away from the window to see where her husband was. She didn't see him. Rushing back to his shop, she jerked the door open.

"Buck!"

He swiftly wrapped newspaper around the magazines he was rolling up in his hand. "What do you want, woman? You startled the devil out of me!"

She glanced at the newspaper. "What have you got?"

He shrugged. "Why? What do you want?"

She had almost forgotten when she saw what he was doing. However, the movie star was more important at the moment.

"I want you to come see the movie star. He's coming down the hill." She hurried out of the room ahead of him.

Buck took a minute to put the rubber band around the magazines and toss them in his toolbox.

"Oh, shucks, Buck!" Emma said in disgust when he reached the window. "The car has already gone. *I* didn't even get to see him!"

## ⟡ CHAPTER 17 ⟡

Mia spent most of Wednesday planning the dinner party, deciding what she would serve. She had the Friday-evening arrangements worked out before her Thursday appointments, and she was quite pleased with them.

Yet despite her dinner plans, she had been more than a little preoccupied with the girl's murder, more uptight than usual. She tried not to let it keep her from having the dinner party or influence the guests she would invite.

Next week she would be involved in getting ready for her trip to California. She wanted to have her plans complete so that she wouldn't be in a last-minute rush. She had even hand-written place cards. It was almost like the old days when she invited guests to dinner. Almost. Except then she had had a cook. And she had had Troy. But it would do her no good to dwell on either fact.

Today's massage clients included Garson, Nora, and Donevan Raitt.

She frowned. She had mulled over Donevan's problems for a week, but she hadn't come up with any concrete solutions. Part of the problem was that she simply didn't know him. She suspected it would take a long, long time to break down the wall around him, and she could do nothing until that began to happen.

Inexplicably she seemed driven to call the police and ask about the murder. Wondering at her own obsession with an unknown girl's death, she dialed the station and asked to speak to someone about it.

The man answering seemed more than eager to arrange for her to talk to somebody. She waited just a moment, then another man came on the line.

When he had identified himself, he asked who she was and how he could help. Oddly, Mia felt as if she were a suspect about to be grilled.

She told him who she was, then said frankly, "I'm nervous about the murder. I—I suppose I just want to be reassured that it's really drug-related as I've heard."

"What murder?" he asked.

"What murder?" she repeated. "Why, the young girl who was strangled!"

He sighed. "Yes, that one. I thought you might know about another one."

"No," she said quickly. He was making her feel terribly uncomfortable.

"You don't know anything about this one?"

"Really," she said, exasperated. "I called hoping you could relieve some of my anxiety. You're hardly being helpful."

His tone seemed a little apologetic. "We get all kinds of calls. Sometimes we get lucky and catch a killer that way. Forgive me. I'm sure you're concerned and rightfully so. We don't really expect a repeat of this kind of thing. This is a quiet town, but we've got a drug problem like everywhere else. We're sure it was drug-related."

Mia felt somewhat reassured. At least he had confirmed what she'd heard from her clients. Still, the situation made her uneasy. "Thank you," she said before hanging up.

Garson's appointment went smoothly, despite his compulsion to discuss the murder. Mia couldn't seem to get away from the topic. Nora was obsessed with it, too, when she came.

It was only natural that Donevan should also talk about the strangling, but Mia didn't realize how tense she still was about it until Donevan spoke about it.

"Did you hear about that girl getting snuffed?" he asked as soon as he'd come into the house.

Mia looked into his blue-blue eyes and tried not to shiver under his piercing stare. She reminded herself that everyone had discussed the same subject. Why should it be any different with Donevan?

Yet it sounded different coming from him—somehow cold and coarse and unemotional. But then, this man had just come from prison.

She realized that part of her unease involved that fact. That was natural. She couldn't help recalling his criminal record in view of the murder. However, she did trust the police officer's belief that the crime was drug-related.

"I heard about it," she said. "It was a terrible waste of life, regardless of the situation."

"I guess so." Donevan wondered if he sounded like he meant it. Maybe he was saying too much.

Mia drew in a breath and tried to get some kind of control. The girl hadn't been raped, and no one else had accused Donevan. She vowed that she would treat him as any other client as she had agreed when she accepted him. But then, she told herself, Garson, too, had made her uneasy. Then there had been the matter of Lane and the scarf. She shook her head. She was battling shadows again, and that was unfair to Donevan.

He fell silent as he went with her to the massage room. Still, she didn't miss the fact that today Donevan seemed so expectant, so eager, so—she couldn't even describe it.

He was nervous, yet he seemed to be filled with some kind of anticipation she couldn't understand after the difficult, distant way he'd behaved last week.

He was tense, but not in the way he'd been before. She didn't know what to expect. She started working on his back, but she could tell from the way he shifted and moved about so restlessly that he had something else on his mind. He seemed to be all worked up internally.

He looked back at her. "Who do you think did it?"

Mia was surprised by the question. "I have no idea."

"Drug people," Donevan said simply.

"That's what the police think," Mia responded.

Feeling a little better, Donevan nodded and tried to settle back on the table. He laid his head down, but then he began to worry that he shouldn't have said anything at all. He'd expected to hear fear in the masseuse's voice, see it in her eyes, but that hadn't happened. He had wanted to know he was in control here.

Maybe he'd just been stupid. He didn't really want her to connect him with the murder, but in a way he did want her to. He wanted her to know his power.

He shifted and wiggled unconsciously. He didn't know how to deal with this bitch. Why was it when he came in here she seemed to have the upper hand?

Donevan was so restless that Mia thought she might have to stop working on him. She couldn't get any kind of natural rhythm, and she was beginning to feel as if she were failing with him again.

She needed for him to make the effort to relax. "Is something troubling you?" she asked quietly. "Perhaps we could talk about it."

Shit! Donevan told himself. He *had* been stupid! He looked back over his shoulder and gave her a boyish grin.

"Nothing's troubling me," he said. "What's wrong with you? You don't seem to be doing such a great job today— not like last time."

That's good, he told himself. Put *her* on the defensive.

"I'm trying," Mia said, "but you aren't working with me. You appear distracted. I can't seem to reach you."

Donevan forced a laugh. "What do you call what you've been doing?"

Mia sighed, but she was determined not to give up yet. If she could get him to talk to her, she would feel she was making some progress. She put both hands on his shoulders and was surprised to feel him flinch as though she'd struck him. She'd already been working on him for about ten minutes. She made herself slide her hands off his back in a careless manner, as though she hadn't noticed how he started at her touch.

"Reaching you that way is easy enough to do," she said, "but as I explained to you last time, I want to help you relax. I think you're resisting."

Donevan felt his anger rising instantly. She was playing with him again, and he didn't like it. He'd *seen* the way she treated her other clients, but he couldn't tell her that was what he was waiting for. Just fair play. Just the same treatment the others got.

Well, her time would come. He could go along with her game for now.

"I didn't know you were trying to get through my skin," he said, laughing briefly, as if he'd made a big joke. "That's spooky."

He really did find the bitch spooky. She was too damned nosy to suit him. Anybody who stuck her nose in his business just might find herself never sticking it anywhere again. He hated that—nosiness, prying, and snooping. It was worse with this woman who had some kind of control over him just because of the situation. He *had* to be here; he *had* to play along. For now.

Maybe. Unless she really pissed him off. And she had a way about her that irritated him. He really wanted her to know that he could kill her right now if he chose to.

Control, he reminded himself. He had to be in control. He couldn't let her push him. Now wasn't the time.

Mia smiled at him. "Actually, I *am* trying to get through your skin, you know. I want us both to discover what makes you tick inside so I can help you regulate the clock."

Donevan almost told her he wasn't a fucking clock and how he ticked was none of her business. He also almost told her that if she cut the crap and gave him the same kind of massage she'd given the man and woman he'd seen, they'd get along just fine. But he didn't say a word. He didn't trust himself. It'd be too easy to blow it.

He was afraid he'd said too damned much just by asking about the murder. He put his head back down and closed his eyes, shutting himself off from the witch. Maybe she really was trying to see inside him. He'd wondered from the first how much she saw with those eyes of hers. She was worse than a fucking psychiatrist. At least they didn't have you naked on a table, probing and poking all over you.

He felt his dick harden at his word choice. He'd really thought the masseuse might give him a real massage today. He had thought and thought and thought about it, and now the cunt was playing those same old mind games. He would just have to show her that he was smarter than she was. She'd learn it sooner or later, but for now they seemed to be on her turf.

"Donevan?" Mia ventured, wanting him to open up more to her.

He pretended not to hear. She wasn't getting another word out of him. He could can that communication shit by simply shutting up. He smiled a little to himself, feeling that he was gaining some control. After all, she couldn't make him talk.

Mia sighed. End of conversation, she noted, but she also noted that he'd settled down some just by closing his eyes. He lay very still, perhaps trying to get her to think he was asleep. That was absurd, of course; he'd been speaking seconds ago, but she still felt that she had an advantage she hadn't had minutes before.

She began to work studiously, seizing the moment to use all her skills to encourage him to become as still inwardly as he was outwardly.

Donevan settled down on the table a little more, smugly thinking he'd outsmarted the masseuse. She'd find that she couldn't *make* him do anything. Nobody could. Oh, sure, they might lock him up and all that shit, if they had the chance, but they really couldn't get inside him. They couldn't steal his power.

His thoughts gradually began to drift away from the woman as her fingers made circling patterns on his shoulders and back. Unconsciously he inhaled deeply and his breathing became regular and even. In minutes he fell into a heavy sleep.

He was startled awake when Mia called his name. "Donevan."

Almost jumping off the table, he sat upright, staring at her, clutching the towel. "What?"

Mia tried to keep calm, although his intensity disturbed

her. "You were sleeping," she said softly. "I think we may as well end the massage now."

"I wasn't sleeping!" he angrily cried. "What the hell are you talking about?"

Trying not to let his anger bother her, Mia only nodded. "It seemed to me that you were sleeping—snoring in fact," she said with a casual smile.

Donevan was getting very, very pissed. She wasn't getting rid of him this way. She hadn't done anything yet.

Had she?

Shit, he couldn't remember. Had he really fallen asleep? He couldn't believe it, but he couldn't remember anything except her fingers circling his shoulders.

"How long have I been here?" he demanded, glowering at her.

Mia looked at the clock in the hall. "Forty-five minutes."

"You're lying." Then, hearing the hate in his voice, he quickly tried to make amends. He was fucking up all over the place because she hadn't fucked around with him like he'd expected her to. He was beginning to think maybe he *had* fallen asleep. He looked down at his own watch, then back at her.

"I—I'm sorry," he muttered, trying to sound genuinely contrite. "I guess I was sleeping. When I get startled awake, I lose my cool."

"That's all right." She tried not to appear as upset as she was. She knew that he was a troubled man, a man who wouldn't want to be so vulnerable that he slept on the table without even knowing it.

Donevan drew in a deep breath and exhaled. "I do feel relaxed," he made himself say, realizing that it was the truth.

The bitch had really tricked him this time. Instead of stirring him up sexually, she'd used some kind of sorcery to put him to sleep. He would *never, ever* let that happen again. It wouldn't have happened this time if he hadn't been wired and tired. He hadn't been sleeping well since the strangling. He hadn't been eating well either, for that matter. He had so many things on his mind.

"I'll be going away soon to California," Mia said casually, deliberately not telling him when or how long she'd be gone. She might be overreacting, but she wasn't at all sure she wanted to continue to work with him.

She couldn't deny that she'd made some progress. Otherwise, he never would have fallen asleep and allowed her time to really work with his body.

"Going away?"

She nodded. "You'll need to call to discuss rescheduling."

Donevan sat on the table and waited.

"You can get dressed now," she briskly stated, wanting him to leave. She had too many things on her mind at the moment to even continue to be civil, much less as caring as she knew she should be.

"Dressed?" he repeated in confusion.

"We're through for the day. You really did have a good massage. Don't you feel relaxed?"

He *had* felt relaxed—until he had sat there like a fool waiting for the same dinner invitation the others had gotten. It was clear that she wasn't going to invite him. He wanted to believe that she'd just forgotten, but inside he knew that wasn't true. She didn't want him to come.

He slid off the table, keeping the towel wrapped around his body. Maybe he'd come anyway. He knew the night and the time. She wasn't going to get away with this. Her day was coming, and it might be sooner than even he planned.

On the way back to his rooms, Donevan stopped at a car wash and washed his car. He had muddied the tires when he had parked in the woods, and he hated anything dirty. Other people might be pigs, but he didn't have to be.

Pigs. The slang word for cops triggered the memory of the murder. He was both pleased and disappointed that he hadn't been singled out by the police. They hadn't even questioned him. He smiled to himself. That's because he was smart. He hadn't raped the druggie bitch.

Still, now that the papers and the news carried the murder, he had expected some attention for the crime. The law usually rounded up suspects like cattle when something like this happened. Of course, they did it to soothe the public, but he hadn't heard a word from anybody on it. It had to be because she was a druggie, he told himself. Nobody really cared.

After he had parked in the garage of the house where he roomed, his landlady came around back, startling him as he got out of his car.

"What the hell—" he muttered, seeing only a shadow.

"I'm sorry if I scared you, Mr. Raitt—Donevan," the old woman quickly apologized. "I just wanted to make sure it was you, and when I saw your car, I wanted to tell you how grateful I am that you're living here. That terrible murder has been constantly on my mind."

Donevan heard the fear in her voice. He swelled up with pride. He might not have scared the masseuse, but he had plenty of other people shaking. Fooled, too. This stupid old hag didn't even know she was talking to the murderer.

He smiled one of his rare, genuine smiles. "You don't have to worry, Mrs. Smith. Nothing is going to happen to you that I don't know about."

He thought that was clever and looked her right in the eyes. She was clearly very frightened.

"Don't be getting upset about that girl," he comforted. "They say the crime was drug-related. You're in no danger. Like I said, nothing's going to happen here that I don't know about. Nobody messes with me."

Seeming a little more reassured, the landlady smiled. "I had five sons," she said wistfully. "Two of them are gone now. It's a terrible thing to lose a child. A terrible thing."

Her mind seemed to wander for a moment, then she looked at Donevan again. "I wish my boys had stayed closer by. They drifted down to Southern California, one by one, leaving me all alone. I'd like to think of you as one of my boys, Donevan, and I just wanted to let you know I'm glad I rented the rooms to you. I think you're a good boy who got caught in a bad situation."

He'd gotten caught in a bad situation all right, but that wouldn't happen again. He'd told the old woman when he rented the rooms that he hadn't really raped the bitch he had done time for. She had seemed to doubt that then, but had agreed to take a chance because she needed money so badly.

"Good night," he said, moving toward the back steps.

"Will you have dinner with me?" she called after him.

"Not tonight."

He had too much on his mind to waste more time with the old woman, even though he was well aware that she might come in handy in the future. "Just call out for me if you get scared by anything," he added, hoping he wasn't opening a can of worms with the invitation.

It was obviously what the old woman had wanted to hear. "Thank you," she said, relief in her quivering voice. "Good night."

As Donevan watched her hurry back around toward the front, he wondered how it would be to rape some old bitch who hadn't had it in years. Maybe the old ones would be so grateful to get some after so long without it that they wouldn't even report it. He smiled. They wouldn't be alive to report it anyway.

The memory of how easy it had been to kill the girl rushed to his mind, and he hurried up the steps. He had so many things to think about. Killing was so much more exciting than rape.

# — CHAPTER 18 —

The table was beautifully set for Mia's dinner party. This evening she had forsaken her sari and had dressed in a simple long black dress. She turned in front of the mirror and was surprised by her appearance. It had been so long since she'd made the effort to look glamorous.

When she heard a knock on the door, she went down the hall in velvet shoes that hardly made any sound. She opened the door to find Brett standing there with a bouquet of flowers and a bottle of wine.

"Finally," he said, pretending immense relief. "I thought you'd never ask me to dinner." He held out the flowers and wine. "This is to soften you up. Three drinks into the evening, and I'll bet you'll be ready to give me that"—he paused—"special massage."

"Brett Williams," Mia chided, "you know this evening is a dinner party for several of my clients. It's not just for you and me!"

His face creased and he broke into boisterous laughter.

"You're so easy, Mia!" he said. "I'm not brain-damaged, you know. I never got hit in the head—at least, not with the football. I know this isn't a quote, unquote, date!"

Mia shook her head and opened the door wider. She'd been "had" again. And she realized that she absolutely adored him and his humor.

"Come on in here. Save some of that fun for the party. I don't know how well my guests are going to mix."

He grinned at her as he handed her the flowers and carried the wine to the kitchen himself. "It'll be fine. Everything you do is fine, Mia."

There was another knock on the door. Mia was reaching for a vase to put the flowers in. They would look lovely as a centerpiece on the table.

"Will you get that for me, Brett?" she asked. "By the way," she said, "thanks for the flowers and wine. That was very thoughtful of you."

"Thoughtful, hell," he said with a grin. "You owe me one."

"I'm sure," she said, smiling.

"Aren't you going to ask one what?" he murmured.

She shook her head as the bell rang again. "Go on and answer the door. I don't want to know one what!"

Still chuckling, Brett went down the hall. Mia heard his exclamation very clearly in the kitchen. "Well, hello," he said in an animated voice.

The giggle that followed could only belong to Frannie Welch. "Hello to you," she replied in a deliberately sultry voice. "Is Mia home?"

"Forget Mia, baby," Brett said. "Let's me and you run off and skip this dinner. It'll probably be a drag anyway."

Stifling her laughter, Mia went to the door. "You stop that, Brett," she insisted. "You're trying to sabotage my dinner party."

Looking sheepish, Brett grinned at her. "Damn, woman, you've got good ears."

"You're an awful flirt," she retorted.

"Wait a minute," he said. "I thought I was pretty damned good at it."

Both women laughed. "How are you tonight?" Mia asked Frannie.

Batting her big eyes at Brett, Frannie answered breathlessly, "Much better than I was minutes ago."

Brett and Frannie were still making eyes at each other as

Mia led the way into the living room, where a fire burned and the lamps had been lit. The setting was decidedly cozy.

Nora squinted into the darkness, nervous about the twists and turns of the winding road lined by thick trees. She kept glancing from side to side, expecting something awful, something frightening, to burst from among the shifting branches. She was just thinking how silly she was being when she thought she saw a dark vehicle parked in the woods.

She slowed down, trying to get a better view. It looked like a black truck, half-hidden by the drooping branches. Her fingers tightened on the wheel. She must be letting the darkness and the road and the skeletons of trees get to her.

Then, through the chill of her fear, she had another thought. Maybe she shouldn't be afraid at all. Maybe this *was* a black truck—the one that belonged to the man who had the appointment before hers. The man she had wanted to meet for so long. Maybe, just maybe, he was as nervous as she was about this evening and had actually pulled off the road, trying to get up his nerve to continue.

Biting her lip, she tried to think. She couldn't decide what to do. She didn't want to do something foolish, but if it were the person she thought it was, this might be the perfect opportunity to meet him. She backed up a little, trying to get a better view. In the climate of fear surrounding the town, she knew she shouldn't take any chances. Undecided, she hesitated, then started forward.

To her surprise, when she looked again, there was no sign of the truck. She must really be losing her mind. There probably hadn't been anything but her overactive imagination. Feeling silly and a little shaken, she drove on toward the cottage.

Donevan slowly eased his truck backward into the denser trees. He didn't know what that stupid lesbian bitch thought she was doing, but she was making him nervous as hell. Jesus! Didn't these bitches have any brains at all? He knew she was the one the masseuse had played with.

If she hadn't gotten her pussy on down the road, she would have been in for one hell of a shock. In fact, if he got stuck in this damp ground, she was still going to be in for it.

The doorbell rang again, and Mia looked obliquely at Brett. "Don't you want to answer this time, too, just in case—"

His gaze traveled boldly over Frannie's tight red dress and down her legs to her red heels. "And leave this beauty alone? Not on your life."

Mia laughed softly. "Brett, I realize this is after the fact, but the beauty you're ogling is Frannie Welch. Frannie, Brett Williams. If you two will excuse me, I'll be right back."

Both paid little attention as Mia left the room. Suddenly Mia's spirits lifted even higher. Maybe this would be a good evening. A little relaxation would help them all, and who knew where the evening and the introductions would lead?

Mia could sense Nora's unease the moment she opened the door.

"Come on in," she warmly invited.

Nora's hands fluttered nervously. "I almost called and said I couldn't come," she admitted, glancing down at her black dress. "I'm very nervous about this," she blurted. "Look at you. You look so beautiful. We're both in black, but what a difference!"

Mia took her hand. "You'll be fine. Really. You look lovely."

"Are the others already here?" Nora asked. She had seen two cars, but she hadn't seen the black truck she was looking for. She frowned, confused, wondering if she had really seen it at all. She was being silly again. Nerves. If it *had* been the man, he had circled out of the trees and gone back down the road. He certainly hadn't come here.

"Two of my guests have arrived."

Nora blinked and forced her thoughts back to the present. "Is the man in the black truck coming?" she asked.

"I hope so. He seemed rather undecided."

Nora frowned. Now she didn't know what to think. She began to wish that she had gone back to town.

When Mia guided her into the living room, Nora's heart began to pound. A young couple on the couch, clearly enamored of one another, were talking. Nora felt out of place. She shouldn't have come, but it was too late to change her mind. Mia was already introducing her.

The heavy blond man stood up and held out his hand. Nora felt she had no choice but to shake it. Her fingers trembled as he clasped them.

"How are you, Nora?" he warmly asked, still holding her hand.

She smiled, somewhat mollified by his friendliness. "I'm okay."

"Okay?" he questioned. "Woman, you'd better be *wonderful!* This is a splendid evening. We're going to have a great time!"

Nora glanced at the blond woman who was sipping a glass of wine. The woman smiled brightly at her. Maybe, she told herself, it was going to be a good evening. This pair certainly seemed nice.

"Are you married?" she asked, then instantly felt silly. What a first question!

The couple laughed together. "Not yet," Brett answered. "Actually, we just met."

Nora felt foolish until Brett set her at ease with his aimless chatter and offer to get her some wine. Nora hadn't even noticed that Mia had left the room until she returned with another man.

The man who drove the black truck! Nora's heart began to beat rapidly again. She held her wineglass in both hands to keep it steady.

She wasn't very hopeful about her chances with him when

Mia introduced all of them. Garson Hundley's eyes strayed time and again to Frannie.

Trying to muster up a little courage to start a conversation with Garson, Nora bravely murmured, "I thought I saw your truck when I drove up."

Mia noticed that he looked at Nora oddly, but then so did she. She'd already told Nora that Garson hadn't arrived when the woman came to the door. Mia didn't think Garson was the kind to sit outside gathering courage to come to a party, but who knew? She awaited his answer as expectantly as Nora.

"My truck?" he repeated. "I just drove up."

"I know," Nora said, growing more and more flushed, "but I thought I saw you."

"Where?" Garson asked, his brows drawing together. He really didn't know what she was talking about. He hadn't seen anyone else on the road, and there had been only three cars here when he parked. He could tell she was getting flustered, and he felt a little sorry for her. She'd obviously mistaken him for someone else.

The hand that held her wine trembled and the other fluttered nervously. "I guess I imagined it," she said, sounding even more ridiculous. She wished she could sink into the floor.

Garson found himself thinking that his wife—ex-wife—Eileen would get herself out of this awkward position with all the smoothness of creamy butter. He couldn't seem to think of a thing to say.

Another knock at the door made Mia excuse herself once more. That had to be Frank. "I'll be right back."

Both Garson and Nora seemed relieved, and they immediately wandered off in different directions.

Outside, squatting in the trees, Donevan had patiently watched the guests arrive. While it was apparent to him that the masseuse hadn't invited everyone she gave massages to, it didn't matter. She hadn't invited *him*. And that was what counted. She had invited these other people, and she had spurned him. He hated her for that.

She had closed the living room blinds. Donevan wanted to see what was going on in there. Badly. He could hear music and talking, but he wanted to *see.*

What he had already seen had interested him. That blonde. While he wasn't real big on blondes himself, there was something about this one that intrigued him. It wasn't the sexy way she was dressed or her blond hair. There was something about her—something that triggered a memory in his brain.

Who was Frannie Welch? There had been a girl—*the girl*—in high school. Frances something-or-other. He was sure of it. He had thought about it a lot. But she had had huge breasts. He didn't even know why he was even thinking of her. After all, it was this Frannie Welch who fascinated him. Somehow he was going to find out where she lived.

The sounds from inside faded as the guests shifted to another room. Prowling around the back side of the house, he peered in again. He could see nothing but the bathroom where he himself had left the blinds open fairly wide and no one had closed them. He couldn't see the room where the people were.

Fucking assholes! Here he was on the outside again. He was getting sick and tired of it, and he was getting that feeling again. The bad one. Getting it real strong, too. It was like there was something running wild inside him, racing and roaring around his brain and his prick.

Reaching for the thin cord in his pocket, he fiddled with it, wrapping his fingers in it. It wasn't fair the way they treated him, excluding him like some kind of disease they were afraid to catch.

Somebody was going to pay for tonight. Let them learn what it was like to feel this bad. Let them learn that his anger was real dangerous. It wasn't smart to mess with Donevan Raitt.

\* \* \*

To Mia's disappointment all three men seemed devoted to Frannie Welch as they went into the country kitchen for dinner. They actually fought over who would seat her.

*"Boys!"* she said, trying to keep her voice playful when she was actually feeling extremely exasperated. "There are two other ladies present, if you want to be mannerly."

Everyone laughed and Frank quickly started toward Mia. Garson attended to Nora, who was looking more and more uncomfortable.

Mia was sure she had lost her touch. Dinner parties used to be so easy for her, but this was proving different. Frannie had been the center of attention from the very beginning, while Nora seemed to shrink further and further into herself.

Mia sighed and put a big smile on her face. "Frank's a writer, too," she announced. "Why don't you tell them about some of your songs while I start serving."

Conversation started to flow then, and Mia moved around the room with ease, making sure everyone was comfortable and well fed. Maybe tonight wouldn't be such a disaster.

Donevan bided his time outside the house. He had no other choice. He could hear muffled sounds from inside, but he couldn't see a damned thing. It seemed like an eternity before the first person finally left the party.

His anger had been at the boiling point for hours. Now it mingled with excitement when he saw Frannie Welch step out onto the porch, a big smile on her face.

The smile seemed to tease him, like she was gloating because she'd been inside and he'd had to crouch, unseen, in the trees. He stared at her hard and long, eyes narrowed in rage. All at once he knew what he was going to do.

He slowly made his way back through the woods to his truck.

## CHAPTER 19

Mia was weary by the time the last guest had left. But she was pleased, too. The evening had gone well, even though Frannie had remained the center of attention. All she wanted to do now was clean up and get to bed.

Donevan drove carefully, maneuvering his truck well out of Frannie Welch's view. He saw her slow down and pull into the drive of a real fancy house. He smiled to himself. So, she was rich. That only added to his interest. He hated snobby rich bitches as much as he did wealthy assholes.

He was so revved-up that the roaring began in his head, and he almost didn't see the sleek Corvette slink up behind his truck. He glanced in the rearview mirror when he heard someone gun the motor. Shit! It was that big bastard who'd been at the party.

Donevan drove down the block slowly, as though he were looking for addresses. When he saw the man pull in behind Frannie's car, he gritted his teeth. The son of a bitch was going to spoil everything. He watched as the couple greeted each other and went toward the house together.

Parking far down the block, Donevan tried to decide what to do. Fear and excitement were roiling inside him. He'd made his plans and waited to follow Frannie Welch into her huge, ritzy house, and she'd let that other man inside instead. No matter. He wasn't going to be put off that easily.

Sneaking silently from the passenger side of his truck, he

returned to the house. The smart thing would be to check things out. Maybe the big bastard had done him a favor. Maybe. But he'd wanted the woman all to himself! He'd wanted to see the look on her face when she realized why he'd come.

He edged along the side of the house, trying to see into the windows. Every one of them had the shades pulled down. Donevan couldn't see a fucking thing. Nothing! For the *second* time that night!

Furious, he slipped away from the house. This night had turned to shit. He might as well go home and try to figure out his next move. He wasn't finished yet. He could feel himself swelling and he had to deal with it somehow.

Back in his rooms he lay naked on the bed, playing with the black scarf he'd swiped from Lane Ross's car. He liked the feel of it sliding across his dick. It was smooth and cool. He wrapped it around his penis and pulled it free, time and time again. He felt himself growing bigger and bigger. More and more powerful.

He made a slipknot in the scarf and put it around his neck. A picture of Frannie Welch in his mind, he grasped his penis in one hand and the scarf in the other.

Mia had decided to take only her Tuesday clients the week following the dinner party. She was leaving for California on the weekend, and she wanted to be refreshed when she arrived. She was going to see Troy. She wasn't going to be put off this time. A confrontation was long overdue, and she wouldn't let him avoid it.

Garson and Nora were coming, but she hadn't scheduled Donevan. She frowned as she stood in her study trying to get ready for Garson. Donevan disturbed her.

But then, so did Garson. And Lane. And Frank. Almost all her male clients disturbed her, but she was trying to rule out any tie between the men and the murder of that girl. She told herself she was being ridiculous, yet suddenly their furtive behavior and their secrets made them suspect in her mind.

Brushing it all aside, she tried again to get in the mood to work. Each of her clients had his or her problems. That was why they came to her. She had handled much more serious cases than the ones she was involved with now. She assured herself that she was letting her personal unhappiness get in the way of her judgment.

By the time Garson came, she was in a better frame of mind. They had a good session, as did she and Nora. She jumped when the phone rang and realized that she wasn't as relaxed as she had imagined.

"Hello?"

There was no response on the other end of the line.

Angie Esterbrook carefully replaced the phone on the hook. She was breathing hard, livid with rage because Mia hadn't invited her to her dinner party.

Angie had heard all about it, of course. She heard about everything social that went on in this town. She was usually there in person, but this time it had come to her secondhand from silly old Nora Simpson at the Senior Center. How that had galled her!

She dialed the number on Mia's business card again. Again she listened to the woman answer without responding. And again she quietly put the receiver back in place.

Donevan had decided that Tuesday was the night. He knew how totally engrossed the masseuse became in her clients—he snorted at the thought of just how engrossed—and he wanted to do it to her while she was distracted.

Not that he expected any trouble. He'd been surprised at how easy it was to murder the girl. So easy. And so exciting.

He began to quiver deep inside. He needed this in more ways than one. For the first time ever he hadn't managed to get rid of his rigid dick when he tried to jerk off after the party. He guessed that his anger was just too great. Or maybe it was because he'd been double-crossed by the bastard who'd showed up at Frannie's.

He didn't know what had happened really. He just knew he needed this night with the masseuse. The poison was still in him and he wanted to get rid of it. And her. She would learn a good lesson, although it would come too late to do her any good.

He hadn't been able to sleep Monday night because he was thinking about what he was going to do. She was going away. Probably nobody would miss her until that redheaded queer came to check on the house. Donevan had discovered that he acted as caretaker.

Donevan carefully drove to the cottage late that night. He had all his necessary stuff. He didn't want her to recognize him. Just in case something went wrong. He had put in his brown contacts. Just in case. It didn't hurt to be cautious.

Mia roamed the house restlessly, nervous about the voiceless phone calls. On top of her concern about the murder, it was just too much. She was relieved that she was leaving soon. She was really getting spooked by this whole situation; it had never been like her to overreact this way.

The first person she thought of was Donevan Raitt. She knew that wasn't fair. She had had hang-ups before. There was no reason to assume automatically that Donevan was the culprit.

It was just that the murder had her upset. No matter how much the police had tried to reassure her that it was drug-related, she hated the way they had dismissed the importance of the case just because they suspected the dead girl had been involved in drugs.

Mia went to the phone and dialed Troy's number. When Daniel answered on the second ring with a crisp but hearty hello, Mia felt a flicker of hope.

"Hello, Daniel," she said, mustering cheer she didn't feel. "I want to speak to Troy." She hoped that her voice sounded firm enough that she wouldn't be put off this time.

She was wrong. When Daniel realized who the caller was, he assumed a long-suffering tone that instantly irritated Mia.

"I'm sorry, Mrs. Jorgenson, but I'm afraid Mr. Jorgenson isn't available at the moment."

"Why not?" she demanded with uncharacteristic bitchiness. "Just what can a paralyzed man be doing that keeps him from accepting a call from his wife?"

There was silence on the other end of the line. It seemed to last forever. Mia nervously ran her fingers through her hair. "Daniel," she prompted, trying to gain control and failing.

Daniel sighed deeply, making Mia feel like an exasperating child he had to deal with severely. "He's in the hot tub at the moment."

"There isn't a phone nearby? Come on, Daniel, stop being a barrier between Troy and me."

There was another lengthy pause before Daniel spoke. Mia knew the house, and Daniel knew that she knew there was a phone available to Troy anywhere he happened to be on the grounds.

"Just a moment," he said in an aloof voice.

The moment stretched interminably while Mia held the receiver to her ear. She realized that her hand was shaking and her breathing was labored. God, how she despised being in this position. Troy was her husband, for heaven's sake. She wanted—she needed—to talk to him.

Daniel was even more remote when he spoke again. "I'm sorry, Mrs. Jorgenson, but Mr. Jorgenson isn't accepting calls right now."

"Damn it!" she cried bitterly.

Before she could think coherently, she slammed the phone down. Not accepting calls! She tried to calm herself by breathing deeply. This wasn't the first time Troy hadn't taken a call from her, but it was the first time in a long while she'd let it disturb her so deeply.

She paced the house again, wanting to walk the beach, but knowing that wouldn't help. She finally decided a hot bath might be beneficial.

The phone rang again, startling her from her thoughts. She answered with a hopeful hello. Maybe Troy had relented. Maybe he had decided to talk with her after all.

"Hello."

There was no one on the line. Soon she heard the sound of the dial tone. She stared at the phone for a moment. Who was doing this and why?

As she stood there, every noise around her seemed amplified. The wind sounded eerier than ever; the rain seemed to send secret messages as it tapped on the cottage roof; branches brushed against the windows.

Shaking her head, she determined that she would not let her imagination run away with her. The sounds were the same ones she'd always heard, the same ones she'd loved to hear in the past. She went to the bathroom. It would do no good to speculate and worry. She'd done enough of that.

She prepared her bath, liberally sprinkling colorful, scented oil beads into the water, then piling her hair on top of her head. She had to relax or go crazy. She was really reaching the end of her rope; she hadn't felt so desperate in a long time. She was as close to the edge as she'd been since Troy had asked for a divorce.

When she had put some soothing music on the stereo and turned it up loud enough so she could hear it in the bathroom, she stripped and slid into the warm water. In the glow of a single lavender-scented candle, she settled deeper into the enveloping warmth and closed her eyes.

Donevan parked his truck deep in the woods close to the cottage. He couldn't afford a mistake this time. Everything was ready for the big occasion. He'd packed two suitcases for his getaway to Southern California. He'd brought along a mask and gloves. This time he was going to do it right. He'd even phoned the masseuse minutes ago, and she'd been home. He was so excited he could hardly contain himself. Control, he kept repeating to himself. Control. *He* had to remain in control.

He slipped silently through the woods and made his way up on the sun deck. As usual, it was easy enough to get into the stupid woman's house. He'd been afraid that the druggie girl's murder would make her beef up security. He grinned cruelly. She didn't even have that much sense.

Tonight was the night he was going to strike. He had the scarf he'd taken from the realtor's car. He loved the idea of using it on Mia.

It had occurred to him that maybe the realtor or his girlfriend or whoever the scarf belonged to would get the blame for the murder. He liked that. He liked it so well that he started to get excited just thinking about it.

But now was the time for control. He couldn't let the whirling excitement and fear overtake him yet. He had to beat the masseuse. He had to have the final triumph over her. She would never be able to use her power on him again. She would never look at him with those big eyes. He snickered a little. She wouldn't be looking at *anyone* anymore.

## ⟳ CHAPTER 20 ⟲

Mia lost herself in the caressing warm water surrounding her. The bath had been a good idea. She was finally beginning to relax and put the unpleasantness of the past few days behind her.

Soon she would be in California, where she would feel more in control of her destiny. Daniel wouldn't continue to be a wall between her and Troy. She was determined to see her husband when she got to Palm Springs if it was the last thing she ever did.

Suddenly she sensed a presence in the bathroom. It was so startling and unnerving that she came up out of the colored water with such force that it sloshed over the side of the tub. Her eyes instantly open wide, she was shocked to see a figure rush toward her.

She bolted out of the water to get a better chance to defend herself. To her horror, she saw that the man wore a dark uniform and mask. In his gloved hands he held a piece of material.

"No!" Mia shrieked, unaware that the cry had come from her own throat.

The madman didn't stop. He tried to loop the cloth around her neck. His gloved hands slid over her skin and she shuddered. She fought desperately to keep him from getting the noose over her head, yet she seemed to feel it tightening before it ever touched her throat—tightening and cutting off her breath and her heartbeat. Fragmented thoughts raced through her mind, but foremost was the desire to save herself, to survive, no matter what.

The attacker struggled to get the scarf around her neck, and Mia was terrified of losing her footing in the slippery tub full of oily water. Her heart thundered in her ears and her breath came in panicked gasps; the fear was filling her head, engulfing her. She could smell sweat on the man's body, hear his ragged breathing, and feel the raw fear that filled the air like a foul odor.

She clawed at the man's masked face, but her hands were shaking so much they were useless. Hysteria rose in her throat, choking her as surely as the scarf that filled her sight.

She battled to catch her breath, to gain control of her trembling hands, to push down the fear and think, but it was hopeless.

She was cold—so cold that her blood seemed to slow in her veins. The man's body was hot and damp with sweat and soap. He gripped her hair and wrenched her head back, holding her pinned while she pushed at his bulk and futilely tried to force him away.

Then, without thought, she raised her knee and jammed it into his crotch. He groaned, releasing her hair for a moment. She frantically twisted away, trying to escape him.

Water plunged over the side of the tub as Mia struggled to stay upright. Bent over from the pain, the man slipped backward on the wet floor, but he took her with him, dragging her by the scarf still caught around her neck.

Mia instinctively shoved the heel of her hand into the man's face and tried to slip by him. He caught her arm, and the rubber gloves he wore held her fast. She tried to override the panic that spread inside her in rising swells. She couldn't let him win. She had to save herself.

Donevan was stunned and unprepared for the battle taking place. He hadn't expected Mia to fight. Rage swelled in his head, and he could smell bitter fear in his nostrils. He was soaked in sweat, and the spinning inside was so great that he could barely stand.

He tried to hold on to Mia's flailing arms, but he couldn't keep his balance on the wet floor. The struggle only made the excitement more exquisite. His blood was hot and flowing in his veins, and his prick was so stiff he thought he might explode.

Even though he managed to hang on to her with one hand, Mia succeeded in shoving her attacker against the cupboards. He lost his footing and almost went down, only staying on his feet by forcing his weight against her.

Mia slipped on the wet tile and hit the floor with a sickening thud. The light dimmed and blackened, flickered from black to slivered silver to black again. She fought against the darkness, knowing if she gave in, she was lost.

Dead. Murdered like that young girl in town. She reached up, grasping at empty air.

His breathing labored, his excitement and fear at a fever pitch, Donevan leaned down, striking Mia repeatedly. Everything was boiling and building inside him, filling him with that feeling that drove him like a demon.

She would not win out over him, even if he had to kill her with his fists. This was not how he had meant it to be, and that made him fierce with fury, but it wouldn't stop him. Nothing would.

The pain of the blows across her face made the darkness retreat in Mia's head. The light wavered once, twice, then grew bright. She would not let this lunatic murder her while she had a breath left in her body. She knew she had to get up off the floor, but she wasn't sure how. She was confused and hurting; the blows were relentless.

Yet she knew that she was strong. Not only mentally, but physically. She often worked with weights to build her upper body for the endurance needed to give massage for long periods of time. She *had* to survive.

She found the strength to bite down on one of his hands. The rubber glove almost gagged her, but it served her as well as it had him when he had grasped her wet arm. He grunted with a mixture of rage, pain, and surprise.

The unexpected counterattack gave Mia the chance she'd needed. When he momentarily stopped pummeling her, she grabbed him by one leg and wrenched him down to the wet floor on his back.

Donevan felt the breath rush from his body, and for an instant he wondered if the bitch had broken his back. He hurt real bad but had to get up. He couldn't see straight, and colors and shadows flickered across his eyes. He was losing control.

He had no idea what she would do next. Fear began to

override the fury and excitement of the danger. She stared down at him for a moment as she scrambled to her feet, then vanished.

He told himself that her gaze meant nothing. Her power was not as great as his, no matter what she saw with those eyes. He struggled up from the floor sloppy with bathwater and oil.

He almost lost his footing in his haste to follow the masseuse. He clutched the counter until he could reach the safety of the rug in the hall. From another room he heard the woman's voice, high and frantic. She was probably calling the fucking cops.

Caught in a moment of indecision, Donevan hesitated. He was all worked up—wet, in pain, covered in sweat, with his fury still like poison inside him. In fact, he'd never known such sheer excitement. But he couldn't risk losing the game. If he did, it meant prison.

The scarf trailing from one hand, he instinctively raced for the back door. His single thought was that he had to get away. He *would*. He wasn't going back to prison, and that was all there was to it.

At the bottom of the hill Buck turned away from the television set when he heard an automobile roaring down from the masseuse's house. By the time he reached the window, he was almost too late. The automobile—car, truck, whatever it was—didn't have the lights turned on.

"Come look at this, Emma," Buck called out.

Emma stubbornly shook her head.

"Emma!" he called, glancing away from the window. "There's something strange about this."

"I don't care." The old woman adjusted her glasses. "It's almost time for Randolph Mason. I told you this is his first movie, and his part ain't long. I ain't going to miss it."

"Fool woman," Buck muttered, turning back to the window. He didn't know why he'd bothered with her. She'd caused him to lose sight of the driver entirely. From what he could gather—and he was only guessing—it was a dark truck, but hell, it could have been anything.

He snorted in disgust. "You made me miss it," he accused.

"I didn't make you do nothing," she retorted. "I told you all day I was going to watch this show. Don't bother me till it's over."

He plopped down in his rocking chair and stared at the cowboys on the screen, still wondering who'd come down the hill hell-bent for leather. He smiled to himself. Apparently somebody hadn't liked his treatment tonight.

Donevan couldn't decide who he was most angry with, himself or that fucking woman on the hill. Shit, she'd been strong! Nothing at all like that stupid druggie girl. He hadn't been prepared, after all. He was sweating like a damned pig, and his heart was pounding. As he turned the corner to leave the winding road behind him, he heard sirens.

Automatically he felt a new surge of adrenaline. He'd beaten those bastards! They'd never connect him to her now. By the time they got to the top of the hill, he'd be home.

He frowned as he crossed the street toward the other side of town. He'd outsmarted the cops, but that bitch had beaten him. He reached down to his crotch without thinking about what he was doing. He had one hell of a hard-on, but then, it had been one hell of a night!

There was no reason tonight should be a total waste. No reason at all. The police would be busy with the masseuse, screwing around with questions and looking for finger-prints. His heart began to beat wildly again. Thank the fates for Oregon rain. His tire tracks wouldn't even show in the woods. With all that water and mess in the bathroom he was safe from ID there. He and that cunt had been all over the bathroom floor, scrabbling and struggling.

No sweat. Nothing to worry about. He was too smart for them all. This had just been a delay, not a defeat. Hell, he still had time to find some entertainment. He was much too wired to go home. Wired and mad. Damn that bitch!

There would be another time for her. And he would be ready. Now he knew what to expect.

Her fighting had turned him on. He could have conquered her at any time if he'd only known what to expect, but he'd gotten too stimulated in all the brawling and battling and slipping and sliding. Next time would be different.

He waited until the sirens began to fade, then drove slowly down the road. He wasn't sure where he was going, but he knew he couldn't go home yet. There was only that old haggy landlady, and he didn't want to see her tonight. Unless, of course, he needed her for an alibi.

Mrs. Ginnby sat on the couch next to her neighbor, Mrs. Oslow, both sipping hot tea while they stared at the western on television.

"This isn't really my kind of show," Mrs. Ginnby said, looking at the other woman over her half-glasses.

Gazing at her landlady a little oddly, Mrs. Oslow managed a tight smile. "Sarah, you might own the building," the feisty gray-haired woman said, "but this is *my* apartment."

Sarah Ginnby seemed startled for a moment. She was in no position to complain about what Grace Oslow watched on her own TV set. She was so grateful that her tenant had let her move in with her until the building could be sold that she wouldn't open her mouth ever again if it was going to upset the other woman!

"Sorry," Sarah said. "I was just making a comment. I'm indebted to you for letting me stay. I've been too terrified to stay in my own apartment since that girl was murdered, and I don't have anywhere else to go."

Grace smiled faintly. She was also scared living here herself since that girl's death, and she had been more than glad to let Sarah move in. She was also hoping the other woman would want her as a roommate when she sold the building and found a better place to live.

Reaching across the distance that parted them, she patted Sarah's hand. "I didn't mean to sound cross, dear. I've found that I enjoy your company very much. I wish we'd become friends before this terrible thing forced us to be companions. I've always admired you."

"Thank you," Sarah said. She'd never thought much about Grace Oslow. She was just another renter and as poor as Sarah's other tenants. However, she was growing fonder of the woman every moment.

"I only wanted to see this program because Randolph Mason is listed in the credits," Grace said. "It's one of his first movies. Actually, I don't like westerns either. As soon as his part is over, we'll switch the channel."

Grace smiled broadly this time. "I'm sure our interests are more similar than you think. I think our life and destinies are very much alike."

Sarah returned the smile, and they gave their attention to the television set.


When the police arrived, Mia was dressed in a sari, the first and most comfortable thing she could find. She had no idea or interest in the fact that the police were more than a little curious about her, or that they found her beautiful, despite her flushed face and the lacerations and bruises that were already beginning to show.

"Really, I don't want to go to the hospital," she insisted.

She felt foolish and out of control. If she hadn't had such a bad night and gotten so angry at Troy, she felt she never would have been at such a disadvantage with the attacker. However, she knew the logic of this was absurd.

What defense had she had? The reason she was really annoyed was that she was such a weak witness against the man who'd tried to strangle the life out of her. She, who was used to working with people, used to sizing up body types and paying particular attention to details, had been so shocked and unsettled that she could tell the police very little, despite the lengthy scrabble she'd had with the man.

"Let's just go down to the emergency room and get you checked out," one officer said in a soothing, encouraging voice. "If we can get you calmed down a little, maybe you can remember more. We've got to catch this pervert. We need all the help we can get."

Mia sighed. She really didn't want to go, yet she couldn't argue with his reasoning. She felt ridiculous. She could remember so little. She tried to explain it away, telling herself it had been dark in the bathroom with only the candle for light, but there was more to it than that. The surprise of the whole scene had shocked her until she was almost numb, mentally and physically.

"There's a very nice nurse who handles these cases in the emergency room," the same officer said. "You won't feel uncomfortable at all with her."

Mia felt reassured, and she realized that she'd been absurdly uncomfortable with the two officers. One of them had come to investigate her months ago when a neighbor accused her of running a brothel here in the cottage.

The nicer of the two officers smiled at her. "You'll need a jacket. It's cold out."

Mia looked around her house. It was cold in, too. In fact, she thought it must be cold in the very pit of the world tonight.

Donevan wound up at Frannie Welch's house without even knowing how or why. His mind was whirling and he still had that damned scarf clutched in one hand. It had gotten wet when he battled with the masseuse, but it had dried in the heat inside the truck.

He switched off the heater. He was already hot. Much too hot. Inside and out. Something had to give. When he realized where he was, he eased down the street a short distance and looked around. Her car was parked inside the fenced grounds, but then, so was another car.

The huge man's—what was his name? Brett something or other—from the masseuse's client list. The man who had followed Frannie Welch home from the party. Donevan glared at both cars. He could just imagine what was going on inside the house.

He was suddenly very, very angry. He had been foiled once tonight, and he wasn't about to engage in another fight. Not that he was afraid; he just didn't have the inclination. He wanted some action. Some real action.

He put the truck in gear and started away. He was automatically drawn to the druggie girl's house. Everything had been so easy when he offed her. Everything had gone so well. He felt better when he parked in front of the apartment building.

## ⤙ CHAPTER 21 ⤚

After meeting with the nurse at the hospital, Mia was in a calmer state of mind when it came to talking with the officers in the emergency room.

The older officer turned to Mia. "Do you think it was one of your—clients?"

She resented the deliberate pause, but suddenly a vision of the man in the uniform and mask rushed to mind. He'd had brown eyes. She remembered that because she, too, had subconsciously been set in the belief that the man might have been one of her clients: Donevan Raitt!

The only two clients she had with brown eyes were Lane Ross and Frank. Either body type might have fit the man who attacked her. She couldn't believe it was Frank. She wouldn't believe it, no matter what the secrets in his past. And she didn't think it was Lane Ross, either. She couldn't bear to think it.

However, he had mentioned the murdered girl. And he had mentioned a client's missing scarf. Mia shook her head. She wasn't about to mention her own doubts. They were too vague and insubstantial. She refused to believe that either man had been involved.

Maybe she'd mistaken the eye color in the darkness of the room. Maybe the candle had added to the deception. Yet she knew that she had seen brown eyes. She had been accustomed to the darkened room before the attacker entered. He had been at a much bigger disadvantage than she.

"Mia," the younger officer said more kindly, "do you think it could have been someone you were treating? We checked you out when we got that complaint from your neighbor, and we know that you deal with troubled people."

Mia looked evenly at him. "I want to do everything I can to help, Officer Reardon, but I don't think we should start pointing the finger at my clients. After all, when I called about the young girl who was murdered, I was assured that it was drug-related."

"Things have changed," the man said. "We don't know exactly what we're dealing with, but the situation's gotten a lot more dangerous. Maybe we've got a serial killer. Who knows how many other people might get hurt? I don't need to tell you that we have to explore every possible lead, and we start with the most likely suspects—those with records."

Mia nodded. She knew he was making a reasonable request. "I'm treating a paroled rapist, but I don't think he's into murder."

The two officers exchanged a glance, then began to jot down information. They stepped outside the examining room when the doctor arrived. Mia knew they were already considering Donevan as a prime suspect.

Donevan sat in front of the aged apartment building in a line of other vehicles. The black truck didn't stand out in this dark, ratty section, and even if it did, he didn't care at the moment. He was busy reliving the girl's murder. It had been the highlight of his life.

When he came to the crucial point, where he had stifled the life out of her, he unconsciously began to play with the scarf. He was aware that his dick was harder than ever. He was going to have to do something about the poison tonight. He couldn't go home this way. Shifting his erection to the left side, he got out of the truck and slipped down the stairs to the back of the building where the girl had lived.

Everything was quiet. He stood outside the main door for a few minutes. He found that he could recall every detail of the murder with vivid clarity. He reviewed it over and over until he thought he couldn't stand any more.

He was jarred from his thoughts by the sound of guns firing. For a moment he stood still in sheer panic, his heart hammering, his breath bated.

Then he realized that the sounds came from an upper apartment. The droning noise of men's voices followed the gunshots. Donevan stared at the upstairs windows. Dingy shades shielded the occupants from him, but didn't deter him. He wanted to know who was watching somebody get shot. He wanted to know real bad.

Slipping up the steps to the second floor, he furtively made his way toward the apartment. He paused outside the front door just as someone switched the channel.

"Will this do, dear?" an old woman's voice asked over the sounds of laughter, apparently from a comedy show.

Another old woman's voice replied, "Anything you want to watch, Grace. Anything at all."

Donevan's pulse began to race.

"Bingo!" he muttered aloud.

It sounded like two old broads. He'd check them out. What better luck could he have tonight? Two old broads for one masseuse. It wasn't a bad trade-off. Anyway, he'd had good luck in this apartment building. He saw it as an omen.

"Are you sure you don't want us to call someone to stay with you or take you to a relative's house?" the young officer asked when they had driven Mia back to the cottage and gone inside with her.

She shook her head. "No, thanks." She had resisted their advice that she spend the night in the hospital, and she didn't have anywhere else she wanted to stay.

"You will be available if we need to talk to you again, won't you?" the other cop asked.

"I'm leaving for California soon," she said. "In a matter of days, in fact."

"Is there an address where we can reach you?"

She hesitated only a moment. "Yes, at my husband's house."

They both looked surprised, but she avoided their eyes as she gave them the address and telephone number. She would be there. She was determined. And Troy was still her husband, after all.

But even she wondered for how long.

When she entered the house, she had that same chilled, numb feeling she'd had once before. The cottage had always been a refuge for her; the fact that an intruder had defiled her home upset her more than anything else about the horrible, nearly fatal evening. She felt as if not only she, but everything she held dear, had been violated.

She shuddered as she went to the bathroom to view the aftermath of the battle with her would-be killer. There was evidence that the crime lab people had been there. Suddenly it was more than Mia could bear. She didn't want to stay here another day.

Instead of cleaning the bathroom, her natural inclination,

she went to her bedroom and packed. She hadn't scheduled any appointments for the rest of the week anyway, and even if she had, she knew she couldn't work with anyone. She was in a state of barely controlled hysteria. Her whole world was collapsing, and she felt as unsettled and unsure as the reckless waves throwing themselves at the rocks at the foot of the cliff. The wind howled outside and Mia trembled. A full-fledged storm was brewing; she felt like the whole world was in turmoil.

She had lost her way as surely as if the crazy man had done her more harm than the obvious physical injuries. She realized how vulnerable she was. She knew she would be until she worked out her life with Troy. And Rand.

For some inexplicable reason a new thought struck her. She had missed her period. She had never missed a period in her life. The possibility that she could be pregnant had never occurred to her. Now she didn't know whether to be despondent or elated. She wouldn't know until she had resolved her situation with Troy.

With gloved fingers Donevan eased the credit card along the edge of the back door of the apartment. He could hear the canned laughter, and it made him smile. The door gave way to a chain that stretched so wide he could easily unhook it.

Pulling his mask into place, he sneaked into the kitchen lit by the light from the single lamp in the living room.

For a moment he studied his surroundings, making sure he had an escape route when the time came. Not that he expected any trouble; on the other hand, he didn't know for sure. Maybe there was someone else in the house. He'd only heard two old women, and he was betting they were the only ones home. But he was too smart not to be prepared. Just in case.

He'd fucked up with the masseuse. But what the hell? Somebody would pay, and it wouldn't be him. Anyway, her turn would come. The excitement was only heightened by the delays. His anger had cooled a little, but that whirling inside him was full-blown. The poison was pushing his prick against his zipper.

He eased down the hall as stealthily as a cat, never making a noise. Although the building was old, it was obviously solidly built, and the carpeted floors muffled any sounds. Besides, the old women had the television up so loud he was surprised the neighbors didn't complain. One, or both of them, must be hard of hearing.

He could feel that churning feeling that he loved so well. Fuck the masseuse. This might be a hell of a lot more fun. He'd thought about killing his landlady a couple of times and knew how risky that was. These old women just might satisfy that urge. At least for a while.

Moving silently into the bedroom, he waited a minute for his eyes to adjust to the darkness, then assured himself that no one was there. He paused long enough to admire the neatness of the room. There were two single beds, both tidily made up. The dresser and highboy were orderly, too. He liked that.

Easing out of the room, he checked the bath and found it in order. And empty. Two broads all alone, waiting like overripe plums to be plucked.

He got very, very excited. Two of them! This was going to be a challenge, but he was determined there would be no fuckup like with the cunt masseuse. He was betting these old bags would be as easy as the druggie girl. And twice as much fun.

Suddenly he entered the living room. "Evening, ladies," he announced.

Both women gasped and one cried out. Donevan was across the room with his hand over her mouth before she could make another noise. In the process he knocked the other woman off the couch with his open hand. She lay on the floor, weeping silently, her broken glasses beside her.

"All right now," Donevan advised, "just be quiet, and I

mean *quiet,* and maybe everything will be okay. Do you understand?" He looked from one terrified woman to the other.

When they both nodded, he removed his hand from the woman's mouth and grinned. He couldn't wait to get started!

⇐ **CHAPTER 22** ⇒

Mia picked up the phone, intending to call Frank to tell him about her change in plans. She wanted him to know what had happened and have him keep a closer eye on the cottage than he usually did. Yet her hand trembled as she reached out to dial his number.

"This is ridiculous," she said aloud.

Frank was her friend. He hadn't tried to kill her. She was coming unglued. Before she could waver again, she dialed his number.

Donevan was so high that he could barely contain himself. He'd tied up both women's hands and legs with their own bras taken from their bedroom, had gagged them and removed their robes. Other than a few whining whimpers and pleas that he not hurt them, they hadn't resisted at all. He grinned at them as he recognized the blatant terror in their aged eyes.

He'd flung their robes back around them, more because they repulsed him than for any other reason. Now he sat down between them on the sofa and looked at the TV set. But he was simply too wired, too fidgety, to drag this pleasure out. He looked from one to the other. He was having such fun. He could almost believe that this was better than the masseuse.

Yet when he thought of her, he began to get sick inside. He didn't like that. No matter how he felt now, he knew he'd failed with the masseuse. It was like a little cancer somewhere inside him, eating at him, reminding him that this wasn't the way the evening should have gone at all.

Control, he reminded himself. He was in control of *this* situation. And that was what counted.

"Girls," he said, savoring the phrase for the two old broads, "I don't like this show."

Actually he didn't give a shit about TV of any kind; he just wanted to toy with the women, liven up this party. They looked at each other helplessly, then at the television set as if they could will it to change channels.

Donevan felt such power, such strength. They could do nothing, even if they wanted to please him. They were totally helpless.

The feisty one, the one who had tried to scream when he plunged into the room, finally attempted to speak around her gag.

"You got something to say?" Donevan asked, looking right into her watery eyes. When she nodded, he jerked her gag down. He noticed that her lip tore a little with the rough movement. A thin line of blood oozed from the small tear.

"Please change the station to whatever you want," Grace Oslow said, her voice filled with fear and desperation. "Do whatever you want. Take whatever you want, but please don't hurt us."

Donevan yanked the gag back in place. God, he hated blood. If only the old bitch hadn't started bleeding. He just couldn't stand it. He was getting that bad feeling. This wasn't really where he wanted to be. These old women weren't even as much fun as the druggie girl. He despised whiners.

Abruptly he struck the old woman across the face, knocking her against the end of the couch. Then he got up. He didn't want to be here anymore. He pulled the black scarf with the initials from his pocket and looped it around his hands. When he saw a strange look flitter across the other woman's face, he paused.

Fear quickly replaced the peculiar look, but Donevan was sure he'd seen it all the same. He undid her gag. She was shaking all over.

"You like this scarf?" he drawled tormentingly.

"Where did you get that?" Sarah Ginnby whispered in a barely audible voice.

Donevan looked at the sleek cloth. "Why?"

"It's—it's mine," she said, her voice cracked and wispy. "I lost it."

Donevan was taken aback for a moment. Talk about coincidences! Suddenly he laughed. So! It was the old bitch's own scarf! What a fine turn of events! This was meant to be, after all! The irony of stealing a scarf from the realtor's car and then strangling its owner—a total stranger who happened to be in the same apartment building where the girl had lived—amused him as nothing had in a while.

He began to feel a hell of a lot better about the masseuse. The bad feeling was giving way to a good one, blending and merging inside him now. In fact, he decided that it would be the ultimate irony if he strangled the masseuse with her own necklace, just like he was going to do the old woman. He liked that idea.

He stared down at his victim. Her robe was red and black. "Where did you lose it?"

Sarah shook her head. "I don't know. I thought I left it in the realtor's car. It's very expensive. I—I reported it to the police."

"Do you want it back?" Donevan taunted. "It's a good match for your robe."

She shook her head. "No, please, you keep it. Just take whatever else you want and go away."

Donevan laughed again. He intended to do just that. He

lay the scarf across the old woman's shoulders and tied it in a knot.

Then he stood back and looked at her. "Not bad, but not good. Let's see how it looks on your friend."

To his surprise, when he turned around, the other woman had struggled off the couch to the floor and was inching her way around the end, her saggy naked rear exposed because her robe had fallen off.

Donevan watched her laborious struggle for a moment. She didn't turn around; she had no idea he was observing her pitiful attempt to hide. On her hands and knees she could only drag along a little at a time, like a hobbled creature. She couldn't possibly escape.

"Grace!" Sarah called out.

Donevan glanced at her, and she seemed to slink down into herself.

When Grace turned around, there was a pathetic, helpless look on her face. Donevan motioned for her to continue, waving his hand toward the back of the couch. When the old woman stayed where she was, immobile with fear, he kicked her in the butt, causing her to sprawl forward in a most humiliating position.

Then he went back to Sarah and pulled her gag up.

"I guess that means you want to go first," he said.

Sarah shook her head, but it was too late for protests.

"Here's your scarf back, old woman," Donevan said, swiftly untying the knot, then wrapping the cloth around his hands and looping it about the woman's frail neck. He tightened it more and more. More and more.

Her eyes wide, Sarah seemed to be trying to scream, but there was no sound as her face contorted. She reeked of fear, the smell sickly sweet as she began to go slack and slip down beneath Donevan's crushing hands.

He felt his power rise. Jesus, that feeling, that incredible feeling! His penis pushed against his pants. He thought he might explode.

Suddenly the other old woman was at his side, trying to push him away from her friend with her bony body against his legs. He kicked at her as if she were a dog while the last gagging breath left Sarah Ginnby's body. He heard a cracking sound, but he was too preoccupied to pay much attention. Grace moaned in pain.

Donevan finally turned to the horrified woman who had begun to cry and mumble against her gag. Her leg was at an odd angle. Tears streamed down her face as she stared at it.

Donevan's fury grew. He wanted to stop those tears forever. Just like he'd wanted to stop his mother's. Shit, he hated crybabies!

He yanked the scarf from around Sarah's neck and quickly looped it around Grace's. To his joy, she bucked and flinched and fought death every inch of the way, just as she'd tried to escape it by pointlessly dragging herself toward the back of the couch.

No one could escape Donevan Raitt. *No one!*

The struggle only added to his pleasure. He felt his power swell to the bursting point as the old woman died in his strong hands. Jesus, he loved the feeling. He was sweating through the mask. The front of his pants was getting wet.

He looked down at the woman at his feet, toppled over now, her face twisted, her eyes bulging slightly from their sockets. Swiftly he unzipped his pants, grabbed her robe from the floor where it had fallen, and tossed it over her. Then he ejaculated, spewing his semen, his power, over the front of her pink robe.

When he turned back to look at the other woman, he was driven by something inside him to pull her red and black robe away from her body. He stared at her for a long time.

Then he dropped down on his knees and began to suck at one drooping, empty sack of a breast.

"Mama," he rasped hoarsely around the dry nipple. "Mama."

* * *

Mia packed like a crazy woman. She just couldn't seem to slow down. She had never felt so vulnerable, so violated, in her life. She'd never imagined feeling this way—as though she would never be safe again as long as she lived.

She wanted someone to hold her. She wanted someone to understand the fear and the hurt. She wanted Troy.

Frannie Welch giggled as Brett Williams lifted her up in his arms and carried her into his house. "It ain't much, sugar, but it's paid for."

"Oh, Brett," Frannie said, her arms around his bull-like neck as she looked around the living room, "it's wonderful and you know it."

He laughed loudly and deeply. "So I lied. It's not bad for a little boy from the Bronx who made the big time, lost it, and then made it again in commercials, is it? I'm leaving for California tomorrow to do a new one."

"It's incredible," Frannie gushed, suddenly wishing with all her heart that he would offer to take her with him to California. "But you deserve every bit of it, Brett. *You're* incredible."

"Do you think so?" he murmured, his green eyes assessing her face.

She nodded as he stood her on her feet. "I really do think so. I really do."

Brett had made all the difference in her life. She hadn't been able to do it, and God hadn't been able to do it, but Brett Williams had come out of nowhere and changed her whole world.

He chuckled deep and low. "You *really, really* do think so?" he teased.

Frannie nodded and tossed back her frizzy blond hair. If he only knew how much, but she was afraid to tell him, afraid to scare him away. She needed him desperately in her life now, and she was clinging as hard as she could without smothering him.

"I've started a new book," she confessed shyly. "You're the hero."

"The hero! I'm impressed. In fact, I'm so impressed that I think we should go upstairs and let me show you how good a hero I can be," he joked. "You ain't seen nothing yet."

Frannie pretended to widen her eyes. "I hope you don't mean what I think you mean, you bad boy!" she retorted playfully.

Actually, she hoped he had in mind exactly what she had. They had gone out a couple of times, but he hadn't made love to her yet. She was starving for some physical attention. She knew she would need it worse than ever with the masseuse going out of town.

Brett whisked her back up in his arms and made his way up the steps to the bedroom. "Girl, you got a good thing coming," he murmured, scattering kisses across her face.

Frannie hoped so. God knew she hoped so.

"Arrogant, aren't you, and just a little too sure of yourself," she protested all too lightly. "We hardly know each other."

Chuckling, Brett nodded. "I know. I intend to change that last part right now. When this night is over, we're going to know each other like you've never imagined knowing a man."

He laid her down on the bed, stretched out beside her, and undid her blouse and bra. "Beautiful. Simply beautiful," he whispered.

He began to tantalize her with his tongue and lips. "Mmm, tasty," he murmured between sucking on her nipples and tracing them with his tongue.

Frannie pressed his head closer. She was slowly slipping into heaven and loving every second of it. She felt sexy and sensual as she hadn't in far too long.

Brett slipped off her bra, then finished undressing her. "I've got to see more of you, you lovely, lovely thing," he said thickly.

Frannie was dying to see more of him, too, but she didn't want to be too aggressive. She was terrified of losing him, even as she eagerly longed to have him. She just wanted to feel his pulsating penis push up deep inside her, driving away the pain and the loneliness, the rejection and the hurt.

Slowly, surely, she guided him in, then began to ride the engorged flesh that gave her such incredibly satisfying sensations.

Donevan was seething when he returned to his rooming house. He didn't know what was wrong with him these days. He should be feeling real high because he'd offed those old bags. Instead, he had a splitting headache and felt somehow disgusted. He didn't like the feeling. His head was reeling when he should have been having that roiling mix of fear and pleasure that he savored so much.

Something had gone wrong in his mind. Somehow his mother had crept in like cancer and crashed his party. That was just like the prissy cunt. She'd ruined everything all his life. It was her fault that nothing went right for him. If she hadn't gone off to California with that sleazy bastard she was screwing—

Suddenly he rolled over on his back and unzipped his pants. Usually when he thought of his mother, he could get a real good hard-on. But not this time. All he could think of was that dried-up old prune he'd killed. The taste of her withered nipple was still in his mouth.

He wished he'd bitten the pukey thing off and spit it out. He was feeling sick to his stomach. At least he'd been smart enough to take the other bitch's pink robe and get rid of it, destroying the evidence of his cum. That had been smart, but he wasn't feeling very smart now.

And his dick wasn't doing a damned thing. It was as useless as some old fart's. He shoved himself off the bed and went in search of the masseuse's hemp necklace. Damn that cunt for fucking him over!

\* \* \*

Mia arrived in California the next afternoon. She was bruised and battered from her brush with death, and she was in no mood to be put off by Daniel again. She rented a car to drive to the house in Palm Springs. She knew she was earlier than expected. That was exactly what she intended.

When Daniel answered the door, Mia realized she had succeeded in surprising him. She had never surrendered her electric gate opener; consequently, Daniel thought she was someone who was welcome and used to coming to the house.

"Hello, Daniel," she said, forcing a smile.

He was clearly taken aback for a moment, but he soon regained his stoic countenance. His face became as impassive as if he were greeting a casual acquaintance.

"Mrs. Jorgenson. We weren't expecting you today."

Mia nodded. "Yes, I know. I'm tired of playing games, Daniel. I want to see Troy."

"I'm afraid I have strict orders—"

"To hell with your orders! I'm his wife! Who do you think *you* are, for heaven's sake? We—Troy and I—hired you as a nurse and companion, not a bodyguard."

For the first time Daniel seemed to notice Mia's appearance. "Have you been injured?" he blurted, more out of surprise than anything else.

"I'm all right."

She opened the door and tried to shove past him. When he grabbed her arm, she cried, "Let me go! I will not allow you to bar me from my own home—and this is my home, lest you forget."

With a long-suffering sigh that was all too familiar, Daniel gave way. "Go ahead. He's in his bedroom." He released his grip only slightly, then murmured in a low voice, "I suppose it's past time for this meeting, Mrs. Jorgenson. I've felt very sorry about the way things have gone."

"I don't want your pity!" Mia exclaimed, exasperated.

Daniel shook his head. "You really don't understand, do you? I'm trying to prepare you, to tell you that Mr.

Jorgenson's not the man you once knew. He's not even the man you saw the last time you visited."

At Mia's stunned expression, Daniel said in a low, tense voice, "Do you understand me? Can you compose yourself when you go in there? He's deteriorated more and more over the weeks."

Tears welled in Mia's eyes. "You had no right to prevent me from speaking to him, Daniel!" she accused, hurt and shock twisting her usually serene face. "No right. He's my husband. I should have been notified about his condition. I should have been here with him."

For the first time Mia saw undisguised compassion on the huge man's face; it moved her more than all his warnings and refusals to let her speak with or see her husband.

"It was never my idea, Mrs. Jorgenson. I've been sympathetic to your cause from the first, but don't you understand that the man is dying? He deserves to be left with some dignity."

"Dying!" she cried, the tears building. "And you've kept me from him? Oh, Daniel, why didn't you tell me?"

Without allowing him time to respond, she brushed past him, her high heels clicking on the expensive Moroccan tile. She was dressed beautifully, in a red suit and red and black shoes with matching purse.

Troy had always liked her in red. He had always said the color made her look sensual. She had wanted to look especially good for him today.

Mia rapped twice on the bedroom door, then opened it. "Troy! Troy, it's Mia!"

She gasped audibly when she saw the shriveled man lying on the king-size bed they had once shared as man and wife. He seemed much too small and weak for such a large bed. Tears sprang to Mia's eyes as she tried desperately to remember Daniel's warning to compose herself.

At the moment it seemed more than was humanly possible. Troy was but a shell of the man she had known, a wasted, pitiful creature with pain distorting his once-handsome features. He was clearly as shocked by her appearance as she was by his.

Racing across the massive room in an attempt to close the gap between them, the gap she now realized was a hopeless chasm, she sat down on the side of the bed and took Troy's trembling hands in her own.

"I'm so sorry, love, I didn't know you were this ill. I tried to call. I tried to come——"

With great effort Troy raised one of her hands to his quivering lips and gave it a dry, fragile kiss.

"I know," he whispered. "I didn't want you to see me like this." He looked down at his atrophied body. "God knows I didn't. It won't be long now, and I clung to the hope that Daniel could keep you away until it was over."

Tears slipped unchecked down Mia's face. She had been wrong to come here. She had done this man an unpardonable injustice. Daniel was right. Troy deserved to die with dignity; she had stripped that from him.

"I'm so sorry," she murmured. "I didn't know."

His hands were shaking so badly that Mia didn't know if he could hang on to hers.

"I wanted you to remember me in better times, my precious," he half-moaned. He tried to smile and failed. "I wanted to remember *you* in better times. What happened?" He gestured to her battered face.

The words seemed to cost him greatly; he was visibly upset by her appearance. She had managed to cover most of the bruises with makeup or clothes, but the terror had taken its toll.

She shook her head. She had rushed here seeking comfort, seeking her husband's support; now she knew that there was none to be found. This man couldn't even support himself.

Troy had been right. She should have let him go a long time ago. She could have saved them both this humiliation and agony, this final unforgettable heart-wrenching memory.

"I was always clumsy," she whispered, finding the

strength somehow to force a smile through her tears. "I fell down the steps at the cottage."

Troy shook his head. "I never have liked you being there all alone. I wish you would come back to California where people can look after you."

His watery eyes met hers, and he laughed bitterly. "Not me, of course. You can see that I can't even look after myself. Cancer. Any time now."

Mia squeezed his quaking hands. "I'm fine in Oregon," she murmured. "I have a good practice, and I'm happy."

His eyes searched her face. "Then maybe it's not so bad you came after all, Mia," he whispered hoarsely. "All I've ever wanted was your happiness. And I could no longer give it to you. You understand that now, don't you?"

She nodded, and tried her best to stem the streaming tears, but it was just no good. She needed to cry. She had needed to cry for—and with—Troy for so very long. Laying her head on his emaciated chest, she sobbed for all that had been and could never be again.

As Troy ran his frail fingers through her hair, she felt his tears dripping off his chin and slipping down on her arms. She held him tightly, knowing this would be the last time.

She was both sorry and glad she had come. The ending of anything that had been so beautiful was both bitter and sweet.

## ☛ CHAPTER 23 ☚

Donevan prowled his rooms, filled with nervous energy. He hadn't slept much at all last night, and he'd been careless at work today. Sure enough two cops had come sneaking around, checking him out, just needling him enough to put him more on edge. He knew they didn't have anything on him, or they would have taken him in for questioning again. He'd sure as hell been through that enough.

But it wasn't only the cops. He didn't know what was the matter with him. He seemed tormented, driven by something inside which his usual methods of release couldn't ease. His hatred for the masseuse grew and grew inside him like a cancer. She had eluded him, but not forever.

He was eaten up inside with his need for revenge. Some evil he hadn't felt before gripped him like a vise. He was simmering with shame and humiliation for letting the masseuse escape. The two old women hadn't been a fair trade, after all. He'd never felt so cheated. His memories weren't good when he reexplored them; that made him feel real bad, like he'd wasted his time.

Unable to stay in his rooms any longer, he left by the back way, as always. When he heard someone call out to him, he looked over his shoulder to see his landlady coming around the side of the house.

"Donevan, you aren't going to be gone long, are you?" she asked in that aged, whining voice he'd begun to despise more and more.

He shook his head. "Just going to get something from the truck," he said more civilly than he felt.

It was none of her fucking business what he was doing, but now wasn't the time to get on the bad side of her. She had been such a good alibi when he'd unexpectedly been taken in for questioning about the druggie girl. Time had passed and he'd been sure he wasn't considered a suspect. Then, out of the blue, the cops had turned up! But he didn't want to think about that.

"Good," she said, clearly relieved. "I'm not trying to pry into your business, son. It's just that I'm afraid alone here at night now."

Donevan smirked. He couldn't help it. "You don't have a

worry in the world. Just keep your doors locked," he said as he went to the truck. After pretending to find what he was looking for, he went back up the steps to his rooms.

As if door locks would keep anybody out, he thought, opening his back door. When he saw the landlady hurry off, he crept down the steps. Mrs. Smith had disappeared into the house as fast as she could. Stupid old bitch.

Suddenly Donevan smiled. At least he'd put the fear of God in some people. Still, that was little consolation just now.

Emma stayed far back from the window this time when she heard an automobile go up the road. Her curiosity had been dampened considerably by the young girl's killing and the attempt on the masseuse.

Rumor had spread fast in the neighborhood. Some of the other neighbors were asking the handyman, Frank, to put better security systems in their houses, but Emma didn't trust that man for a minute. She wasn't about to let him near her house.

But she wasn't about to get too near the window, either. She didn't want to be killed.

"Buck, somebody's going up the hill," she whispered, even though no one outside could possibly hear her.

"What?" he called, absorbed in a TV show.

"Shh!" she said, glaring at him. Why did he have to be deaf at all the wrong times? "Somebody's going up the hill."

Buck left his rocking chair to peer out the edge of the curtain, looking over Emma's shoulder.

"You've done it again," Emma declared, forgetting to whisper. "The car or truck or whatever is already gone. I don't even see taillights now."

Buck glared back at her. "Then we're even," he said petulantly. "You wouldn't look last time I asked you."

"I told you Rand Mason was on TV," she snapped.

He shrugged. "Well, you should have just looked for yourself this time. You didn't need to call me over."

Blinking behind her glasses, Emma murmured, "I'm scared. The killer ain't after men, but he might decide to kill me if he sees me looking."

"Ain't nobody wanting to kill you," Buck growled sarcastically. "You're too much trouble."

Donevan parked the truck in his favorite spot in the woods. He knew the masseuse was supposed to be leaving soon, though he wasn't sure exactly when. Not until the weekend, he thought. Maybe he was a fool to come back here so soon after the attack, but he seemed possessed tonight.

He promised himself he'd take a look around, see what was going on. That was all. Nothing drastic. Just some movement to take off the edge. He still had plenty of time to kill her.

He didn't want to put a scent on his tail, but on the other hand, the police hadn't really seemed to doubt him when he told them how he was never going to fuck up and go back to prison again. When they talked to him at work, they hadn't been real bent on pinning something on him.

Of course, there was the possibility that the old women hadn't been found yet. After all, he'd just killed them last night, and sometimes old people weren't checked on for days.

Anyway, he was betting the police would start with that realtor, Ross. No doubt the old lady had said where she thought she'd left the scarf, if she really had called the police. That pleased him. The realtor just might be in for a little surprise.

When Donevan reached the cottage, he put on his gloves, his mask, got his flashlight, and went around to the sun deck, his favorite way of entry. He slipped the sturdy plastic from his pocket and discovered to his anger that the credit card no longer worked!

Some son of a bitch had put a dead bolt on the door. No doubt that queer shithead who wore the earring and did odd jobs for her.

He fingered his own earring. He'd been stupid to put one in, but he'd thought it would be a good foil, making somebody think the handyman was the killer. He was probably right. It was just that the damned thing had hurt like hell; it still wasn't healed.

Making his way silently around the house, he looked for new ways of entry. His anger was building; he was determined to get in somehow.

Finally he gained entry through the bathroom window. He should have known the dumb cunt wouldn't have thought to secure that. Anyway, even if she had, he would have come back with a glass cutter. She wasn't outsmarting him a second time.

When he had eased into the house, he carefully combed every inch of it. The fucking bitch was nowhere to be found. He looked around her bedroom, then began rummaging through the closet and chest of drawers. He could tell that a lot of things were missing from the last time he'd searched the drawers. She had already gone!

Fury pulsating through him like the heartbeat of a wild beast, he stalked through the house, trying to find some clue, some idea of her whereabouts in California. She had said she would return, but he didn't know if he could wait. Ever since that druggie girl, he'd known he'd never be right with himself until he killed the masseuse.

Suddenly the black cat darted out from under a chair in the bedroom. So, Donevan thought to himself, the woman would definitely come back. He was sure she wouldn't leave the cat forever. That earringed fruit was probably taking care of the animal while she was gone.

Abruptly Donevan decided he would save the man the trouble. He'd take care of the cat himself. For good.

He looked under the chair the animal had fled. For a few minutes he looked everywhere. He wondered if the cat had escaped somehow, too. He refused to let that happen. He couldn't have the masseuse, but he was going to kill that damned black cat if it was the last thing he did tonight.

He paused for a moment. He was really superstitious. What if he did kill the cat and that was the last thing he ever did? He would be cheated forever out of his revenge on the masseuse.

He shook his head. No, the cat's time was up. His nine lives were over. Black or not.

There was a flash of midnight as Soot dashed out from under his mistress's bed. This time Donevan was quick enough to grab him. Soot yowled in terror and writhed and wiggled, trying to get free of his tormentor's grasp, but Donevan wasn't about to let him go.

When the cat bucked and twisted, trying to sink his teeth and claws into Donevan's flesh, the man became enraged. He was going to get this over with as quickly as possible. After all, it wasn't nearly as much fun as killing a woman, and this damned animal was dangerous with those sharp teeth and claws.

The cat was struggling so hard that Donevan hurried down the hall to the bathroom and threw the animal inside. Then he flipped on the light, stepped in, and closed the door.

When he looked down at his hand, he saw that the little bastard had already clawed him. Three red dots were forming on the back of his hand where the glove had been punctured. Blood. *His* blood!

The sight made him reel. He felt a blackness down deep inside him. The cat was going to pay for that. He was really going to pay.

Soot had darted into the shower. Donevan opened the curtain to see where he was. When the cat hissed at him and reared up, Donevan turned the hot water on full force, then directed the scalding spray at the animal.

Trying frantically to flee, meowing in fear and pain, Soot clawed his way up the plastic shower curtain.

Seeing his chance, Donevan caught the animal in the heavy plastic, balling it up around the cat. The hot water had made the fabric stretchy and pliable and Donevan's own rubber gloves stuck to it. If he hadn't been so furious, he would have simply crushed the cat right then and there between his own two hands, but the animal had been a real pain in the ass.

Yanking the shower curtain down from the plastic hooks that held it to the rod, he threw it and the cat to the floor. He saw the thin, wet form of the animal trying to get out from under the cumbersome cover. Donevan grabbed its body again.

Then he tossed back the shower curtain enough so that he could tell one end of the animal from the other. When he saw Soot's black head, he held onto the body with one hand and reached for the cat's wet, scrawny neck with the other.

Unexpectedly the cat opened its mouth wide and bit down with its last bit of strength on Donevan's index finger. The man flung the creature down.

"Fucking son of a bitch!" he cursed.

Soot headed back under the shower curtain, searching for safety, but it was too late. Donevan was past rage. He was boiling with fury, totally freaked out when he saw the blood spurting from his finger.

He stomped down on the moving form and kept stomping and kicking, stomping and kicking, completely out of control. Soot shrieked and howled in pain, but Donevan was oblivious to anything but his own wounds and the blood seeping from him.

His heart was pounding wildly. His head was reeling. There was no mix of good and bad excitement, only horror at what the cat had done. Deep inside, he wondered if he'd been cursed by the black motherfucker.

When the cat's last terrified cries died away, Donevan kicked back the blood-soaked, fur-matted shower curtain. He turned off the hot water, which had steamed up the room, then gathered up the bloodied curtain and battered animal.

He was feeling panicked when he dumped the mess on the sun deck. A haunting refrain in his head kept repeating, "If only the cat hadn't been black, if only the cat hadn't been black . . ." What if the motherfucker had cursed him?

But hadn't he lifted the curse by killing it?

He was suddenly shaking all over. He went back inside the house to the vanity table in her bedroom. Recalling that he'd seen a tray of nail polish there, he carefully picked through the colors with the help of his flashlight. When he had found the brightest pink polish he could find, he took two bottles and carried them out of the house with him.

Out on the sun deck he shined his light on the putrid remains of the cat. He hated all those guts and crushed insides and blood. He thought for sure he was going to puke, but he knew he had to do everything he could in case the cat had cursed him.

He unscrewed the bottles of pink polish and tried to pour them on the body. The contents were too viscous. In a moment of inspiration, he took the nail polish brush and hastily dabbed pink dots here and there on the cat where there was enough left to paint. The stench was beginning to get to him; still, he felt that he had to ward off the curse.

The cat wasn't black now. He was pink polka-dotted. Donevan wished he could smile about the whole thing, but it wasn't in him right now.

As he left the house, he threw the entire mess over the sun deck into the ocean, shower curtain, cat, polish, and all. Then he took off the mask and gloves. He was feeling real weird. He wanted to get out of here.

Emma had stood at the window a long time, barely peeking out, but her vigil did not go unrewarded. Eventually the automobile that had gone up the hill came back down.

"Buck, now!" she hissed.

At his leisure Buck left the comfort of his rocking chair, but he was in time to see the end of a dark truck.

"I'm calling the police," Emma said. "Ain't nobody supposed to be up there at that house. She's gone away."

"Nobody 'cepting Frank," Buck agreed. "Are you sure it wasn't him?"

"He don't drive no truck," Emma said, as if her husband had lost all the good sense he had.

"He does, too, woman. He drives that old truck to haul his gardening stuff in."

Emma shook her head. "It wasn't that old wreck. It was one of her clients. I've seen that truck before."

Buck shrugged. "So maybe it was somebody who didn't remember the woman was leaving town. You didn't see his face, did you?"

Emma shook her head. "No, but it ain't nobody's regular appointment time. I know 'em all."

She suddenly frowned. "Seems like I did see something about the man. Maybe it was Frank. You know that stupid gold hoop earring he wears. It kind of seemed to catch in the floodlight we put up in the front yard yesterday. I seen something bright and round. Maybe," she mused aloud, "he got a new truck."

"Huh," Buck scoffed. "With those eyes of yours? You saw a earring?"

She nodded. "I did, Buck. I'm sure."

He waved her away. "Why don't you just stay away from the durned window, Emma? You're scared to death as it is, and you've been brain-dead since the masseuse moved up there."

Emma put her hands on her hips and glared at her husband. "You're stupid, Buck Carson. Stupid! You might not be on the lookout for a maniac that might kill you, but I ain't about to stop watching."

He shrugged. "So call the police if you think you know something."

She stared at him. "You think you're just daring me, but I'm going to do it. So there!" She marched across the room and picked up the phone. "You know you ain't so smart, Buck. You really ain't."

He laughed and Emma glared at him again.

Frank was running late. He'd given a music lesson to his most promising student, and when he found out the girl had written some of her own material, he had been favorably impressed.

As they worked on her originals, he lost all thought of time. He didn't want to take his work to Nashville, but he thought his student surely had good prospects with hers.

He hurried up the hill, knowing Soot would be fit to be tied because his dinner was late. Mia had spoiled that cat horribly. Frank grinned. He supposed he'd done his share of spoiling, too. He really enjoyed Soot's independent personality. He was a good cat and, like his mistress, sensitive to strangers.

When Frank had parked in the drive, he used his new key and entered the house. "Soot! Soot!" he called. The little devil usually came running to meet him. "Come on, boy! Chowtime!"

Suddenly he sensed that something wasn't right. He couldn't put his finger on it. It wasn't just the fact that the cat hadn't come out. There was a strange feeling in the house, a feeling that something had been spoiled or sullied.

He sniffed the air. There was a deathly stench. His pulse rate increased. Mia had told him she was leaving early, but what if she hadn't managed to get away?

Frantic, he rushed down the hall. "Mia! Mia! Are you here?"

He came to a dead halt at the bathroom door. God, what a mess. Water and cat fur and blood. Frank stood there, appalled. Who had done this? What kind of crazy man was running loose in the town? What was happening around here?

He spun around when he heard footsteps behind him.

Two burly policemen, their guns drawn, pointed directly at him, took a defensive stance.

"Freeze, mister!"

"Wait a minute," Frank protested.

"Face the wall, hands flat, legs spread!"

Frank sighed wearily. He'd been through this before. When would it ever end?


Donevan couldn't stop staring at his bleeding hand. Blood had dripped down on the steering wheel and was making a mess. He stopped the truck long enough to take off his T-shirt and tear it into strips.

When he had wrapped his hand, he drove toward the emergency room. He wanted something done for his pain, but mostly he just wanted them to take away the blood. After he stopped, he was suddenly afraid to go inside. He'd left a mess at the cottage, a stupid mistake; he'd freaked when he found the masseuse gone and the cat so mean.

He sat outside the emergency room for a long time, wishing he knew what to do. Jesus, he hated blood. And he hated his own worst of all.

He was growing angrier and angrier. He didn't know what to do. He'd lost control. Damn it to hell, he'd lost control again!

He really shouldn't have killed the cat. He hadn't even particularly enjoyed it. Not that he wasn't glad to be rid of the little motherfucker. It had happened so fast, just like with the old women, that he hadn't taken any real pleasure in it.

He was finding his relief harder and harder to come by. Only killing the masseuse would keep him satisfied.

Donevan started his car, deciding to return home. Fuck the emergency room. He'd take care of his wound himself. And then he'd plan the masseuse's impending death.

* * *

Mia hadn't known where to go when she left Troy's house. She knew in her heart that she had left a very important part of her behind. She also knew that her life had changed forever. Troy would always be alive for her in her memories, but she knew she would never see him again. They both knew that.

It made her sad deep in her soul. She felt a blackness come over her like nothing she had ever known. She seemed to be riding around aimlessly, drifting about the city she knew well, when she stopped in front of a long, expensive-looking ranch-style house.

Rand's. She hadn't been roaming without direction at all. She had known exactly where she was going.

Instead of heading home, Donevan wound up at a drugstore. There he purchased some peroxide and Band-Aids, and then left.

When he had bound his injury, he felt a little better, but not enough to know what to do with himself. Jesus, he was at loose ends tonight. He didn't know what he wanted to do. He just knew he had to do something. His mind was a blur of conflicting thoughts. His lip started twitching. He knew he was in a hell of a bad way when that happened.

He pulled on the cheap earring he'd put in his ear. He had to get some relief somewhere. He reached down to his crotch, but nothing happened. He couldn't seem to override the strange despair inside him. He pulled on his dick until it hurt, then he drove on through the night.

He didn't know where he was headed, only it wasn't home. Home, hell! To those rooms that the old hag rented him. For the first time in a while, he smiled. The old broad was probably sleeping like a baby, thinking he was upstairs guarding over her.

Dumb bitch! Nobody had a bodyguard. Except maybe the blonde the masseuse worked on, the one who had that monster of a boyfriend, the only woman who thought she'd outsmarted him by not listing herself in the phone book.

Well, he knew where she lived. He knew where she lived, and he wasn't ready to go home yet. He felt like lashing out at the whole fucking world!

## — CHAPTER 24 —

Mia sat in front of Rand's house for a long time. It was late. She felt her stomach. She still hadn't had her period, and her spirits lifted slightly. She prayed to God that she was pregnant. It would mean more to her now than ever.

Troy was going to die; she couldn't stop that. But it seemed a miracle to her that she might bring a new life into the world. She hoped she was carrying a boy. A baby would ease the heartache of losing Troy.

And there was Rand. She couldn't deny that Troy had set her free in a way she had never known she could be. Now she could admit how much she cared for Rand.

She opened the car door and walked down the winding walk to the house. She needed someone badly tonight. She needed Rand. She had needed him for a long, long time, well before she had faced the truth that she'd lost Troy, well before they ever made love.

When she rang the bell, Rand appeared immediately.

"Mia!"

Mia shrugged slightly, hoping he couldn't see her injuries in the muted light. "I—I should have called. Are you busy?"

"No," he said. "You're always welcome. Come on in."

Unexpectedly, Mia burst into tears the moment she

entered the house. She had thought she was all through crying, but a new well seemed to have filled up inside her.

"I'm sorry," she murmured. "I'm sorry."

"Don't be," Rand whispered, gently lifting her in his arms. "You're going to be all right, Mia."

She hid her face in his shoulder and continued to weep as though an ocean of misery still swelled inside her while Rand took her to his bedroom.

His mask on, his rubber gloves covering his wounded hand, Donevan sat cross-legged in the bedroom where Frannie Welch was sleeping. She looked so peaceful, so content, while he was seething with wild, hateful emotions that would give him no peace.

His whole evening had been a disappointment, a fuckup, and he was determined to do this cunt right so he could get some relief. He'd never known these totally uncontrollable feelings before.

If he couldn't jack off with something around his neck, if he couldn't kill something, if he couldn't get rid of the poison inside him, if it wouldn't come out his dick anymore, he didn't know what he was going to do. He was beginning to fear for his life.

What if the poison swelled up his whole body? What if it no longer confined itself to his penis? How was he supposed to get rid of it? He was feeling panicked, and the more peaceful Frannie looked, the more furious he became.

He had lost all track of time. He didn't care. He knew he couldn't go back to the boardinghouse until he got himself taken care of. What good would it do? He would just pace and go madder inside.

The blond woman stretched and the upper half of her body came free of the covers. Donevan stared, trying to decide what to do. He tried playing with his dick, but nothing happened. At least his hand had stopped bleeding.

He got up. He was just too restless to sit there any longer. He began to roam through the house. It was pretty, in a gaudy kind of way, as if the woman had more imagination than taste. But then, what the shit did he know?

He wandered into her study, and suddenly he became more excited than he had been all evening. Seconds ago he had been as low as he could ever recall being. Now he was as high. The room was huge, but it wasn't the size that impressed him.

It was the crap on the walls. He despised cluttered walls, but his own imagination went nuts in here. He knew he was at a disadvantage with his wounded hand, but the bitch had provided him with everything he would need.

Just as if she were expecting him. Just as if she were listening to the plans inside his head. There was a huge picture of a pirate and a partially dressed woman hanging on one wall. A book cover with the same picture was framed by it.

But it was the other stuff that interested Donevan. Jesus, he felt like he'd stumbled into a gold mine. The most bizarre assortment of weapons and contraptions and some things he'd never known existed filled the walls.

He recognized guns, swords, shackles, leg chains, handcuffs, and a whip. This cunt must really be kinky. He was getting turned on. He grabbed his dick and felt such immense relief that he almost howled in glee. It was as stiff as a rod. He had that racing feeling again. He embraced it wholeheartedly.

Looking around the room, shining his flashlight on first one set of bookcases, then another, he scanned titles of all kinds, from the very old to the very new. His light stopped on a big leather-bound book on erotica. He was reminded of the massage book he'd taken from the masseuse's house.

When he went over to pull the book from the shelf, it was so heavy that he dropped it. All kinds of things spilled from it. Donevan stood there and snickered. It wasn't a book at all. It was a front for sex toys: there was a vibrator in the shape of a penis, a French tickler, some silver balls, and several packages of rubbers.

Donevan laughed aloud. He couldn't help it. Jesus! He *had* removed the curse by killing the black cat. He'd just hit the jackpot, and he meant to have himself one hell of a night!

Frank had been grilled before, but never for such serious matters, and never had he been so insulted, not even in Boston. A girl had been murdered, the masseuse had been attacked, the town was scared and angry. These cops were out for blood, too. Anybody's.

It didn't take a genius to figure out they thought they really had something on him. With his past record—no matter how minor—cocaine and possible fondling of one of his students, he was a prime candidate. Being found outside the bathroom door where obviously some serious damage, probably even death, had occurred to the cat, had been the clincher.

They had asked the same questions over and over, hour after hour. Frank was getting weary and disgusted.

"I'm not your culprit. Mia and I are friends. I work as her handyman, I went there to feed the cat, I had just arrived when you did," he said by rote, trying to keep his temper. "Please call her in California, and she'll confirm it. I've told you that a dozen times already."

The smart-ass cop smirked. "We can't reach her in California. We've told you that a dozen times. She's not at her husband's house. He's frantic—says he doesn't know where she went."

"But she did arrive there," Frank reminded them. "She did go to California, and she did leave me in charge of her house, as she always does. Christ, man, use your brain. Why would I go to the cottage to kill her when I knew she was gone? Why would I hurt the cat?"

The other half of the team, the nice-guy front cop, straddled a chair and faced Frank.

"Come on, Frank, make it easy on yourself. We know your drug record. We know all about Boston. We know you're hiding up here in Oregon with all those diplomas not worth a damn. We know you like young girls. Something went wrong with the drug buy and you lost your cool, didn't you?"

Frank shook his head. "I don't use drugs anymore. Check me out. I'm clean."

"Don't play us for dummies, okay? You and the girl had a sweet deal, but it soured. Then you got a taste for killing, didn't you? That's why you went to the masseuse's house and attacked her."

"She's my friend!" Frank exclaimed passionately. "I wouldn't ever harm her."

The cop went on as if the other man had never spoken. "When that failed, you took your frustrations out on that miserable cat, for all the reasons you just gave. You figured you wouldn't be a suspect, but that old woman saw you go up the hill. She saw your black truck."

"I told you I don't own a black truck. It's an old navy blue wreck."

"Blue, black." The policeman shrugged. "At night what's the difference?"

Frank sighed tiredly. When he spoke again, his voice was filled with the pain of mistreatment and unhappiness.

"I want a lawyer."

## ☞ CHAPTER 25 ☜

Mia was still sobbing when Rand laid her down on the satin spread of his round bed. Without saying anything, he lay down beside her and drew her into his arms.

Although he had seen the bruises, he didn't ask for an

explanation. He wanted to comfort Mia. Were it possible, he would reach inside her and lift out her heartache, easing her misery. But he could only hold her. It seemed like hours, and perhaps it was. Eventually she fell asleep.

Rand removed her shoes and his own. Then he got a lightweight cover and pulled it over both of them. For a long while he lay gazing at her in the faint light. He loved her. But that was hardly a surprise.

Donevan was in a frenzy as he picked up the false book and began to shove things into it. He would wear a condom. It had been very smart of Frannie to provide them. No semen stains. No diseases.

He lovingly caressed the chains of the shackles, wishing he were unfettered by his rubber gloves, but he didn't dare take them off. Things were heating up in town. The old women would surely be found soon, even though he'd heard nothing about them. On the other hand, he'd been busy himself. Very busy.

Things were heating up in him, too. He had never seen his penis bigger than it was right now. He knew it had swelled so huge because he hadn't been able to get rid of the poison since he'd jacked off on the old woman in the pink robe. The stuff was festering inside him, harming him, but tonight he *had* to be clean again, no matter what it took.

He stole four pairs of handcuffs from the wall and put them in the book. Then he pulled the smallest of the strange-looking curved knives from the wall, mainly because it seemed to be one that would fit in the box.

Creeping back down the hall to the bedroom, he made sure all that metal in the book box didn't rattle. He stood just inside the blonde's bedroom door, studying her, looking for any signs that she might be aware he was there.

He saw nothing but a contented look on her face. He watched for a while longer, still as a shadow. The blonde had conveniently left a small night light on; he could see her fairly well once his eyes adjusted. Sometimes the brown contacts irritated him, but he wasn't wearing them tonight.

That rush he loved so well shot up inside him as he watched the woman. Jesus! He hadn't felt this good in a long time. He moved closer to the bed. The sleeping form didn't stir.

He quietly set the book box down beside the bed, then quick as a snake striking, he clasped his hand over the blonde's mouth and pulled her toward him.

Garson Hundley stared at the policeman in surprise. "Answer some questions?" he repeated, as though he couldn't quite grasp the statement.

"That's right. You own a black truck, don't you?"

"Yes."

Garson didn't know why his heart was acting so strange. He hadn't done anything wrong. He had an impeccable record. He was a military hero. So he owned a black truck. So what?

"Can we come in?"

Although Garson couldn't recall the last time he'd been so insulted and put on the defensive, he decided to let the policemen in.

He faced them angrily, rigidly. Did they think he was a suspect in a crime? He couldn't believe it! They had to be joking! Suddenly he recalled telling Mia that he could have killed his ex-wife with his own hands. *And* that boy she married. His heart began to do double time.

Donevan stared at Frannie Welch, relishing his power. He didn't think he'd ever seen such terror in anybody's eyes. He needed to feel good about himself right now, and this bitch was doing a good job of making him feel like king of the mountain.

He wanted to see her expression more clearly. "Keep

quiet and I won't kill you," he told her harshly. "Do you understand?"

Frannie nodded. She was so terrified she didn't think she could utter a single word if her life depended on it. She stared at the man.

He removed his hand from her mouth and tossed the covers away from her body. Of all times to be sleeping in the nude, why had she picked this night? She had never slept without pajamas until she made love all night with Brett.

Brett! How she wished he were here, that he would turn up like a hero in her book and rescue her from this nightmare. But Brett was in California making a commercial. And he hadn't asked her to go. But he had left her feeling loved and secure. He had left her with hope for the future.

And now this.

She rolled her eyes toward the ceiling. Oh, why, God? Why? Why did she take one tiny step forward and fall back into the abyss? Where was the justice? Why did she have to pay for each moment of pleasure with pain?

The intruder suddenly moved away from the bed to switch on the light. Frannie desperately looked for something to help protect herself, but she was surrounded by nothing but beautiful white wicker furniture and lovely pictures. She had wanted her bedroom to be the prettiest room in the house, and it was beautiful. Beautiful and useless. Just like she was.

Donevan closed the distance between them and squatted down by the bed. Frannie gasped when she saw that he had the shackles and handcuffs from her writing room. She had collected them when she researched her historical romance. Her romance which had become such a hit. Her romance written from her own misery.

She looked at the ceiling again; she couldn't stand to watch that masked face. Suddenly she wondered if she would ever see Brett again. She shivered and tried to reach for the sheet to cover herself, but the mask-faced monster ripped it from her hands and flung it to the floor. He stood there staring at her nakedness, and she felt like an ugly teenager all over again. She couldn't shake the feeling that all the physical changes had been in vain.

She was sure she was going to be hurt by this maniac—maybe tortured, maybe raped or killed. And she didn't think she could bear that. It reminded her of that other time—the first time. And this would be the last. She choked back a hysterical scream.

She wanted to speak, to ask him why he was doing this, but she was afraid he would tell her the truth. Blessed—or cursed—with more imagination than most people, she could guess why he'd brought the torture equipment into her bedroom.

Donevan continued to stare. There was something familiar about her, but only faintly. He had felt that all along, but maybe that was just because she had been the only one on the masseuse's list to try to hide from him.

"Why aren't you listed in the phone book?" he asked suddenly, startling Frannie so badly that she jumped.

She felt so exposed, so vulnerable, so desperate. "I'm a writer. Sometimes the public can . . ." Her words tapered off.

She'd almost said sometimes the public could be a nuisance, but that hadn't happened in a long time. She'd kept her phone unlisted because she wanted to be left alone in her despair.

"Can be what?" he said. "A pain in the ass? Is that what you started to say, bitch?"

She shook her head. "No. That wasn't it."

"Liar!" he shouted, his rage and excitement building. Jesus, he felt high tonight! This big-deal writer was about to discover who had the real power in this world. Donevan Raitt. That's who!

"What makes you think you're so fucking important?" he asked. "What makes you think you're better than I am?"

"I don't. Honestly, I don't," she protested, near tears.

"Don't start sniveling, bitch. I don't like it. I'm in control here. Understand?"

Frannie nodded, trying her best to hold back the tears.

"Do you know who *I* am?" he asked, thumping his chest as though he were some great man.

She shook her head.

Suddenly Donevan ripped off his mask. This cunt wasn't going to live to identify him anyway.

"I'm Donevan Raitt," he proclaimed loudly, enunciating very clearly as if he were a person of extraordinary importance.

Frannie hadn't really needed to know his name. Once he ripped off his mask and she put those blue, blue eyes with that face, she had known.

She had known that he was the blue-eyed nightmare who lived on in her dreams after all those years. She had been only in her teens. She had never been hurt so badly in all her life as she had when he beat her. She didn't think she would live through it again.

He stepped closer to the bed. Frances Wachasky fainted.

It was the middle of the night when Mia first stirred from her sleep. Her clothes were restricting and she felt uncomfortable. There was an unfamiliar warmth against her. She opened her eyes.

"Rand?" she murmured.

"Hello, Sleeping Beauty," he said softly.

She looked around, confused. "What time is it?"

He shrugged. "Oh, I don't know. About midnight, I suppose. Are you hungry?"

She smiled. "I don't know. How long have I been here?"

He winked. "Not nearly long enough. A few hours. Do you feel better?"

She touched her puffy face. "I must look a mess."

He shook his head. "Impossible. You're beautiful. You've always been beautiful."

"I feel like I need a shower." She ran her tongue around her mouth. "And a toothbrush."

"At your service, madam," he said, assisting her from the bed. "Come right this way."

When he had led her into the master bath, he helped her undress, murmuring again and again how beautiful she was. There was no way to miss how battered and lacerated her body was, but Rand had no intention of even asking about her condition until she was ready to talk to him. It was enough that she had come.

Mia was embarrassed, but she didn't say anything. She needed Rand. And he was here, like a long-awaited answer to a prayer. God only knows what she would have done, where she would have gone, if she couldn't have come to Rand after she left Troy's house.

A twinge of pain and regret shot through her, but she closed her mind to it. She'd had enough pain; she'd known enough regret. It was time to put it behind her. More important, she felt free to go forward after being stuck for so long in one hopeless position.

Rand adjusted the water and helped her into the shower. Mia looked back at him, her eyes filled with love. "Will you shower with me, Rand?"

He chuckled. "Do I look crazy to you? Just give me a minute to get out of these clothes."

He was stripping as he spoke. Mia smiled. It felt good to be smiling again.

Frank was finally released after several grueling hours at the police station. They hadn't had enough evidence to hold him, but he was still considered a suspect. He knew he was in serious trouble. Very serious trouble.

While he had been interrogated, news of two more stranglings had come in. Two elderly women. Frank could sense the heightened tension and excitement crackling through the station as he left. He was sure they were going to call him back in on those two cases, but he and his lawyer walked away from the building.

He was shaking when he got out on the street.

"Are you going to be okay?" the lawyer asked.

Frank shook his head. "I don't know, man. I'm really scared, and that's no lie. I know Mia will vouch for me, but that doesn't help me much with the girl's killing, and what if they try to tie the two old women to me?"

The lawyer gave him a sympathetic look. "Fortunately for you, and unfortunately for some poor other bastard, they're going to try to tie the old ladies' deaths on a realtor."

"A realtor?" Frank asked, puzzled. "How do you know?"

The lawyer shrugged. "One of the detectives is a friend of mine. Seems the scarf the women were strangled with was lost in the realtor's car. The old gal called the police about it because she'd paid a lot of money for it. Since the girl was strangled, the attacker attempted to strangle the masseuse, and the women were strangled, the police think they have a serial killer on their hands. Some bastard is going to be in deep shit, I don't need to tell you. Just be glad you're not the one at the moment."

Frank shuddered. He was glad. More glad than the lawyer could imagine, yet that didn't ease his mind.

"Want to stop for a drink? You really look like you could use one."

Frank shook his head. "No, thanks."

The lawyer shrugged. "Stay clean, stay around, and stay in touch."

"I will."

His lawyer didn't have to worry about that. As soon as he got out of this mess, Frank was moving on. There had to be some way to escape his past. Other people did it. Other people with a hell of a lot worse on their records than he.

# ~ CHAPTER 26 ~

When Frannie opened her eyes, she was sorry she was still alive. Donevan was slapping her repeatedly across the face.

"Wake up, you fucking cunt! You're not going to cheat me out of tonight!" he roared.

Frannie blinked and flinched as the pain registered. Oh, god, if only she were dead already. She wasn't nearly as afraid of death as what might precede it with this psychopath.

She had gone to a psychiatrist in search of peace, and it had been easy enough to blame her wretched life on Donevan Raitt, who had raped her at such a vulnerable time. Yet, it wasn't that simple. Nothing ever was. That hadn't been the whole answer.

Most of the answer had lain in her lack of ever feeling loved: by her parents, by her peers, by herself. Then Brett had come into her life. Just like that, just that easy, everything had changed for her.

For the first time in her life she had self-esteem, she had hope, she had love. Real love. Brett had told her. And she believed him.

Now, like the bad dream he was, Donevan Raitt was back. Why, God? Why? She didn't understand. She didn't know what she'd done to deserve this.

She tried to get away from his fists, then realized to her horror that she was handcuffed to the bedposts. Her feet, in the ancient shackles, were handcuffed to the footboard.

Moaning from the pit of her soul, she sank into utter

helplessness. This was like no other depression she had ever known. The hopelessness, the fear, was incomparable.

"Why did you pass out?" Donevan demanded when he saw that she was awake.

Frannie tried to think of the right response, but she couldn't contain her panic. Should she admit that she knew him? It had been so many years ago, maybe he would believe that they had been friends.

After all, she thought dismally, she had wanted to go out with him because he was the only boy she'd thought might be interested in her. She had been nice to him every time she'd seen him, trying her best to win his friendship. She had felt that he, like she, was an outcast, and they had a tie because of that.

But she couldn't forget how he had physically and emotionally hurt her. Then. Now. She didn't know what to say, how to answer.

"I asked you a question!" he bellowed at her.

Frannie drew in a shuddering breath. "I do know you," she said, hoping that just maybe that would flatter him.

If she could boost his ego, try to get him to like her, as she had done in high school, maybe, just maybe, he wouldn't hurt her. She had never told a soul about the rape or the beating. Surely, if he remembered the night at all, he would remember that she hadn't reported him.

Donevan seemed to puff up with pride. Frannie felt the slightest tremor of hope go through her.

"You really do know me?" he asked, grinning strangely.

She nodded and when she moved the chains rattled. A new rush of terror went through her, but she tried not to show it.

"My real name is Frances Wachasky," she offered tentatively. She saw immediate recognition in his cold eyes. "We were—were friends in high school. Do you remember?"

She was hoping desperately that he wouldn't recall the rape and the violence all those years ago, the terror that lived on so vividly in her own mind.

Donevan stared at her. He had thought there was something familiar about her, but he couldn't reconcile this woman with that bosomy, big-nosed girl.

"You're lying." His heart was hammering and his dick was getting even more rigid. Could this be? How? His luck couldn't be *that* good to run into the cunt that had started all his trouble with women!

Frannie shook her head, and again was made aware of the chains. "When I sold my book, I had plastic surgery."

She was lying naked before him, helpless, a captive. There was no reason to stop at anything that might save her life.

"Look at my breasts," she said in a quivering voice that she tried her best to steady. "Most men can't tell they've been reduced, but you were always so smart, so different from the other boys, Donevan. You'll be able to see the thin scars that run beneath them."

Donevan was breathing hard; he couldn't help it. He reached down and lifted one perfectly formed breast. There was a thin, faded line right down it, just as she had said.

"Frances Wachasky, Frances Wachasky, Frances Wachasky," he repeated like a litany. F.W., F.W., the initials he'd puzzled over. He couldn't believe his luck. It must have been that damned black cat. What were the odds of him and her turning up here?

Of course, they had gone to school a few miles down the road, and both had obviously gravitated to a smaller town for reasons of their own, but it seemed like an omen to him. Justice was finally going to be served.

"Do you recall that we were friends in school, Donevan?" Frannie asked, fighting to speak at all. She couldn't seem to breathe. It was as if the chains on her wrists and feet went around her throat and chest, too, even though she knew that wasn't possible. She tried to control her terror, but she didn't know how.

Donevan didn't seem to hear her. Jesus! After all these years he was finally going to get his revenge on the bitch who'd bloodied his dick so bad that he'd been afraid for it ever since. Everything would be different for him after. He knew it would.

"Donevan?"

He was still holding her breast; abruptly he reached for the knife in the box. Frannie held her breath, her mouth open in horror as he traced the thin scars on each breast. Then he tossed the knife aside, bent down, and savagely bit a nipple.

Frannie cried out in agony. She was afraid he'd bitten it off.

If she had known Donevan, she would have known he hated blood too much to actually carry out such an act. But he had other ways of meting out his own brand of justice.

Lane Ross had never known such humiliation.

The police were looking for a serial killer. They were breathing hot and heavy on this one, even trying to tie their suspects into some of the other killings of women that had been going on in Washington for years. They had a plum and they wanted the prize for picking it.

What had shocked Lane most of all was that he knew every man on the force. They had smiled at him, winked at him when they should have ticketed him, and asked him for special deals on houses. And now he had been treated like scum. He had been insulted and embarrassed. He had been questioned and grilled. He had been treated alternately with pseudo respect and then innuendos that he was the most despicable person alive.

And all because Sarah Ginnby had left her black scarf in his car. He couldn't believe it. He couldn't make his mind register that his entire fate could turn on such a simple matter.

He looked up when his wife and daughters came running toward the car as he pulled into their driveway. He shut off the motor and got out wearily. Once they were inside the house, Davida dismissed the girls and spoke to him privately in their bedroom.

"Was it awful, Lane?" she asked gently.

He felt tears well up in his eyes, and he didn't want to humiliate himself further. "It was worse than awful, Davida. I felt disgraced. I didn't do it. I swear. But I'm ruined all the same. We're *all* ruined. My reputation is irretrievable. The business is lost."

She put both her hands on his face and made him look into her eyes. "Lane, none of that matters. It's only a business. You've been putting too much time into it anyway. It doesn't matter. Your reputation doesn't matter. The girls and I know that you've done nothing wrong. *Nothing*. We're behind you all the way. If this really gets nasty, we'll spend every penny we have to clear you."

Lane seemed surprised. "The business really doesn't matter to you?" he asked, shocked.

"No, it doesn't," she answered matter-of-factly. She kissed him lightly on the mouth. "You're all that matters."

"But your father started this business. You and I—we've been poor before—we've been nothing. Could you really face all that again?"

Davida seemed almost cheerful when she replied. "I could face it with you. I don't think you've realized how much you've shut me and the girls out, Lane."

"Davida—"

She held up her hand. "Please let me talk. You and I have been married for years, and the more successful you became, the more driven you became. You're almost never home."

"Davida," he had to interject. "There was never another woman."

She smiled slightly. "I know that. I never thought there was; your only mistress is the business. What good is it? You don't have time or energy for anything else, and I know it's been getting to you."

He nodded, and the look in his eyes told her that he was amazed she knew. He'd tried to keep his problems from her.

She shook her head. "Lane, I couldn't have lived with you

all these years, been as close as you and I once were, and not know how troubled you've been. It hurt that you wouldn't share, let me help you with whatever was bothering you."

He drew in his breath. "I didn't think I had the right to burden you. I wasn't even sure I understood what the problem was myself."

She touched his lips with her index finger. "All that's in the past now. This situation we're suddenly caught up in is horrible, terrifying to us all. It just seems so unreal that you're even a suspect in this—this nightmare, but in my heart, I feel that nothing but good will come from this in our personal lives. The police can't pin a crime on you."

"They sure seem to think they have a good chance of it." He ran his hands through his hair. "Davida, I thought they were my friends. That disappointed me as much as being questioned shocked me."

"You've made money your God, Lane. Everyone knows it. They liked you for your money and prestige, but the situation is so absurd it would be laughable, if it wasn't so tragic and traumatic. Still, I believe it's made us all look at what's really important in life. The girls and I have spent the entire time while you were away discussing it."

Lane exhaled. He didn't realize he'd been holding his breath. Questions the masseuse had asked him about what good money was whirled around in his head. Now Davida had asked the same thing.

What *was* important in life? He was down to the very basics now, and he saw answers to questions that had plagued him for months.

He pulled his wife down on his lap. "I love you so very much. Please believe me that I've done nothing wrong. You and the girls are my life. I would never do anything consciously to harm any of you."

"We know that, Lane," she said with such certainty that he didn't doubt it.

"Thank you," he murmured.

Then he sought and found comfort in her arms.

# ➤ CHAPTER 27 ➤

Garson Hundley stood looking out the window at the pitch black of the night. He missed the masseuse already. She had been his one social contact, for what it was worth. He thought about the dinner party she had arranged and the women who had come.

The writer had been exciting, but the ex–football star clearly had mesmerized her. Then there was the other woman—Nora.

She wasn't really his type, yet he couldn't deny that something about her called out to him. He wasn't sure what. Maybe the insecurity which matched his own. Maybe the loneliness that was as apparent as a neon sign.

He shrugged. Perhaps it was time for him to step out into the world a little. He knew that Nora went to the Senior Center. That wasn't his scene, either, but he felt extremely restless tonight. And he hadn't gained enough confidence to face just any woman.

Yes, Nora would be a start. Who knows? Who ever knew about life? He could always say that he thought perhaps she might be afraid to drive home alone because of the rash of recent killings. God knew that was legitimate enough. He'd been stunned to be questioned himself—stunned, and strangely afraid. And he hadn't even done anything.

Donevan was so high that he was actually prancing around the bed. Frannie followed him with eyes filled with stark terror.

Donevan knew that he shouldn't stay too long. He hadn't been with it on his job recently, and he sure as hell couldn't afford to lose it, for more reasons than one. Those damned cops hadn't helped any, and they were sure to be back, even though he thought he'd convinced them he'd rather die than go back to prison.

But he was savoring this so much. And he owed her. How he owed her after all those years! Why let the cunt off easy like he had the old ladies? They had been such a disappointment. He didn't want that to happen again.

He unzipped his pants and shook his penis at her. "See this?" he asked. "Have you ever seen anything so big in your life?"

Frannie shook her head. Donevan's proportions were certainly no more than average, but she would agree to anything, anything if he just wouldn't make her suffer.

He looked down at his penis, not realizing that he was automatically stroking it with the hand the cat had clawed. It really was huge! All that poison that had built up over time had settled there in his dick.

He was going to feel so much better when this was over, but, Jesus, the roaring and reeling was mixing in his head with such fucking good feelings that he couldn't seem to make himself do anything yet.

He shook his dick at Frannie again. "This is power, bitch. Power! Do you understand?"

She nodded again.

"Say it," he commanded.

"Yes," she murmured.

"No, cunt," he said, slapping her with his free hand. "Say how huge this dick is, say how much power it has in it."

"It's huge," she mumbled. Her face hurt where he had been striking her, and her bonds were beginning to cut into her wrists and feet.

He struck her again. "Say just what I told you to say."

Frannie bit back tears and tried to remember. "Your dick

is huge," she said more audibly, although her voice quivered. "It has great power."

"You're fucking right, it does," he said, finding that her words turned him on even more. "Look at it again," he ordered her. "You want it, don't you?"

When Frannie didn't speak, he struck her again. She felt as if one of her teeth came loose, and she was afraid she might swallow it. She found the strangest, most disjointed thoughts going through her head. She was helpless, so utterly helpless.

If he was going to kill her, she couldn't prevent it, but maybe, just maybe, if he thought she wanted him, he might rape her and let her go. It was worth the risk. What other choice did she have?

"I want it," she said quietly, almost choking on the words.

"What?" he said, drawing back his hand again.

Frannie saw that he was still massaging his penis with his hand that was bigger than the other one. He had on rubber gloves, but this one seemed to be padded.

"I want your huge, powerful dick," she said quickly before he could strike her again.

"You bet you do, bitch," he said, his voice full of arrogance. "All women want it. I've always known it. They just don't like to own up to it. They like to play games."

He squatted down by the phony book, and Frannie braced herself, watching as Donevan took out her penis-shaped vibrator.

Her face turned red. She had masturbated with it hundreds of times. It had given her more pleasure than she wanted to remember. What was this monster going to do with it?

"What's this?" he asked in a strange voice. "What do you do with this disgusting thing?"

Frannie felt a flush race over her whole body and tried to move, but she was shackled too securely to the bed. This man was invading every last privacy.

His own penis was still jutting out of his unzipped pants

when he came closer again. He turned the battery-operated vibrator on and watched it squirm and wiggle. He frowned severely at her as if he had discovered something very naughty.

"What do you do with this, Frances?" he demanded in that peculiar high-pitched voice.

She was afraid not to answer him. He obviously knew what she did with it.

"Masturbate," she mumbled.

"What?" he exclaimed in mock disgust. "You touch your *privates* with it. How repulsive! How sinful! God will punish you, you wicked, wicked thing. You must never touch your own privates!"

He seemed to be going mad before her eyes, and Frannie's terror rose to fever pitch. He sounded really crazy, like he was applying his words to himself, instead of her, and yet he was standing there with the vibrator in one hand and his own penis in the other.

She tried again to move and was rewarded with a shaft of pain in her right wrist. She was a tall woman, but he had her stretched to the very limit. The handcuffs were tight. The shackles held her legs about two feet apart.

Suddenly she cried out in pain and shock when he reached down and shoved the vibrator up inside her. He began to laugh maniacally, and Frannie felt herself convulsing from fear and pain. She wished she would pass out again. She wished he would finish with her. Just get it over with.

"God," she prayed aloud, "help me."

Donevan switched off the vibrator and jerked it out of her, causing more pain. "Don't pray while you're sinning."

He tossed the vibrator back in the box and picked up a pack of condoms. Frannie watched in new horror as he tried to put on not one, but two, without taking off his clothes. The rubber gloves seemed to thwart him in putting on the rubbers. Finally he ripped off one glove. Frannie saw that his finger was bandaged.

Suddenly he straddled her.

She started to scream, but he struck her again. Then he reached down and got the vibrator. She felt new shame and shock when he shoved it far into her mouth.

"Try to bite this one off, bitch," he said. Then he rammed himself into her. Again and again.

Frannie was in too much agony to know which torture was causing her the most discomfort. She was sure she was choking to death. She kept gagging, and tried to breathe through her nose.

Each time Donevan shoved himself into her, her chains strained and cut. She had pain behind her eyes that was so bad she could hardly see. She supposed it was sheer terror, but she was afraid she was going blind.

Abruptly Donevan climbed off her. Trying to breathe around the vibrator, Frannie dared to search out a single thread of hope that he might be finished with her.

The hope grew a little when he reached down and got the key to the shackles. He fought with the ancient lock while Frannie held her breath, praying fervently. He seemed to grow angrier as he battled the aged torture equipment.

Finally he succeeded. Frannie felt immediate relief when he freed her ankles. She tried to move her feet and legs, but there was very little feeling after the long confinement.

She looked at Donevan hopefully, pleadingly, as he came to the head of the bed. When he jerked the vibrator out of her mouth, she almost vomited. Her heart was hammering. She thought he was going to let her out of the handcuffs.

The hope was short-lived as he unexpectedly wrapped the shackles around her neck.

"No!" she gasped.

Donevan tightened the chains until the last bit of breath left Frances Wachasky's body.

Mia couldn't believe how tender and tantalizing Rand's loving was. She had thought he was incredible the first time, but this time he took her places she had never been.

When their union was over, he gazed down at her. "You

are the most beautiful woman I've ever met. I knew I was in love with you the first time I saw you at a party you and Troy had given."

"Really?" she murmured.

Rand nodded. "Really." He smiled. "I wanted to touch— you can't imagine how much, but I was told you were too much in love with Troy to acknowledge the existence of another man."

Mia's smile was suddenly melancholy. Rand began to wish he hadn't brought up the party, but he'd wanted her to know how long he'd worshiped her.

"I didn't think I could ever love anyone else," she murmured, looking away.

Yet hadn't she known for a long time now that she was in love with Rand, that all she needed was Troy's permission to let that love grow? She thought of the baby she suspected she was going to have, and she had to believe that this was meant to be. She wondered if she should tell him.

No, it was too early. Besides, she needed time to adjust. To everything. Her life was still so chaotic. She decided she would spend a few days with Rand, then go back to Oregon and get her affairs in order.

She needed to rethink her situation, away from him. She needed to confront the fear of the attack, instead of running away as she had. She needed time to deal with Troy's impending death. She wanted to think about the fact that Rand had known her for so long—had cared for her.

"Penny for your thoughts?" he murmured.

She shook her head. "Not yet, but one day I'll tell them all to you."

"Will I be pleased?" His voice was so earnest, his eyes so hopeful, that she laughed.

"I think so. I certainly hope so. If you aren't, I'll be broken-hearted."

"Oh," he murmured, drawing her back into his arms. "That sounds more than promising."

\* \* \*

When Donevan had gotten back in his truck and turned the radio on, he found that the shit had really hit the fan. Somebody had found the old ladies; the police were saying they already had a suspect.

Donevan didn't know whether to be relieved or panicked. Somebody was always peeing on his party. He had been feeling so incredible when he left the writer's house. Now he wondered if he was next on the list to be questioned. Those bastards were sure to drag him in again. He was too good a suspect. They liked to harass him. He began to doubt his acting at the fast-food place. Maybe the police hadn't believed him after all.

Suddenly his wounded hand was throbbing as it hadn't in a while. He felt overwhelmed by the abrupt need to go home and cleanse himself. Frannie had seemed clean enough, but no woman was. He stepped on the gas, then slowed down.

Control, he reminded himself. The cops in town knew him. He didn't want to be stopped. He had all kinds of incriminating stuff in the truck. But, Jesus, was he ever in a hurry to get back to the house!

What if the police had already come? What if the old landlady had gone to his door and let them in when he didn't answer?

He was beginning to get in a foul mood. All the good times were over and the bad ones were starting in on him. He didn't like it this time. He didn't like it at all.

He exhaled a breath of relief when he approached the house and found no other cars. But that didn't mean the police hadn't already been there. Shit, he would sweat this one out!

He couldn't go ask Mrs. Smith; she would know he'd sneaked out. He would just have to get in bed and hope he'd outsmarted them all.

# CHAPTER 28

Nora Simpson was thrilled to see Garson Hundley walk into the Senior Center. It had been another dull night for her, dull and frightening, with the news of the two elderly women who had been found strangled. In fact, if she had known before she left home, she wouldn't have come.

She deliberately made herself look away from Garson. She was working on being independent. She would like a man, yes, but she *could* manage alone. Mia had taught her that in more ways than one. It was funny how much a single individual could influence another.

When her gaze strayed to Angie Esterbrook, she tried not to think unkind thoughts. Angie wasn't the sort of person Nora liked to associate with, but she supposed the woman needed friends, just like everyone else.

Of course, Angie had her share of acquaintances, but friends? No, Nora didn't think so. In fact, she was surprised to see Angie here. Usually she only socialized with those she considered the elite in town.

Oddly enough, the woman had been singling out Mia's clients since the masseuse held the dinner party. It was no secret among Nora's friends that Angie had been furious at not being invited. But that was foolish; all the guests were single.

"Hi."

Nora glanced up when the male voice spoke so near her. She had been lost in her thoughts and was startled to find Garson standing in front of her.

"Hello," she shyly said.

"That music is about my speed," Garson said, smiling at her. "I'm rusty, but I'm willing if you are."

Nora smiled. "I'm rusty, too, but I'm certainly willing."

When he took her hand and led her out on the dance floor, she smiled again. She'd done rather well, she thought. She doubted that he knew how much effort it took for her to extend her hand and walk across the floor, her knees shaking.

To her surprise, she had barely been drawn into Garson's arms when Angie tapped her on the shoulder.

"You don't mind, do you, Nora? My husband is working tonight, per usual."

Nora shook her head, even though she did mind. What else could she do? When she looked at Garson and tried to let go of his hand, he held hers firmly as he looked at the intruder.

"If you'll pardon me, I asked this lady for this dance, and I'd prefer to see it to the end."

Nora knew how angry Angie was, and although Nora tried not to feel smug, she simply couldn't help it. Suddenly her heart sang like a young girl's. She had a feeling about this man. She really did. She had ever since she first saw him on that winding road to the masseuse's house.

Donevan twisted and turned in his bed, feeling self-satisfied now that he was home and apparently the police hadn't turned up here looking for him. He'd washed himself thoroughly and treated his injured hand again. The low he'd experienced a short time ago had vanished, and he was high again, reliving all the thrills of the night.

Jesus, but it had been a thriller! He'd never forget the look on Frances Wachasky's face if he lived to be a hundred. And the way he'd felt when he tightened those shackles around her throat. He was sure she thought she had a good imagination—after all, she was a writer—but he'd bet anything she'd never imagined those shackles being used the way he'd used them.

Just the thought made him wish he'd brought them home with him. But he knew that wouldn't be smart. They were so uncommon, too bizarre. It was dangerous enough having the hemp necklace and the crummy druggie girl's chain.

But those were small items, easy to hide, like his mask. And, of course, he got a constant supply of gloves from work. Nobody counted and he flushed the used ones down the toilets.

Unconsciously he reached down to his crotch. This was the part he liked best. He really did wish he had those shackles to put around his own neck now. What a fucking high that would be!

Suddenly he heard some commotion downstairs. Still caressing his penis, he went to the window and looked out. The cops! He should have known they would show up sooner or later. They must have had to let that suspect go, if there had been one, and here they were for him!

Control, he reminded himself. He would bet his life that the old bag would vow he'd been at home all evening. He could hear her high-pitched voice asking who was at the door. He knew she was talking loud enough to alert him, just in case she was in danger herself. Two heavy-duty voices answered.

Donevan stroked faster. Jesus, the fear and the thrill! The danger and the excitement! He had to be quick. They would be coming up the steps any minute. But he could be quick when he wanted to.

Except, he remembered, for that one time after the old broads when his dick had been useless. He hurried into the bathroom and ejaculated into the toilet, then flushed the foamy matter away.

When the knock came at his door, he was ready. His mask was in the false bottom of his trunk, as was the hemp necklace and chain. Control, he reminded himself as he opened the door.

"Oh, no, not you guys again," he said in a long-suffering tone. He clearly looked as if he had been much maligned already and this intrusion was hardly justified.

The bigger of the men made a wry face. "Save the suffering act, Donevan. We need to talk to you."

"What druggie got snuffed this time?" he asked. He held up both hands. "I swear I did my time, and I don't do murder at any rate."

"Who said anybody had been murdered?" the thinner cop asked.

Donevan shrugged. "That's what you tried to put off on me last time. I swear, man, how long is this harassment going to last? I had sex with one willing woman and went to prison for that. Isn't there any justice?"

"Don't overreact, Raitt, okay?" the big cop said sarcastically. "A jury believed the woman wasn't willing."

Donevan sighed. "So what is it this time? Another rape? I swear on my mother's head that I haven't left this house all evening." He looked at Mrs. Smith.

She nodded in agreement. "I told the officers, son, but they insisted on coming up."

They looked at each other; Donevan didn't need to read minds to know that they thought the old woman was crazy to be renting to him at all.

Donevan gave her his best smile. "Thank you, Mrs. Smith."

"Why don't you let us come in, Donevan?" the big cop asked. "Let's see how well you live here."

Donevan was getting pissed. He didn't like their fucking attitude. He didn't want to anger them, but he had rights, too, and he was well aware of them.

"Do you have a warrant?"

The bored one shook his head. "No, Donevan, we don't."

"Then you won't mind if I don't invite you in. I'm real particular about who comes into my home."

They looked at each other. "Okay, then, put on some pants and a jacket and come down to the station. If you have nothing to hide, you'll spare us a few minutes of your time, won't you?"

"Jesus! I was in bed, man. Don't you guys ever let up? I haven't done anything. I told you last time, I'll never see the inside of another prison, and I don't like going into that jail."

"Come on, Raitt," the thin one said impatiently. "We've had a long night. If what you say is true, you've been resting."

Donevan exhaled wearily. "I suppose the girl gave a description of a guy who could be me again, huh?"

"Who said it was a girl?" one cop asked.

"It was a girl last time," Donevan said. "The masseuse, of all people. I couldn't believe it. She was supposed to be trying to help me. I couldn't believe she thought I tried to kill her."

"The masseuse never accused you," the big policeman said. "We told you that last time. And the young girl wasn't alive to describe anyone, much less point the finger. The masseuse gave us a description that was too close to you not to question you."

"And this case?" Donevan said.

"Two old women—murdered. Don't tell me you don't listen to the radio, Raitt," the sarcastic one said.

Donevan pounded his fist on the side of the door. "Are you kidding me, man? I'm not into harming old ladies, man. You've got to be jiving me. I really don't believe this!"

"Can it, Raitt, and come on."

Donevan met Mrs. Smith's sympathetic eyes and shook his head, playing on her soft side. "I didn't do anything. I was here all evening."

Donevan went to get dressed, looking the part of the abused, harassed, downtrodden citizen who was trying his best to adjust to society.

"Please be easy," Nora murmured to Garson shyly. "It's—it's been a while."

A while, she repeated to herself. She hadn't had sex in so long, she wasn't sure what to expect. She didn't even think she should be doing this, yet she knew she wanted to.

They'd gone through all the formalities after Garson followed her home to be sure she was safe. They'd made idle chitchat and drunk coffee.

Time had passed quickly. She didn't honestly know how she'd wound up in bed with him, completely naked. She'd certainly never done that with George, yet she felt amazingly confident and sexy with this man.

But scared all the same. It had been a long time.

Garson whispered to her, "Don't you worry, sweetheart. We're going to take our time. You're going to be just fine. Better than fine."

So was he. He just knew it. He'd had an erection when he danced with her. It had excited him so that he'd almost rushed her off the floor right then; however, he'd been sensible. He would go slowly. Try not to shock her. He was confident he could satisfy her. If they could get to that point.

He kissed her lips, then scattered a line of kisses down her nude body. Suddenly his tongue touched that exquisite place Mia had shown Nora where to find.

She gasped in pleasure, arched her hips, and pressed Garson's head closer. Yes, they were going to be fine. Just fine.

# ⟡ CHAPTER 29 ⟡

"Angie, let me explain," James Esterbrook pleaded, reaching for her.

Angie jerked away from him. "Don't touch me!"

He ran his hands through his thick gray hair. The diamonds in his ring glittered mockingly at her. "Angie, it just happened once."

"Get the fuck out of my room!" she screamed at him. "What kind of fool do you think I am? *Once?* And you gave her a three-hundred-dollar gold chain? You lying bastard!"

"Angie—"

"Out!" she screamed at the top of her lungs. "I wish they'd kept you in jail. I wish I never had to see your repulsive face. If I've caught some disgusting disease from you, I'll sue the shorts right off you!"

She watched, red-faced with rage, as her slump-shouldered husband left the bedroom. Then she slammed the door behind him.

"Damned deviate!" she shrieked, twisting her hands in anger. She ripped the chains from her own neck and flung them against the door. Then she pulled the watch off her arm and crushed it beneath her high-heeled shoe.

God! How would she ever live down the shame? The snide remarks? The dirty jokes at her expense?

Damn James! No wonder he didn't want sex with her often. The rotten pervert! How she detested him now! She'd been sure it had been a mistake when the police came to the house looking for him, wanting to talk to him about that first murder—the young girl's—the *prostitute's.*

She'd made quite a show of indignation. Now she wished she'd vented it at him instead of the police. The sick son of a bitch had given that little slut an expensive gold chain that came from the same store where he purchased all of Angie's own jewelry. Some creep had traded the chain for drugs, and somewhere down the line it had turned up in a drug bust.

It had been traced right back to James. God, she couldn't believe it! Not that she believed he'd killed the girl, but it was bad enough that he'd been having sex with the wretched thing right here in their hometown. And him president of the biggest bank in town. And her his wife, the ruling society queen.

She could just imagine how the town was laughing at her expense. She would never get invited to another party, much less give one. All she wanted to do was get out of this place. But not before James paid the price for her shame. She'd take every damn dime he had!

Her head began to pound and she wished desperately that Mia would return. For once she was grateful that the woman wasn't a snoop and a gossip. If the masseuse were in town, at least Angie could go there and get some relief for the relentless pounding at her temples and the pain behind her eyes without being snubbed or snickered at.

Mia had spent three days with Rand, as she planned, but she was glad to set foot on Oregon soil. She'd missed the tranquillity, the gentleness of the earth, the rain and ocean. She had even managed to put the terrifying night when she'd almost been murdered behind her.

Or so she thought. She had barely stepped into her cottage when she was inundated by a barrage of information. She had been gone only four days, and the whole world had opened up to scenes from hell. There were notes on her door, messages on her machine, and even telegrams.

But there was no Soot to greet her.

"Here, kitty. Here baby," she called a few times, but she would have to wait to locate him.

So much had happened in such a short time. She responded to each message with increasing horror. The police had been trying to get in touch with her at Troy's house. Daniel had left several messages on her machine, as had numerous other people.

Many of her clients seemed somehow to be connected to the murder—*murders,* she noted with increasing despair. Not only the young girl who had died, but two elderly women and Frannie Welch.

"God, no!" she gasped aloud as the impact of the deaths

hit her. "Not Frannie! Dear Lord, how many more? How many more?"

Her phone began to ring even while she listened to messages.

"Hello," she said in a voice devoid of emotion, so totally shocked was she by the events that had taken place. She might as well be on another planet; she simply couldn't grasp all that had happened in her absence. And somehow it all seemed ironically to involve her.

"Mia, it's Frank," the harried voice on the other end of the line said. "Thank God you came back early."

"I'm still reeling from all this awful news, Frank. I don't understand. There are urgent messages—frantic messages from you, Lane, Garson, Angie Esterbrook, and even Donevan Raitt. Everyone knew I'd planned to be gone about two weeks. The police have been trying to locate me. And, god, Frank, tell me that Frannie isn't dead. Tell me this is all more of that monster's sick joke. I'm overcome by all this madness."

Frank sighed as though he had the burden of the universe on his back.

"I'm sorry to say it's all true, Mia. The murders. The frantic calls. Almost every one of us has been investigated as a suspect. The cops are crazy to pin this mess on anybody they can. They're even trying to tie it into those Washington murders."

Mia sat down in the nearest chair, cold chills running over her body. "How did this nightmare happen?" she asked in disbelief. "Poor Frannie. She was so lost and lonely. Why my clients, Frank? What's it all about? Have they caught the killer? Is it Donevan Raitt? Have I brought this hell down on us all?"

She could hear the grief in Frank's voice. "They haven't nailed anybody for it yet, Mia, and I honestly don't know why you're in the center of it. After all, you were almost a victim. The killings seem random, but the fact that your clients are implicated is no coincidence."

"I don't understand," she murmured.

Frank's voice trembled. "Maybe I should drop by and talk to you, Mia. It really is a nightmare."

"That would probably be best. I'm terribly shaken up. I suppose I'd better let the police know I'm home."

"Don't call them until I see you," he said tensely. "Wait for me to get there."

Mia felt more shivers up and down her spine. "Why?" she blurted before she thought. Why would Frank want to come here before the police were notified she was home?

She suspected from the pause that Frank knew she was frightened; she was sorry she'd blurted out the question so quickly, but she *was* frightened. Of everything. And everyone.

"The police caught me at your house right after—" Frank hesitated, then pressed on, "right after Soot had apparently been killed in the bathroom. There was blood and fur on the floor. The cat hasn't been seen since."

Mia began to weep. Not Soot, too. Not her precious pet. Did the depraved man wish to destroy everything?

"The police speculate that the killer came back for you, Mia, not knowing that you were going away."

"I left early," she said, dazed. "Otherwise I would have been here, Frank."

She could hear the cracks in his voice. "Then thank God you were spared. He's a madman, Mia. I can't begin to tell you the sick things he does to women. I know because the police accused me of all of them."

He seemed unable to continue for a moment. Mia didn't know what to say. She had lost all perspective. This was her friend, Frank, but the madness had permeated her perceptions of everyone and distorted reality.

"They knew about my past, Mia: the cocaine, the student-fondling accusation in Boston," he finally continued, his voice breaking repeatedly with shame and humiliation. "One of your neighbors reported possible suspicious activity at your house when a truck went up the hill. I was in the house to feed Soot when the police arrived. I was standing at the bathroom door. I own a truck."

"Oh, Frank—"

"Mia, I swear that I never killed anyone. Please believe me. I couldn't hurt anyone. I didn't kill Soot. I loved that cat almost as much as you did. I told the police you would vouch for me, Mia, if only you could be found."

Tears were streaming down Mia's face. Frank was her friend. She knew he hadn't harmed anyone. But she was overwhelmed by the atrocities that had been committed in the brief time she was gone.

"Mia," he said plaintively. "Please say something. Please believe me."

Through her own anguish, she responded to his. "Come on over, Frank. Then I'll call the police."

It wasn't necessary. Emma and Buck, the old couple who lived down the road, apparently never missed a thing. The police arrived before Frank could, and Emma and Buck Carson weren't far behind.

Mia went to the door to find two policemen trying to shoo the persistent couple away without antagonizing them too much.

"But you wouldn't know nothing if we hadn't been good neighbors," Emma was saying.

Still teary-eyed, Mia opened the door for the officers. They shut it behind them before the two old people could push in.

"Well, you left quite a mess here," one of the policemen said. "I thought you agreed to let us know where you were staying in California should we need to reach you."

Mia stared at him. "I gave you the address . . ." Her words trailed off. Of course; she'd gone to Rand's. She hadn't stayed at Troy's. It all seemed to have taken place light-years ago in view of what she'd returned to.

"Please," she offered, "come into the kitchen. I suspect this is going to take some time. I'll make some tea."

They sat down at the table and started right in with

questions and connections. Mia couldn't fail to understand how she'd been caught in the middle, not only as a victim, but in a bizarre way as the hub of the death wheel.

She was stunned as she listened to the reasons her clients were suspects. Lane Ross and the scarf. Yes, she did remember him calling about it. But, no, she couldn't believe he had any part in it.

"He's suicidal," she confessed almost inadvertently.

One look exchanged between the two officers was enough to make her wish she hadn't made that comment.

"In some cases, serial killers suffer extreme highs and lows. For one to come to you full of remorse and guilt isn't all that unusual. Or he could be a hell of a good bluffer. This killer is clearly psycho."

"Lane Ross didn't kill anyone!" Mia protested.

"Oh?" one officer said. "Can you prove that, because he sure as hell needs somebody who can. He's definitely a suspect. Or was the killer your client Garson Hundley? He's impotent, right? Often a common denominator in these cases—impotent or latent homosexual. And he does drive a truck."

"It wasn't Garson," Mia said, surprised that the officers knew of his impotence. They seemed to have down their grilling technique, adequate sources, or both.

"Can you prove that?" the same man asked.

"Or was it your friend Frank, with a record, caught right here at the scene? The fur and blood was your cat's."

"It wasn't Frank, either," Mia said, though her firmness had begun to waver. She couldn't believe it was any of the three men, yet how could she be so positive?

"Garson's too big to be my attacker," she said, suddenly feeling old and tired and soiled by all this.

"Maybe there's more than one killer—a copycat isn't at all uncommon," the other man said.

"Frank wears an earring. So did your attacker."

Poor Frank, Mia thought to herself. He'd wanted to talk to her. She'd needed to talk to him.

If he had come, he'd been scared away by the car. This was harder than she'd imagined. She felt such loyalty to her clients, yet a crazy man had to be stopped. *Had* she been duped by one of her clients?

"You haven't mentioned Donevan Raitt," she said, feeling guilty at pointing the finger at him, yet thinking surely he was the most likely of her clientele. "He drives a truck, has a record, and a pierced ear."

"The most obvious suspect, but with the best alibi, believe it or not," one officer said, shaking his head. "We think he's too compliant, too eager to plead prison panic, not to be involved, but we can't hold him."

Mia couldn't believe that she actually felt relieved. Maybe it hadn't been Donevan. Maybe it was none of her clients. Just crazy coincidences. Those things did happen. Reality was stranger than fiction. That had been proved time and time again.

"What do you know about James Esterbrook?" one of the men asked.

"James Esterbrook?" Mia repeated. "He's a banker in town. He's not my client."

"We know that," the officer said patiently, "but his wife is."

"What has Angie Esterbrook got to do with this?" Mia asked, thoroughly confused.

The bigger of the officers shrugged. "Who knows? Maybe nothing. But there again, she's a tie to you. Her husband gave the first murder victim a very expensive gold chain, which was traced right back to him at a local jewelry store. Must have traded it for sex. We questioned him."

Mia covered her face with her hands and closed her eyes. This was a nightmare like none she'd ever imagined. She didn't know what to say, what to think. She wished that she had no part in this terrible tragedy, and yet she felt strangely responsible. It was a terrifying thought.

* * *

Donevan knew the police didn't really have anything on him. He was too smart for them. He'd known that all along. Still, he was also smart enough to cool it now. The heat was on, and he wasn't about to get in the fire.

But that didn't stop the poison that raged inside him, building and building and building. The killings had had some real good parts, and he loved to lie on his cot and think about them. Somehow, though, he wasn't in control anymore. He couldn't keep the poison at bay.

He kept thinking back to that black cat. He'd thought that night that it had been a blessing he'd killed it. Jesus! What a night with ol' Frances! His best yet!

Still, it was hard to stay away from the cottage on the hill. He wondered if the masseuse had returned, but he wasn't stupid enough to go find out. She was supposed to be gone for a while.

He slapped his forehead. What the hell was he thinking? He didn't have to go to her house to find out when she returned. All he had to do was pick up the fucking phone. Without wasting a second, he dialed Mia's number.

"Hello? Hello? Who is this?" she asked.

He could tell she was angry by the way she slammed the phone down. No, not angry. Scared. That was better. He had the power now.

# ➤ CHAPTER 30 ➤

Mia talked with the officers at length on several occasions. She was finally convinced to restart her massage sessions after a week of considering her options.

There was no denying that she was a link in all of this, intentionally or not. However, the police's most convincing argument was the fact that she was the only victim who had lived. They strongly believed the killer was a client of hers, and while she wasn't convinced of that, she was both aware and afraid that the killer might return to complete his work.

Her first impulse had been to run back to California. She thought about it a lot, but she felt that she had an obligation to help solve this mystery, help stop this madness before anyone else was harmed.

After much discussion, it was decided that she would have a live-in female police agent in the guise of a roommate. It was logical enough, given the temperament of a town in total panic, with gun sales at an all-time high in an area where guns were common. Single women were especially frantic since they appeared to be the ones most at risk.

Once Mia had been counseled and all possible security precautions arranged for, the new roommate, Lou-Ann, moved in. Although reluctant to do business in such an environment, Mia called her regular clients and set up schedules. Each one, without fail, was eager to resume work, and each one, again without fail, talked about the climate of madness and murder in the town.

On the surface the schedule seemed organized as before.

The policewoman was always at the cottage, unobtrusively, of course, under cover as a reporter working on the murder story; the surveillance crews, doing their work mostly by radio because of the limited access to the cottage, were in evidence no matter how much they wished to conceal themselves. Mia herself had a police radio at the ready and phones in every room of the cottage.

She felt like a prisoner in her own home. She felt sorry for her clients. She felt sorry for herself. She wanted it all to end. And this was the only way she knew to help.

Monday's schedule didn't begin until the afternoon, when Lane Ross appeared at the door. Mia was nervous; she felt like she was betraying her people by luring them back while she tried to help the police uncover the identity of the one who might be a killer. Still, it had to be done.

The moment she looked into Lane's face, she felt better. She would keep an open mind and do what the police had asked. She would be especially diligent in her questions and checking body shapes, trying to trigger her own memory, but she didn't think for a moment that Lane Ross was a killer. Oddly, he looked more rested than Mia had ever seen him. She was puzzled.

"Hello, Lane," she said softly. "I'm glad you came." Her eyes met his. "I know about your ordeal, but I must say that you look fine."

He managed a smile when he entered the house. "I've survived the shock of being a murder suspect," he answered honestly. "I know it's not over until it's over, but I've made adjustments." He laughed with a minimum of humor. "What were you always asking me? If the money was worth all the work and sacrifice?"

She nodded.

He shook his head. "It wasn't. The whole matter was taken out of my hands. Would you buy a house from a suspected mass murderer?"

Mia reached out and clasped his fingers. "Yes, if he were you, Lane. I know you didn't do it. People who know you know that, too."

He laughed again without mirth. "Mia, this whole town knows me, and business is down to less than a third."

She smiled. "You'll be fine, Lane. Who wants to move in the midst of all this tension and fear? At least people *think* they know who their neighbors are now. Things will ease up."

He nodded. "I suppose so, but I've learned my lesson. I *feel* better than I have in years. My wife and I have had some involved conversations, and I've realized that having my worst fears come true, being a failure, doesn't hurt half as bad as worrying about it."

He laughed, and this time his eyes crinkled with inner mirth. "Mia, by damned, that business will never run me again. I just didn't know what a merry-go-round I was on."

She laughed with him. "Then maybe all the misery you've been exposed to is worth it. I guess it's what's called finding the silver lining in the black cloud."

He nodded. "My lining may never be silver again, but I can honestly say I'm on the road to happiness, Mia. I wish I had listened to you months ago."

"You weren't ready," she said simply.

He smiled. "I couldn't hear what you were saying, but I *am* ready for that massage now, a long, relaxing one. I have plenty of time."

They both smiled as they went to the massage room. Mia had no intention of being naive and unguarded again. Still, she was determined that she was going to help every client to the best of her ability, under the circumstances.

Donevan was like a man holding a hot wire. He couldn't keep his mind on his maintenance job at the fast-food restaurant. The gloves reminded him of the wonder and glory of his power. Every time he needed to wear them for cleaning, he got a hard-on. He didn't want to be here. He knew the masseuse was back in town, and that was all he could think about.

She had even called him and made an appointment for Friday. Jesus, he could hardly wait. Not that he was stupid enough to do her that day, but it wouldn't be long. There had to be a break in the game, a cooling-off period, if he was going to be successful. He knew he was a suspect. But then, so were lots of her other clients. He'd listened to the talk in the restaurant, and he'd been pleased by what he'd heard.

Still, he knew the police weren't dumb enough to leave the bitch on her own now. He'd heard prison scuttle enough to know about setups and traps. He'd *lived* long enough to know about them.

But, Jesus, he wanted to off somebody! The poison was building again, and even the sound of Mia's voice as she made his appointment hadn't helped him get rid of his hard-on. He hadn't been prepared with his rope.

He was so antsy that he didn't know if he could stay at work. Yet he knew it was the safest place to be. They were probably watching him. The whole town was probably watching him. But he knew how to be careful.

When Brett came to the cottage door, Mia was alarmed by the pain etched on his rough features. She hadn't heard that he'd been interrogated. After all, he'd been in California when she had. Still, he was clearly upset—as upset as she'd ever seen him. She hurt for him without even knowing why.

"How are you, Brett?" she asked, her eyes searching his face.

He shook his head. "Devastated. Aching. Feeling guilty. I should have taken her with me."

"Who?" Mia asked as she automatically preceded him to the massage room.

"You must know she's dead, Mia. My Frannie's dead."

She turned around and saw the tears in his eyes. "Brett, I'm so sorry. I didn't know you were involved with her."

He heaved a sigh, and his whole body moved with it. "It was love at first sight. I know that sounds stupid from someone like me, but she was *the* woman who finally touched me, Mia. I wanted to take care of her, to be with her, to spend my life with her. We were together only a few times, yet I knew right away that it was forever. She wanted to go with me to California, but I wanted to surprise her with this when I came back."

He pulled a big diamond ring from his shirt pocket. Then he sadly shook his head. "She was probably being murdered while I shopped for an engagement ring."

"Did Frannie know how you felt?" Mia asked.

Brett nodded. "We were in love, Mia. I know how corny that sounds, but she was writing again, making me the hero in her book. I wanted to be her hero. I was happy making her happy."

A trembling smile played on Mia's lips. Frannie's last days had been good ones. There was some satisfaction in knowing that.

"God!" Brett raged raggedly. "If only I could get that bastard, I'd rip him limb from limb with my bare hands."

"You made Frannie happy, Brett. Please take some comfort in that."

"That asshole took her happiness away," he said savagely. "He took it all away in a single night of madness."

Mia held out her arms. She wanted to soothe his anguish, to ease his pain, and she knew no other way. Brett hugged her up against his body as he had done many times before, but this time he was racked with sobs that shook them both. Mia's tears mingled with his.

He didn't have a massage that day, and he left the diamond with Mia despite her protests that she didn't want it. As she watched him drive away, she felt a new guilt when she pondered the fact that she had brought the couple together.

Then she put the unwarranted emotion in the back of her mind. Thank God for Brett. She could only imagine how happy he had made Frannie, and that had been a true blessing.

Donevan went home from work, but he was more wired than ever. He didn't know what to do. He paced his rooms and played with himself. Nothing worked. Finally he got in his truck and drove off. He felt like he was going crazy inside, and he didn't want to make a bad mistake.

Eventually, Donevan found himself back at the apartment where he'd killed the druggie girl and the two old women. He parked in the distance and stared at the building, willing the good memories to come so that he could get some relief, but nothing happened.

No, that wasn't right. Something happened. His dick got harder and harder, but he couldn't get rid of it. He didn't know what to do. What if he really did swell so big that he went crazy with the poison? He looked down at his prick in the semilight of the street. It was grotesquely huge!

He had to do something. He started the truck and drove off aimlessly. This time he saw that it wasn't aimless at all. He ended up in the woods at the masseuse's house. But he'd been smart, very smart. He'd driven his truck as far up the beach as he could, then walked from there.

The cottage had lights on. He began to grow excited. He'd expected to catch the masseuse alone. However, maybe she'd switched the schedule all around. He didn't know. On the other hand maybe she was alone. There was only one way to tell.

Donevan was surprised to find the bathroom blinds he'd so often peered through still partially open. He'd expected them to be closed tighter than a drum. Didn't anybody learn anything around here? Jesus! These people were stupid. It was almost too much to believe!

Still, he didn't know why. Everybody he decided to off was just as unprepared to be killed as if they'd been invited out to a party. Only he was the party. And what a party.

He peered through the window. Shit! That fuck-face banker's wife, Angie.

Donevan hated her on sight. He'd seen the patched-up bag prancing around town in her expensive clothes and gaudy jewelry with that tight-ass banker husband of hers. Big shit. He was no expert on plastic surgery, but he could see that her face was stretched too tight to be the way she was born with it.

He sure as hell wasn't interested. Or was he? That jewelry she wore was worth a fortune, and wouldn't it be a charge to choke somebody off with a diamond necklace? He wondered if it would hold up for a strangling.

Mia had seen Angie drive up in the big fancy black Cadillac that belonged to her husband, James, and she'd been prepared for the woman's usual arrogance. Yet, to her surprise, the woman on her massage table was humble—and quiet—for the first time ever.

Mia wondered if Angie was having one of her awful headaches, but that had never stopped her from talking before. Then she suddenly recalled one of the policemen telling her that Angie's husband was a suspect in the young girl's murder.

To say Mia had been shocked was an understatement. But she was sure she hadn't been as shocked as Angie must have been. Mia could only guess at the pain it had caused this hard, class-conscious, egotistical woman.

Finally, tightly, coldly, Angie began to talk. "I suppose you know about James."

Mia nodded. "I'm sorry. Are you managing all right?"

Bitter tears slid beneath the woman's closed eyes. She looked as if she had aged ten years in a few weeks. "I'm managing just fine, thank you. I kicked his sorry, philandering ass out of the house, and I'm suing him for every dime he has."

Mia tried not to absorb the woman's hatred. She tried to

shield herself from it and think of something that would help. Angie had always been difficult; now she'd turned her cruelty in a single direction.

Silently Mia endured Angie's ranting and raving about what a fool James had made of her. It seemed that once she started venting her hostility, it spewed forth like a fountain.

"We all make mistakes," Mia managed to interject.

"Don't start that forgiveness shit with me," Angie snapped. "I came here because—because—"

Abruptly the woman turned over on her stomach, put her face in the pillow, and sobbed. Mia waited while Angie wept. She knew the release would be good for her. So would talking about the situation if she could be objective.

"I'm sorry," Angie said at last, never looking up.

"You needed to cry," Mia said. "And you need to talk, not just shriek out your humiliation. Why did you come here today? Why did you make the appointment?"

Angie's mascara was streaked, her face ravaged by grief and tears, when she turned over on her back again. She rested her head on the pillow gingerly.

"I don't have a single friend in this town," she said in a drained, miserable voice. "I'm the latest joke. The laughing-stock. My husband, James Esterbrook, with a cheap little whore. I can't even talk to my psychiatrist about it. I know he would laugh, too."

Mia had no doubt in her mind that the town was glad to find a reason to take this woman down a peg or two, but clearly she was suffering and needed nurturing. For the first time it was easy for Mia to provide it. Angie was acting like a human being with a conscience and weaknesses and failings like everyone else.

"Do you still love James?"

A string of muffled curses came out of Angie's mouth. Mia waited for the bitterness to abate.

"Do you?" she repeated.

Angie clutched the towel to her face like a huge handkerchief and began to weep again. Between sobs, she muttered, "That cheating wimp! He's all I've ever had, and even though I knew he was stingy with sex and it irked me, I merely thought he was a workaholic. To learn that he was with that—that . . ." Her words tapered off and more oaths followed. Then more tears.

"What does James say?"

Angie waved a hand and closed her eyes. "The usual drivel, that it only happened once. That was why he gave her the gold chain." She laughed harshly. "He'd bought it for me and was mad at me because I'm never 'there for him,' to use his term. So he picked up this creepy little slut and gave her *my* chain. After I worked my ass off all my life to make sure he could climb up the career ladder, giving dinner parties and making connections. Well, the bastard will get his just deserts, and you can bank on that."

"I'm not going to start that 'forgiveness shit,' as you phrased it a few minutes ago," Mia said, using Angie's own words, "but you might try counseling. You might find that there's something of your love left to salvage. Something you both want."

"Not on your damned life!" Angie raged. "I'm going to find the same kind of consolation he did when I wasn't 'there for him.' I'm attractive, too, you know. I'm going away tonight. My bags are in the car. I'm not letting a soul know where, but you can bet your ass that when some man makes the right advances to me, I'm going to screw my twat off, too. James isn't the only one who can play that game! And you can bet on something else, too. *I* won't have to pay for it!"

Mia shook her head. She didn't know what to say. Instinctively she knew there was no point at all in trying to reason with this raving shrew.

Donevan was being extra careful. He would have bet his life that the police had worked out some scheme with the masseuse for entrapment, but maybe they weren't as sharp as he gave them credit for. Shit, everybody else around here was stupid. Why should they be any different?

Still, he wasn't about to be a reckless fool. He waited until the old black-haired bag came into the bathroom, then he vanished around the side of the house.

Down low on his belly, lest someone should be watching from somewhere, he slid inch by inch in the damp soil and vegetation toward the big Cadillac. Damn, he wished he had one of these! Barely reaching up, he tried the door.

Son of a bitch! He couldn't believe it! The cunt had left the door unlocked. Who was he to turn down such an invitation? Wouldn't it be a riot if he stole the car and drove it down the hill with the police watching, thinking the old bat was at the wheel?

Unexpectedly he heard Mia and Angie talking. Quickly he held the button to keep the overhead light from coming on, then slipped into the rear of the car. Shit! The whole fucking backseat was filled with big suitcases. The bitch was planning to travel.

Lying down as flat as he could on the floor, he waited for her to come to the car. His heart was beginning to pound and his dick was trying to keep the same rhythm. He'd never done anything like this before, and he was getting all geared up for some kind of fun.

Bigger than life, the cunt strutted out to the car. Donevan listened, trying to contain his breathing, as Mia walked with Angie, telling her to be sure to lock her doors. Mia wasn't at liberty to discuss all the police precautions being taken since no one knew who could be trusted, but she wanted Angie to be careful anyway. The woman wasn't behaving rationally at all.

"I'm not afraid of the big bad wolf," Angie said arrogantly.

She got in the car and slammed the door. Donevan lay so still he could have been a statue, but then, he'd learned over the months how to remain absolutely motionless. He'd even learned how to control his muscles when he could use enough restraint to do so.

After the woman started the car and roared off, Donevan realized that he didn't have a plan. Sure, he could get a ride down the hill to his truck, trick the police if any were about, and scare the bitch half to death, but that wasn't enough to take care of his problems.

His dick. Always his dick these days. He was beginning to think it ruled him. And that made him very nervous. What—just what—if his mother was right about him playing with it so much?

He dismissed the notion with a wave of his hand. That crazy, puritanical old witch. She was the biggest cause of his problems, and he wasn't going to let her preaching spoil his night.

Suddenly he recalled how he had stood on the cliff and watched the water spewing and churning. He remembered thinking that if he could throw one woman off into that foaming, frothing, endless dark depth, he might be rid of all his problems forever. He could visualize that particular day he stood at the edge of the cliff, dizzy and excited and feeling wonderfully giddy.

The plan. Ah, the plan began to form. *This* would be the woman. Who would miss her anyway? He'd heard the gossip about her husband, and clearly she was going away. Chances were she wasn't too eager to say where. He'd bet his ass she was running in shame, and he knew how that was.

Suddenly the whine of a siren filled the air. Donevan thought his heart would stop. The fucking cops! His luck couldn't be that bad. Instead of stopping, the bitch began to speed like a wild woman, taking the curves so fast that the suitcases all fell toward him.

Shit! He didn't know what to do. On the one hand, he sure as hell wanted the cunt to outrun the cops, but on the other she was about to get both of them killed. Her, he didn't give a shit about. He was going to kill her himself. That was a given. But he wanted the chance. And he didn't want to die himself. He had plans. Big plans still on the horizon besides this useless cunt.

Abruptly the woman skidded to a halt, causing more luggage to pound Donevan. He almost cussed out loud. Damn, she was going to pay for this. He was about to piss his pants. His dick was still a problem, but it had shrunk up so small with fear that he didn't know if it would ever become erect again.

He was sure the cops would hear his heart bang, but maybe they would think it was the woman's. Clearly nervous, she rolled down her window and said in a whining voice, "I know I was speeding, but I'm just so scared. I've not been well. I'm Mrs.—"

Angie licked her lips. "I have migraine headaches that can only be relieved by massage, but I was terrified to come all the way up here to this isolated spot, and once it got so dark, I just wanted to get home as fast as possible."

Donevan held his breath, praying right along with Angie that the cops would let her go with a warning. He wanted to get the hell out of here.

"License, please," one man said.

Hands shaking, Angie pulled it out of her purse. She didn't want these policemen to know she was James Esterbrook's wife. Donevan could hear the two men murmuring, then they lectured Angie as they returned her license.

"I know you're scared, but you could get killed just as fast the way you're driving as by a maniac," one said. The other added, "We saw you go up and you were driving too recklessly then, too."

Angie pressed a hand to her head as one of the cops held the flashlight on her. "Please," she murmured, "my head still hurts. I just want to get home and get in bed. I'll drive more slowly. I promise."

The cop was more observant than Donevan had thought. Suddenly he shined the light briefly in the backseat. It was all Donevan could do to keep still and not curse the bitch for driving like a fool and putting them both in the frying pan.

"Looks like you're going somewhere besides home," he noted.

Fuck! Angie thought to herself. She found a smile from somewhere. "Yes, but I don't want anyone to know."

"We need to know," the cop said. "Your husband is under suspicion for murder. Is he going, too?"

"He most certainly is not!" Angie said indignantly. "I'm leaving under doctor's orders to rest. Do you want to see the order?"

"No, but if you want to get where you're going, you'd better slow down or you'll find yourself resting longer than you want."

Angie flung her driver's license back in her purse and snapped it shut. "Thank you," she said a little too sharply.

Donevan listened as other car doors shut and Angie cautiously started the car. Jesus! That had been close. She was going to pay for that one! If the cops had discovered him—well, let's just say this bitch had put him in jeopardy and she was going to know just how that felt any minute now.

He waited until they were well away from the cops who were hidden in the trees, then swiftly shoved the suitcases away from him and wrapped an arm around Angie's throat.

"Uhh!" she gasped, startled.

"Shut up, bitch, or you die," Donevan said, tightening his arm around her neck.

Angie was sure he was going to cut off her air supply. She almost swerved off the road.

"Pay attention to what the fuck you're doing and pull over down there where those pines are," Donevan ordered her. "I see from your suitcases that you want to go places." He snickered. "I plan to take you."

"Listen, I'm very wealthy," she said, trying to sound cool when she'd never been so frightened in her life. This had to be the murderer. She didn't want to get murdered. God knows she didn't want to die.

"Shut up and pull over," Donevan said, tightening his grip so that her words were slurred and she was getting a little dizzy.

"But you don't understand," she tried to say. "My husband is very rich. You could hold me for ransom."

Donevan broke into such maniacal laughter that Angie was chilled to the bone. If he didn't want money, what could she do? What else could she offer him? He would take what he wanted, she realized, so how could she help herself?

Impatient with her stalling, Donevan whipped the car to the side of the road. Angie barely managed to brake before they rammed into some trees.

"Get out!" he ordered, banging suitcases around with one hand, then sliding out himself, his arm still around Angie's neck.

When she didn't budge, he reached in and dragged her out. As she started to scream, he cold-cocked her, knocking her to the ground.

"Shit," he muttered.

He thought he'd knocked her out, and he wasn't about to carry her to the cliff. They'd have to work their way through the bushes and brambles as it was now. He was sure they were well below the place where the cops were parked, but they were also far below the masseuse's house. He'd have to settle for whatever they found.

Bending over the inert form, he slapped her several times.

"Please don't hurt me," Angie murmured.

"Playing possum, were you, cunt?" Donevan said, thoroughly pissed now. She was turning out to be more trouble than she was worth. Still, he was excited about throwing her into the ocean. The spot they found wouldn't be as high up as the masseuse's cottage, but it should still work.

"No, no," Angie stammered.

"Shut up and get up," Donevan ordered, eager again to get on with his plan. "Have you got a flashlight in the car?"

Angie got one from the glove compartment. As she climbed back out of the car, her first instinct was to smash this man over the head with the light, but he was too fast for her.

Smirking, he yanked the flashlight from her hand and pushed her in front of him.

Donevan turned the flashlight on, but he kept the beam low to the ground, grasping Angie's arm with the other hand, with fingers that felt like steel. She felt briers and bushes scrape at her legs as she literally made a path. Once she hit her head on a tree branch, and she was sure she heard Donevan snicker.

She had thought she'd felt hatred before, when she found out about James's betrayal, but she'd never known such anger as she felt at her kidnapper. How dare he treat her so? How *dare* he? Suddenly she felt the strangest longing for James. He would never let this man hurt her. He loved her; she had to believe that now, needed to believe it, in spite of his adultery. Maybe she'd acted too hastily, but what could she do now?

She didn't know what to do. She wanted to whimper and beg someone to help her. She wanted to demand that someone do something to get her out of here. She wanted— she just wanted not to be here in this awful situation.

Perhaps this fiend had listened to her after all and was taking her to some secret hideout where he would hold her for ransom. Maybe he wouldn't murder her. Maybe.

They came to the ocean so abruptly that Angie almost went over the edge. They both stopped when she gasped. Suddenly she could sense the change in the man. He began to smell of musk and sweat. Maybe she simply hadn't noticed before, but the smell scared her more than anything now. She was reminded of a wild animal.

Donevan shined the pitiful little beam of the flashlight over the cliff. Shit, it was only about twenty feet down. Still, there were plenty of big boulders at the water's edge and the waves were washing up on them. This old bitch would probably splatter on one before she drowned. He smiled at the thought.

Angie's heart was hammering fiercely. There were no steps down to the water that she could see. She and James had a beach house, but it wasn't in an untamed area like this, and wooden steps led to the beach. Surely this madman didn't expect her to scramble down the hill with him. To what point? She was already scratched and aching. But fear overrode all her other pain.

Donevan shined the flashlight into Angie's face, and she blinked at the blinding yellow color. "Are you ready to go on that trip now, bitch?" he asked, his voice very high and strange. "If you've been good, the angels will take you to heaven, but if you've been bad, the devil will get you for sure."

"Oh, no! Oh, no, please!" Angie cried out, realizing what he had in mind for her. He wasn't planning to rape her. He had no intention of holding her for ransom.

"Shut up," he hissed. Before Angie could fight at all, Donevan picked her up with amazing strength and held her high over his head, preparing to hurl her into the angry waters below.

"Oh, God," she whispered. "Oh, God. No!"

"Yes!" Donevan cackled with glee, releasing his hold.

Then Angie was plunging through the chilly night air.

Donevan followed her with the beam of light, his hand on his cock, ready to shoot off the minute Angie landed in the water.

To his disgust, she hit a huge black rock just as the water receded. He hadn't really thought about what would happen to her when he imagined her splattering. The sight was nauseating as she bounced off the boulder and vanished in the water, blood and guts going in every direction before the water claimed them.

Dry-heaving, Donevan turned around to retch. He didn't want to see any more. This hadn't worked at all. Nothing was going to work until he killed the masseuse, and now he was stuck with this putrid cunt's car. He'd have to drive it down to where his truck was parked, hide it, and call somebody he knew who dealt in stolen cars. At least she'd done that right; even the police knew she was going away. He didn't even want a piece of the action. He just wanted to go home and puke. Jesus! When was something going to go right for him?

# ⟶ CHAPTER 31 ⟵

Tuesday's clients included Nora and Garson. Mia was surprised to see them arrive together, hand-in-hand as they got out of Garson's truck. Clearly something had happened between them in Mia's absence. Something good. She smiled.

"Hello. Have I made a mistake? Did I double-book you?"

They both laughed. "We double-booked ourselves," Garson said. "This little sweetie doesn't go anywhere by herself these days. I don't want a pretty hair on her head harmed. She'll wait inside while you work on me, if you don't mind."

Mia laughed with delight for the first time since her return. "I don't ever do business this way, but then, these are unusual times. I don't mind at all. Come on in."

Still holding hands, they entered the house. Mia found them both easier to work with than she ever had. She was pleased and made a point of telling them so. She was feeling happy when they left.

\* \* \*

Frank was a nervous wreck when he arrived for his appointment. Mia grieved most for him; he was the most likely suspect, and though she intended to be as good as her word, she could not find anything in poor Frank to condemn, anything that looked suspicious.

She wanted to take him in her arms as she had Brett and let him relieve himself of some of his anguish. But that wasn't Frank's way. She had to leave him with his dignity. She'd learned that from Troy.

She let him talk. It seemed so strange to have Frank talking instead of falling asleep on her table, completely relaxed as he had always been. Her heart hurt for him as she pried more and more into his past and what had taken place while she was gone.

Her pain for him did not lessen until he told her about one of his students—one of the few he still had left.

"She's got real talent, Mia. Real talent. We've already made some connections in Nashville, and I'm going there to be with her—when this mess clears up. She's going to record one of my songs."

"Frank, that's wonderful," Mia said, confident that was the best place for him. She was also confident he would become a singer in his own right, once he settled in.

Friday was the day Donevan's appointment was scheduled. Mia was visibly strained, no matter how she cautioned herself that she could help no one if she were not in control and objective. She had tried her best to convince herself that Donevan wasn't the man who had tried to murder her, but some sixth sense went contrary to all her attempts at rationale.

She despised herself for thinking so critically of him when she herself had defended him to the police. She had been almost sure the man had brown eyes. Almost. But almost wasn't good enough.

His sharp rap on the door startled her from her thoughts. She remembered the same thing happening on their first meeting, and she tried to put her fears behind her. She was still working out her own problems, but at least the worst with Troy was behind her and Rand was in her future. Of that, she had no doubt.

When she opened the door, Donevan smiled. "I'm so glad you agreed to see me."

Mia didn't miss the fact that his lip was twitching. It was revealing, but of what? He was nervous. So was she. She reminded herself that the policewoman was only a call away. Mia had a two-way radio hidden in the massage room, and she was fairly confident that she wouldn't be taken by surprise again. Ever.

"I told you I would reschedule," she said easily, amazed by her own glibness when she was shaken by just seeing this man.

"I sure need a massage," he said, following her down the hall. "Man, I don't need to tell you that the police have been all over me. Jesus, I hate that. I paid my debt, even if I didn't owe one. But let something happen anywhere in the area, and every cop in phoning distance comes after me. It's not fair," he lamented with so much earnestness that Mia was tempted to believe him.

Once again she was caught in her own war. When she was in Donevan's presence, she honestly didn't think he was a murderer—for several reasons, she realized. He simply didn't seem savvy enough. On the other hand, the attempt on her life hadn't succeeded; perhaps that was because of inexpertise. Her mind began to swirl with thoughts.

Maybe Donevan needed more stimulation than rape, as the police had suggested. Psychopaths generally grew progressively dangerous. Yet perhaps the attack on her was one random attempt that had failed, thereby curing him, especially if he was a copycat attacker.

Obviously he wasn't as skilled as the killer who had murdered four women without leaving a trail the police could follow.

Enough! she told herself, readying her supplies while

Donevan went into the bathroom. She would focus on massage and wait until he was relaxed to see if she could learn anything.

On the table Donevan found that he detested the masseuse's touch more than ever. She was the symbol of his failure, a living testament to his lack of power. He kept repeating the word *control* until he thought he would go crazy. He didn't even care about raping her now. All he wanted to do was kill her and get it over with.

"Donevan."

When she called his name, he actually jerked on the table. Mia shook her head. He hadn't relaxed at all. He hadn't even seemed to hear her when she tried to talk to him. It was as though he had erected some kind of interior barrier.

They were back to step one. She wasn't sure what it meant. Maybe only that they would have to work at trust again because of the break in the bond while she was away.

Or was it something worse? Did the man on her table hate her enough to kill her?

Stop it! she warned herself. How could she help if she couldn't control her own runaway thoughts?

"Please turn over," she instructed.

When Donevan did so, she looked right into his blue-blue eyes. He met her stare and she was sure she saw hatred there—raw and undisguised. She blinked.

Donevan smiled. She couldn't hold his gaze! She wasn't so powerful after all. He drew in a deep breath. He was starting to feel better. He'd just needed to face her down. To establish his position of superiority.

Wondering at the strange smile, Mia murmured, "You aren't relaxed at all, Donevan. Have the police given you such a bad time that you feel massage won't help at this point?"

"No," he answered. "I'm feeling better already. It's just that it's been so long I forgot what to expect. I feel—er—exposed when I'm not dressed. Don't you?"

She managed a smile. "That's certainly not unusual. People do feel vulnerable on the table because I'm the one in control and they have the disadvantage of nudity."

"I don't feel vulnerable," he said sharply, then quickly regretted the words.

She was testing him again, but he'd known from her eyes that *he* was the one in control. He had to get it together.

Now was not the time to get hostile with her. She was stupid, but he was sure she was more alert because of the attack. He wouldn't make another mistake with her. He knew he had to cool it, keep a low profile. But it was hard. Damned hard.

She started to work on his chest. Donevan tried to be patient, but he had a sudden need to feel her hands on his dick. He wanted her to feel the surge, to know the power of the poison.

Mia was well aware of his aroused state. He wasn't a man of large size, but working so intimately with him, she knew he was erect, and she knew he knew she was aware of it. Stay in control, she reminded herself.

"I'm glad you don't feel vulnerable," she said, even though it seemed that he'd made that comment eons ago.

"Hell, no," he said with that cockiness Mia had seen the first time he came to the cottage.

They were having to begin all over. She hated that, though perhaps she should have expected it. He seemed to resent her very touch; she'd hoped they'd gotten beyond that.

She tried to draw on her inner strength. She reminded herself that she had a very serious purpose in working with her clientele again. She might be in the position to prevent another murder.

"Do you think massage has helped you at all, Donevan?" she asked, deliberately repeating his name. "You were very hostile the first time you came here."

He met her eyes again. If she hadn't known better, she would swear that he was trying to intimidate her. Perhaps she was jumping to conclusions, but his eyes seemed to dare her to hold that cruel gaze. And it was cruel. So cruel, and so distinct, that she thought again that his eyes weren't the eyes of her attacker.

"I said I was sorry about that, didn't I?" he asked. This time he wasn't smiling. Nor was his lip twitching. "I didn't know what to expect," he said, as if he were speaking to a child deficient in communication skills. "You said that wasn't unusual, remember?"

She nodded and said as casually as possible, "Yes, I do."

His eyes still held hers. She was determined not to look away. Suddenly he reached out and grabbed her arms. She gasped, and he immediately loosened his grip, but did not let her go. He had that strange smile on his mouth.

"You said the idea was to learn to put me in touch with myself so that I could get in touch with other people, remember?"

Mia's heart was hammering. She couldn't stop it, but she forced a brave front. "Yes, I remember." She hoped her voice didn't sound as weak to him as it did to her.

"Well," he said, the peculiar smile becoming an odd grin, "look, I'm touching you."

They both looked down at his hands tightly holding her wrists.

"Yes, you are," she said with more courage than she was feeling. He was incredibly strong. Stronger than she, she realized, which only made her think again that Donevan had not been her attacker.

God knew he was troubled, but he was so strong that he could have easily bested her. He was playing a game now that she didn't understand—a bid for power or reassurance or self-confidence—but that didn't make him a killer.

A rapist, yes. She could believe that.

A murderer? It was doubtful. Mia's heartbeat slowed with a pain that shocked her. She realized that, after all, she wanted Donevan to be guilty. Because if he wasn't, then one of her other clients probably was. She couldn't bear that thought.

"You're doing very well," she said. "I'm proud of you, but grabbing the therapist isn't quite what I'm talking about. You know the old song—try a little tenderness. That's what we're striving for."

He freed her, easing his hands off her wrists, letting his fingers slide down her arms.

"Well, I want to get it right," he said, as though suddenly contrite and ashamed he'd been rough with her. "I want you to believe that I haven't done anything wrong."

He looked away, his blue eyes hidden by his lashes. "I'd rather die than go back to prison. I'm not going to do anything that puts me in there."

That much was true. He wasn't lying to the bitch about that.

His eyes met hers again. Mia nodded. "It must have been awful for you."

"I can't bear being caged up," he said thickly. "I didn't do anything wrong. That woman wanted it."

"Why do you say that? A jury believed that you forced yourself on her." Mia's words were amazingly even and nonjudgmental.

"I worked with her. She was a prick tease. Do you know what that is?" he asked so softly that Mia had to strain to hear him.

"I've heard the term," she said noncommittally.

"A prick tease sends a certain message to a man—a real man," Donevan replied in a vehemently quiet voice. "She should get what she asks for. In this case she cried rape because two men saw us."

Mia stared at him. Donevan held her eyes. She didn't know what to say. Did he really think the woman had teased him? She'd reviewed the case with the probation officer's permission. Donevan had had a rough upbringing. He wasn't a social mixer, but he had had no previous record. This was his first offense. That's why she'd agreed to take his case.

Now she was thoroughly confused. He was giving her

mixed signals. She felt that he was trying to threaten her somehow. But she also felt he was just trying to convince her he was a real man.

"You really don't think you forced the woman?" she asked casually.

"I don't have to force women."

Pure bluff, more bravado, Mia told herself. She was willing to bet he had no woman in his life.

"Do you have a girlfriend, someone special, Donevan?" she murmured.

He grinned that strange grin. "Yeah, I do. Someone real special."

He did. She was it.

"That's good," she said, not believing him for a minute.

He grinned wider. They understood each other. She was aware of his power. She had actually *felt* it. He was in control. Not her.

"Shall we continue?" she asked, wondering if her hands were steady enough.

"Sure," he said. "I'm looking forward to you working on my front. That's when I really relax."

She managed a smile. He forced a grin.

Mia began to work again.

Donevan didn't relax.

Neither did Mia.

## ～ CHAPTER 32 ～

Donevan left more angry than he had arrived. He repeated the word *control* until he had no patience left for it.

Once he was on the porch, he muttered aloud, "Fuck control!"

Jesus, he was uptight. He'd tried to do the damned thing right. He didn't think the masseuse was on to him, but he was aware himself that he wasn't in control, no matter how much he'd said it.

He wanted to kill the bitch. He wanted to kill her so fucking bad he could taste it. His head began to swirl as he started back toward his truck.

He was too agitated to get in. He had to vent some of this poison. His pecker was still rigid. He'd tried to jerk off in the bathroom on the green towel, as he had done the first time he came to the cottage, but it hadn't worked.

He was really getting scared about the poison. It gave him a headache. A bad headache. The roaring and reeling didn't feel good today. That scared him, too. Minutes ago he had felt in power. But then he hadn't known his dick wouldn't go down.

Involuntarily he walked around the house and stood staring at the churning water. Maybe if he'd handled the banker's wife differently, the ocean would have worked as a purifier. He didn't know. It just seemed that his destiny was the masseuse.

It had been his original plan, and even though he had enjoyed some of the other parts of the killings real well, he hadn't had that thrill, that sensation, that ultimate mating that he craved like candy. He was unaware that Mia and the policewoman were watching him, discussing him.

"He's a weird one all right," Lou-Ann commented.

Mia nodded thoughtfully. "I think he's definitely weird, but I don't think he's the killer." Mia frowned. "Of course, I'm no expert in these things. I'm glad you're here. I wouldn't be seeing clients if you weren't staying in the house."

"Does he usually roam around your yard like that?" Lou-Ann asked.

"Never. He comes for his treatment and leaves. Of course, you must remember that he's a new client."

"What do you think he's doing now? What's the point?"

Mia watched Donevan for a moment, reviewing his session. "I think he wants me to think he's a strong man, when he really isn't. I think he's very troubled. I think he's afraid of returning to prison. This murder investigation has him wired. That's what I think, but that's trying to rationalize. A sixth sense about him frightens me."

The women looked into each other's eyes. "Good," Lou-Ann said. "That might save your life one day."

Mia mulled the words over in her mind. She hoped it wouldn't come to that.

Three weeks passed very quietly. It was amazing how soon the talk of the murders began to fade. Mia could barely believe it herself. When she subtly questioned her clients, she found that they had gotten on with their lives, most of them in a more positive manner, with plans she'd hoped to help influence from the first.

Garson and Nora were a couple; Frank and his new girl were well on their way with his song. Angie had gone to only heaven knew where. Her husband was frantic because she hadn't gotten in touch with him. Mia was grateful she could tell James that Angie had planned to go away. The poor man was horrified to think evil might have befallen his wife because of his infidelity.

At least something positive had come out of the murders: They, with their shock value, had effected what Mia couldn't with her massage.

In fact, she didn't think she was being very helpful to the police at all. They stayed in constant contact with her, but even they were beginning to wonder if the killer had sated himself temporarily, or permanently, been arrested for something else, died, or moved on. They couldn't find a pattern in his killings, which seemed to have stopped as abruptly as they had begun.

In the rooming house Donevan was quietly going crazy. His dick had been rigid off and on for days without relief. He had resorted to going to the writer's house late at night and actually pounding his pud until it pained him before he could get any release. The poison was winning. *He* was losing. That told him that he had to off the masseuse soon for his own safety and sanity.

Yet he knew that was dangerous. He knew the killings had given way to other news, not as colorful or exciting, but life had a way of causing the past to fade quickly. He was buying time, but he didn't know how much longer he could last.

Sometimes his pecker got so huge that he didn't think he could keep it in his pants. On those days he'd been forced to call in sick to work; that entailed a lot of shit he didn't want to deal with. Still, he had held on somehow. He had kept his appointments with the masseuse, and he had gotten through them.

But things were getting bad. He would stand in the shower for long periods of time, washing his dick, trying to get some of the poison out, to purify it, but that had to come out from the inside. His pecker was like a boil, a filthy boil, filling with pus instead of semen. Maybe his mother had been right. He was beginning to feel like he was going crazy. He began to think more and more about the black cat.

He'd even tried killing another cat, but that repulsed him. Blood and guts. It hadn't worked. He couldn't sleep. He was growing more haggard.

The nights were the worst. He dreamed that his prick grew until he couldn't turn over in bed. He would wake up in a cold sweat. He couldn't wait much longer. The time had come. Now he didn't think in terms of cats.

It was the masseuse or him. And he had to win. His life depended on it.

* * *

Despite the constant presence of the policewoman and the vigilance of the police, Mia inevitably began to let her guard down. She wasn't the kind of person to stay uptight. Life did go on.

Also, she was pregnant. She was sure of it. She was more pleased about the pregnancy than she had been about anything in her life. It occupied much of her waking thoughts.

Rand was going to Australia next week. Before he left, he was coming to Oregon. Mia intended to tell him about the baby, not because she expected any commitment from him. She didn't. It was enough to know that he loved her, but she wanted him to know about his child.

Although they had stayed in constant touch over the phone, Mia wanted to tell him about the baby in person. She wanted to see his expression. Of course, she would be disappointed if he didn't want the child, but she would love it enough for both of them. As though he were reading her mind, the telephone rang, and it was Rand. Mia couldn't contain her excitement.

"Hello, sexy lady."

"Hello, Rand."

"Guess what?" he exclaimed. "I'm heading your way early. I should be there in two days. Will that work for you?"

Mia felt a mixture of excitement and uncertainty. She had clients scheduled, and she knew this time that Rand would be staying in her house. She had hoped to block out the week he would be here so that she could spend all of her time with him.

"Oh, I don't know, Rand," she murmured. "I still have my work."

"Mia, we've gone over this a dozen times. I want you to give up massage—"

"Now, Rand—"

She could picture him holding up his hands as he conceded.

"Whoa! Wait a minute before you start in. I want you to

give up massage, at least temporarily. Come with me to Australia. I don't like you being the bait for this killer. You know that. I worry about you constantly. That's why I cut my schedule short."

"He seems to have disappeared anyway," Mia said. "I really don't think you need to worry so much. Let's just let the next week go by as we planned. I'll see you on Saturday."

"God, but you're stubborn," he declared. "Come with me to Australia. You need the break. You know you do. Besides, I want you with me."

Mia smiled. She wanted to be with him, too. But in her heart she still felt that she had so much to offer with massage. Everything was confused now, but once the murderer was caught—

That wasn't all, she admitted to herself. Her work had been draining her even before the murders. They had occurred at a time when she was still dealing with so much emotional turmoil of her own. She did need time to rest, to heal herself, to get over the lingering pain of Troy.

"I'll think about it," she agreed.

"That's my girl!" he exclaimed as excitedly as a young boy. "Pack a bag, just in case you decide in my favor."

She laughed. "I'll see you next week, Rand."

Once she had hung up, she decided if Rand viewed the news of the baby favorably, she would go with him to Australia. At any rate, she was going to inform the police and her clients that she was suspending her practice at least temporarily.

However, when she spoke to Lou-Ann, the policewoman wasn't at all happy.

"We're counting on you, Mia," she said plaintively.

"I know," Mia said, "but this is all getting too much for me. I want to help, yet I don't seem to be doing any real good anyway."

Lou-Ann was pensive for a moment. "Maybe it's not such a bad idea after all," she said thoughtfully. "Let me call the chief and see what he thinks."

Mia was mildly surprised when he agreed that it might be a good idea, but only if Mia would cooperate just a little longer. Perhaps if she announced the suspension of her practice and the fact that she was going away, it might flush out the quarry if he was still around and intent on murder.

All agreed that Mia would be even more of a target, but she was willing to go along for a short time. She wanted to see the murderer caught as much as anyone did, but she wanted to get her own life in order, too. Although she wasn't happy about the arrangement, there seemed to be no other way.

Donevan was livid when he hung up the phone. The bitch had been aware of his power. Now she was shutting herself away from him. Well, he wouldn't be thwarted that easily. He would simply speed up his own plans. He had one week to take care of business. He was up to it. He looked down at his dick.

Jesus, was he ever up to it! The damned thing seemed to grow bigger all the time. Donevan thought it would drive him crazy if he didn't get some permanent relief. That relief was the masseuse. He knew it as well as he lived and breathed.

For two days he worked at making sure he didn't mess this up. True, things had slowed down. The murders were old news. But the cops were still trying to pin them on somebody.

He had seen an occasional odd car following him, and known that he was under surveillance. He decided he would drive his white car the night of the murder. That would throw them off a bit. He spent most of his time in the truck.

He was so wound up on the night he had chosen that he paced the house like a caged animal. He got out his collection of goodies: the hemp necklace, a selection of scarves, the mask and gloves, and something new—a glass cutter. He had driven to Portland to buy it. He was pleased with the way it had performed when he'd tried it out on his back window one night. It worked like a charm. All was ready. Especially him.

Mia and Lou-Ann spent another solemn night at the cottage. Both had been lulled into a false sense of security, despite Lou-Ann's constant warnings that anything could happen at any time, especially now that Mia had, in effect, served notice that she would only be available for a short time. Then the phone call came about Troy.

Although Mia thought she had dealt with his impending death, she was distraught to learn that he had already been cremated when Daniel phoned her. It was Troy's wish, Daniel explained gently, that there be no service and no notice about his death. His greatest wish was that Mia not know until it was all over.

After receiving the news, Mia retreated to her bedroom, her grief lulling her to sleep.

Lou-Ann was drowsing on the couch, supposedly watching television, when she thought she heard something. She'd been particularly jumpy this entire assignment. She was getting very bored stuck at the cottage in the guise of a guest—a guest that never left the place. She'd insisted on a television, a necessity she couldn't believe Mia didn't possess.

She went around the house checking things out, securing windows and doors; nothing seemed amiss. She sat back down in front of the set and stayed alert, the adrenaline pumping for a while. Finally, inevitably, she settled on the couch again, stretching out, and began to nod off.

She never heard the man sneak up behind her. She was aware of nothing but the droning of the comedy series on the set until the sudden attack. It was such a shock that she didn't even cry out.

Donevan had come up behind her, a thin cord in his hands, and he had looped it around her neck so quickly that Lou-Ann had no time at all to think, much less defend herself. Her hands were only halfway up in a protective pose when Donevan succeeded in choking the life out of her.

"Gotcha!" Donevan whispered gleefully to the corpse. "Nobody is smarter than Donevan Raitt. You didn't really think you could guard her, did you?"

He pulled his cord free, stood back, and admired his handiwork. Yes! This was the way to kill! The only way. And he was so very good at it. His faith was restored; his pecker was hard enough to penetrate anything. The old women and the splattered rich bitch were only experiments. This was what he was good at, what he was meant for. It was what he loved. God, how he did love it!

Mia, who had finally drifted off to sleep, didn't stir. She knew that Lou-Ann had made a security check of the house, but that was standard procedure for the policewoman, and Mia was secure in that ritual, for she could no longer trust her own instincts.

She awakened abruptly and rudely, gasping, to find a hooded monster cramming a gag in her mouth. At first she thought she was having a horrible nightmare that seemed all too real. She struggled to wake up, but despite her fear and the rush of adrenaline that sent the desperate alarm through her, she felt so weighted that she could only think of going back to sleep.

Gradually a peculiar odor penetrated her senses, and she knew, suddenly, frighteningly, that this was no nightmare, but a very real horror with which she must force herself to contend. She fought to wake up as fully as possible, against great odds.

She choked and coughed and tried to cry out, but couldn't. She felt as if she were being smothered; when she tried to reach up to pull away the offending gag, she was stunned to realize she was trussed to the bed, hand and foot. How had he done this to her without waking her?

From the far recesses of her brain, she thought she recognized the strange smell as ammonia or chloroform or some other kind of anesthetic. That must have really put her out. That was why she'd had so much trouble waking up, distinguishing the real from the unreal.

The two-way radio stood mutely on her nightstand. Lou-Ann was nowhere in evidence. The house had been bugged, but apparently that meant nothing at the moment, either. Mia shuddered and a film of sweat covered her body as every system warned her of danger. She was at the mercy of a madman, and in her heart and soul she felt that she alone had to save herself.

She could hear the intruder's irregular breathing, feel the heat of his breath on her face. In the semilight the shape of the masked man seemed to loom all out of proportion. Mia prayed for someone—anyone—to come, but she suspected that he had done something to Lou-Ann.

She no longer heard the faint noise of the television set, and she didn't think for a moment that Lou-Ann was safe in bed. The possibilities sent her to the edge of panic. If this man was the killer, the policewoman was probably already dead.

The silence was filled with her pounding heart and her own labored breathing as the figure hovered above her, smiling a smile that froze her blood.

Although her hands were sweaty, her bonds still bit painfully into her wrists when she tried to move. She knew only helplessness and anger that was encased in so much fear that it would serve her little purpose at all.

The reality was so frightening that she almost lost all hope. Then she remembered the baby growing inside her. Rand's baby. Her future.

The madman suddenly straddled her. Mia tried to buck him off, twisting and turning and arching her hips, terrified that she would harm her baby. The man's weight pressed her down into the mattress, tugging at her bonds, scraping the skin until she cried out at the pain. He didn't even pause.

With a harsh laugh he struck her so savagely that he almost knocked her out. Mia lay stunned into submissiveness, unable to fight, and unable to think. She had never known such excruciating pain or such vulnerability. She couldn't cry out and she couldn't move.

The lunatic was sitting on her hips. She could feel his erection. She looked at that awful hooded face and shivered. She couldn't really see his eyes. The room was nearly dark, despite the light from the living room, which cast eerie shadows on the wall through the open door.

Abruptly he climbed off her, and to Mia's surprise he ripped off his hood. Donevan Raitt! She didn't know why she should be so shocked—he had been a suspect—but she was taken aback by the sight of his face and those cold blue eyes.

He grinned at her. "Did you really think you were going to leave me, too?" he asked in a high, strange voice.

Mia went pale with a horror that stuck in her throat and stopped her breath. The man was crazy. She could no longer doubt it. Smiling wildly, madly, he unzipped his pants and exposed himself.

"This is my power," he said in that peculiar voice. *"My* power. *You* have none!" He struck her pelvic area with his fist. "Nothing," he said, grabbing a handful of her pubic hair.

She choked on the gag as bile rose inside her. She knew, suddenly, that she was going to die and that Donevan would not make it easy for her. His eyes gleamed with expectation and a bright, unnatural excitement.

She tried to communicate with her eyes, though she knew Donevan did not really see her. He was caught up in some terrible vision of his own, whose ugliness she could not begin to comprehend.

Abruptly he freed one of her hands. "Feel my power," he ordered. "Touch it."

He forced her free hand down on his penis. "Tell me how huge it is, how powerful my dick is," he demanded.

Mia was shaking with helpless fury and fear and the cold certainty that she could not fight him. She stared at

Donevan, praying that her steady gaze would unnerve him, at least for a moment. He didn't even notice.

"Say it, you dirty cunt!" he ordered in that strange voice. "You massage every part of your other clients. Why not me? Just who the fuck do you think you are?"

Mia tried to talk around her gag, but she only made muffled sounds that caused her to choke and gasp.

Donevan shoved her hand away and ripped the gag from her mouth. When he removed the wadded-up scarf, Mia's first impulse was to scream with every shred of strength inside her. Yet instinctively she knew he would kill her without thought at the first sound.

She struggled to find her voice, playing for time. Surely one of the police backup systems would work. Or maybe the neighbors, Emma and Buck, had seen something. Mia thought about the nosy old couple, and a small flame of hope began to grow inside her.

"Where's Lou-Ann?" Mia rasped.

Donevan grinned that haunting grin of his. "She's gone bye-bye, just like Frannie and the asshole banker's wife."

Mia's eyes grew wide. He had been the cause of Frannie's death! Her heart began to ache, actually ache as if she were about to have a heart attack. And Angie? Had he killed Angie, too?

"Donevan," she said, trying her best to think rationally over her own terror, which had succeeded in forcing her awake, more awake than she thought she might want to be, "you didn't kill Angie, did you?" Her voice, quivering uncontrollably, betrayed her fear.

His grin grew broader. "Yes, indeed, although it was a real bummer of a disappointment. I hurled the old bag off the cliff into the ocean." His lip turned up at the memory. "She made a godawful mess when she hit the rocks. It made me puke. There was no thrill at all in it. Strangling is the only way to kill."

Mia thought she was going to throw up. Lord God in

heaven! What kind of sadistic demon was this man? She felt tears of sadness and despair fill her eyes.

"Donevan, please tell me you didn't do those things to another human being. Please. I wanted so desperately to believe in you, to help you."

Suddenly Donevan struck her, hitting her so viciously that she thought he might have cracked her jaw. "Shit, don't start that sniveling with me, you phony bitch. Help, hell. You can't even help yourself. You want to see what happened to your friend in the other room, you want to see what I can really do, well, okay."

Mia didn't think she could bear it if he had murdered Lou-Ann and was going to bring her in here to prove it. Her stomach lurched at the thought, and she wanted to scream out her rage. She had to get away. She had to tell someone, do something to stop this lunatic.

Yet she found that she was too terrified to move, even if her bonds had not held her so tightly. She could not think clearly; her mind was as motionless as her spread-eagled body. Then she heard what sounded like a body being dragged, bumping across the floor. A black despair washed over her. Oh, dear God. Lou-Ann.

Mia opened her mouth wide to scream, but only a weak cry came out.

The sound of her own voice, the realization that she was still alive, stirred something deep within her. She couldn't give up and let Donevan take her life, let him win so easily. She *wouldn't*.

Working frantically, she tried to untie her other hand. She had succeeded only in loosening the knot when Donevan returned. Mia's blood ran cold in her veins.

"Is this your friend?" he asked, glancing down at Lou-Ann. He was dragging her along behind him by one foot like she was a piece of garbage. "What have you two been doing up here?" he asked in that high, strangely feminine voice. "Have you been naughty?"

Mia didn't want to look, but her eyes were drawn to the

policewoman involuntarily when Donevan dropped her foot. She wasn't wearing any shoes and her heel thunked hard on the floor. Her head was tilted at an odd angle and her blouse had slid up, exposing her pale midriff.

Fighting against the vomit rising in her throat, Mia swallowed hard. She wanted to believe that none of this was happening, to retreat into another world that was safe from this savagery and senseless sickness, but she knew her only chance to survive was to pay close attention to Donevan's every move.

"Guess who's next?" he said in that same high voice. "Guess who else has been bad? I don't know what you've been doing up here in the cottage all alone with this dyke, but I know you've been bad. Don't think I didn't see you playing with your client's dick, you filthy bitch, because I did. I was watching you. I've been watching you for weeks. I know how bad you are."

"You've been sneaking into my house and watching me with my other clients!" she accused, surprising herself with her indignant reaction to his invasion of her privacy.

"Yeah, and I saw how very bad you were. Very bad people have to be punished."

"I only give therapeutic massage for impotency or related reasons," Mia said vehemently, wondering why she was defending herself to a madman. But perhaps if she kept talking she could gain some kind of advantage, or at least some time.

Donevan laughed, and Mia realized she'd never heard him laugh before. The sound was high-pitched and hideous.

"Therapy? How about masturbation? You played with his dick, and you played with her pussy. I saw you. You were very, very bad, and bad people have to be taught a lesson." He repeated it like a litany that gave him strength and purpose. "You can't just run away when you're bad. You have to learn not to be naughty."

Mia's pulse hammered in her ears. She searched the room desperately as Donevan came closer. She saw that he was stroking his penis, but he had a necklace in his other hand. Her hemp necklace.

"You have blue eyes," she said, almost inadvertently. "How—"

Donevan tapped his head. "And *brown* contacts. Very smart, huh?"

Mia's gaze shifted to the heavy statue of the fertility goddess on her bedside stand, next to the useless police radio. She tried her best to hang on to her sanity. Donevan was moving closer. If she could grab the statue before he could get the scarf around her neck, she might have some chance of surviving.

A small chance, but a chance just the same. Her breathing was labored and ragged and her skin damp with sweat and fear.

Donevan seemed absorbed in caressing his penis, though his gaze was on Mia. She'd sensed a change in him since he'd returned to the room; perhaps harming Lou-Ann had vented some of his venom. He didn't seem as vicious, but he still seemed determined.

He climbed back on her body again, grasping the hand he had freed with his gloved one. He seemed reluctant to let go of his penis to retie Mia, but in the end he jammed it down between their bodies. He hadn't removed any of his clothes and they bit into her flesh as he forced her hand back up against the bedpost.

Mia waited until he shifted his weight, until the nervous stench of his body filled her nostrils and made her want to retch. She closed her eyes, said a desperate prayer, then ripped her hand from his and reached out for the fertility goddess. In one swift movement, while he froze in stunned surprise, she brought the statue down on the back of Donevan's head with every ounce of power she possessed.

# ~ CHAPTER 33 ~

When the pottery made contact with Donevan's head, Mia felt as if she had crushed his skull. Instead of the noise she expected, the statue seemed to sink in, as though damaging tissue. Donevan immediately released his grip and toppled over, his body half across hers.

Her mind spinning wildly, her hands shaking, she struggled to get out from under him and free herself of her remaining bonds. She suspected that he was dead, but she was too panicked to think of anything but getting away and getting help.

She had just reached for the police radio when Donevan raised his head and grasped handfuls of Mia's hair.

She felt strands rip from her scalp as she instinctively pulled away, trying to scramble off the bed. Screaming and kicking, she fought to escape. He struggled up from the bed, actually using her body for leverage, pulling her back toward him, as though her blows did not exist, as if he were invincible.

She could see blood running from his wound, yet he appeared oblivious to it. He faced her with single-minded determination. He was going to kill her.

Now! She kneed him in the groin, momentarily causing him to double up, groaning, but when she looked for something else to strike him with, she saw only whirling, useless darkness. He did not release her hair and the pain made her white and weak.

She reached up, trying to gouge out his eyes, but he held

her fingers, bending them backward with amazing strength. He seemed to possess superhuman power tonight. Mia knew that she had to run; it was her only chance. She raked his face with her nails, but they were short and did little damage other than to startle him.

Dragging herself off the opposite side of the bed, she managed to reach the massage room. In disbelief she discovered that Donevan was right behind her.

She had never felt so vulnerable in her life, not even when he'd surprised her in the bathroom the first time he tried to kill her. She knew his strength, and it terrified her. Instinctively she grabbed the phone. It was dead!

Holding the single thought that if she could reach the fireplace, she could bash him with the poker, she raced across the room, bumping furniture and banging her bare feet in her frantic attempt to protect herself. She thought she was safe when her hand fastened around the poker. She spun and raised the weapon, but Donevan knocked it from her hand.

Desperate, Mia didn't know what to do. She succeeded in ducking beneath his grasping hands, but where could she hide?

Almost involuntarily she began to scream. She didn't really know who she hoped would hear. A surveillance team? The bugging device?

Obviously Donevan had destroyed her sources of security as easily as he had ripped out the phone system.

"He's going to kill me!" she cried. "Oh, God, he's trying to kill me!"

Out on the front porch Emma's ears perked up and she grabbed Buck's arm. They had seen a white car drive up the road and had thought it was Rand Mason. Emma felt that the masseuse owed her something for being such a good neighbor. After all, she had called the police and had been the one to put them on to the suspects, including Frank and the man in the black truck.

The woman just might introduce her to the movie star, even though it was very late at night. She didn't see his car, but it was probably hidden for privacy's sake. She knew it hadn't come back down the hill.

Buck had been reluctant to ride up to the house with his wife, but things seemed to happen up here and he didn't want to miss anything himself.

"Did you hear that screaming?" Emma asked.

Buck nodded. "We'd better go back down the hill and call the police."

"We'll do no such thing!" Emma cried. "Where are they? I thought they were supposed to be patrolling around here, but that clearly ain't the case. If we wait for them, he'll be done killed her by the time they come."

She seemed very puzzled for a moment. "Rand Mason a killer? It just don't seem right. I'm so upset to think it. Maybe the police do know he's here. Maybe he'd got permission. Still, that awful screaming—"

As fast as the screaming had started, it stopped. Emma and Buck heard a commotion from the back of the house.

"Let's sneak a look," Emma suggested.

A reluctant Buck followed. He didn't know what to think. Or maybe he was just too scared to want to get involved. The man might really be the murderer.

There was a faint light on the sun deck, and Emma and Buck could see the two shadowy battling figures. Donevan had Mia pressed against the rails, trying his best to get the hemp necklace around her neck.

"That woman's naked," Buck said, stunned by the scene before him.

"Buck, you fool!" Emma cried frantically, her old heart pounding. "This is no time to notice *that!* He *is* trying to kill her."

Still, Emma, too, seemed too stunned and frightened to know what to do. She had truly expected Rand Mason. This man wasn't Rand.

"I'm pregnant, Donevan!" Mia cried desperately. "Please let me live. Don't do this."

Unknowingly, Mia had only revolted Donevan more. Jesus, he despised pregnant women! He paused to look down at her belly to see if she was telling the truth.

As though in slow motion, he became aware that he was growing dizzy and disoriented. He touched the back of his head, and when he looked at his hand, he saw his own blood. The color drained from his face. He felt sick to his stomach. The cunt had cut him. She had stolen his power when she tricked him by saying she was pregnant.

Hate and fury twisted his features as he felt his head again, then ran his hand down his neck. More blood, leaking out of his body, beneath his shirt collar, seeping out of him, covering him in red slime.

He went berserk, wanting only to destroy the source of his anger. With a howl of raw rage, he dropped the hemp necklace and grabbed Mia's long hair in his bloody hands. While she struggled to be free of his iron grasp, he tried to wrap the strands of hair tighter and tighter around her neck.

Suddenly Emma was startled into action. "Stop that!" she yelled, running around to the sun deck. "Let go of her!"

Buck followed, his pulse pounding in his ears. He didn't want a confrontation with a killer, but what could he do when his wife was leading the way?

Donevan stepped back to look at the intruders. All the violent activity had caused the blood to pour from his wounds. He couldn't seem to think.

He'd lost control. Damn it to hell, he'd lost control. In a moment of indecision he looked around in confusion.

People were coming. The police could be on the way. Suddenly he pushed Mia down on the boards of the sun deck, hearing her body hit as if from a very long way away.

Then he ran. It wasn't a conscious decision. It was the survival instinct. There was danger here. And he was in a losing position. The cunt had bested him again. He was filled with fury, but he was impotent. His power was seeping out in his blood instead of through his penis.

He jumped over the sun deck rails in the opposite direction from the Carsons. He crashed to the earth and lay there for a moment, not knowing what to do. Instinct drove him to get up, but he was terribly disoriented. He had left the road and worked his way laboriously through the trees when he came. He found his car by sheer luck and headed back for the road, his foot to the floor even though he knew better.

Suddenly, out of nowhere, a police car appeared. It seemed to explode from the woods themselves. Donevan was way ahead of them. Despite his throbbing head and leaking blood, he began to feel the excitement and fear mingle in him. This was the real thing. If he was caught, it was all over.

He didn't intend to get caught. The adrenaline surged through him, giving him renewed vitality. He reached the bottom of the hill and lost himself on the curving roads. He could hear the screaming siren behind him, and it only served to stir him on.

He reached down and felt his dick. He was on a high, and when he was on a high, nothing else mattered. He began to stroke himself. But that something special was missing. The masseuse had cheated him out of the big death coupled with the little death.

A brilliant idea occurred to him: there was still a way to accomplish it.

All by himself.

He was good at doing things solo. He always had been.

Racing at breakneck speed, his penis still throbbing in his hand, he made his way back to the rooming house.

The laundry room. That was the place to go. It was an added room, and it had exposed beams at the top. The ceiling was high enough and a good sturdy cord was stretched across the room. The landlady used it to dry the clothes she hand-washed.

He thought he saw her peeking out the window when he came to a screeching halt, but he didn't have time to bother with her. He had that roaring inside his head. He had a headache, too, but he was used to that now. It was the roaring that counted. It felt so good. His dick felt so good.

He looked down at it as he slipped into the laundry room. It was huge. His power was back! His blood wasn't destroying him. He would be just fine when he got rid of the poison in his dick. Especially the way he intended to do it this time.

With the sound of the sirens still in his ears, mingling with Mia's pleas for her life, and the shrieking of that old woman, Donevan climbed up on the washing machine, swung one end of the rope around the sturdiest-looking of the beams, then looped the other end around his neck.

He began to stroke faster. The power was at its peak. He'd never felt so good. All those noises began to merge inside his head. He thought he heard the sirens coming closer again.

Suddenly he jumped off the washing machine. The rope tightened around his neck. Donevan's hands still on his penis, he was aware of incredible conflicting sensations, horrible and wonderful and more intense than ever. The mating of the big death and the little death.

He kept stroking. The rope kept tightening. He was going somewhere he'd never been before. The high was agonizing in its pleasure, excruciating in its pain. Hell! It was incredible!

He heard someone scream, but he was already losing consciousness. He tried to open his eyes, but he couldn't. He was too far gone, feeling too good. And he was doing it all himself.

From far, far away, he decided that the scream was his mother's. He felt panic mixed with all the other emotions. Mama had finally caught him.

But it was too late to stop. Way too late.

Mrs. Smith was hysterical when she opened the door to the laundry room to let the police in. She was screaming and crying and pointing. The police took one look at the inert body and knew they'd arrived after the fact.

"Damn," one muttered to the other, "I wanted this one alive. Think of the confessions we could have gotten. I don't know how the smart son of a bitch got to the cottage without us seeing him unless he turned off into the trees before he reached us. Must have been one hell of a tricky trip. Thank God the neighbors turned up."

"Well, he won't hurt anybody else," the other one murmured. "But I guess he went out the way he wanted."

"Comfort the old woman. I'll make the station calls," the first cop said.

The other nodded.

Emma and Buck were in their glory. They had rescued the masseuse. *They* had! Not the police, who had somehow missed the white car and were waiting in the woods while one of their own was murdered and while the masseuse was almost a goner.

By the time the police arrived, Emma had gotten a housecoat for the woman, fixed her a cup of hot tea, and covered up the other body.

She'd also gotten a promise out of Mia to get her an introduction to Rand Mason. It had been such an exciting evening that she and Buck didn't even stand by the window. They went to bed when they got back home.

At the hospital Mia was being interviewed by the police and grasping at the scattered fragments of her sanity. She was bruised and battered, but she was relieved to know that it was all over.

Donevan was dead. Everyone could get on with their lives.

Soon she would be leaving the cottage. God knows she couldn't give a massage with her injured hand anyway. Donevan had almost broken her fingers.

As soon as the police left and Mia was checked into her hospital room for the night, she called Rand.

"What's up?" he asked, sensing her tension before she spoke.

Mia spilled it all, her words tumbling over one another, the attempted murder, the baby, Donevan's death.

There was a pause and Mia caught her own breath. What would he say?

Finally he spoke. "You're sure you're all right?"

"Yes."

"And our baby's all right?"

"Yes."

"Then everything's going to be fine. I promise you that, Mia."

"I believe that's true, Rand," Mia murmured.

For the first time since she awakened to the hooded figure above her bed, Mia did think everything was going to be all right.

"It is, Mia," he said gently. "I know this is an awful time to propose, but you know how much I love you. Will you marry me, Mia? Will you give our child my name?"

Mia smiled. It wasn't an awful time to propose at all. It was just what she needed to hear after the long nightmare she'd lived through.

"Yes, Rand. Nothing would make me happier. I love you, too."

Suddenly she felt secure again, loved, cocooned. After a few more words with Rand she replaced the receiver and then closed her eyes.

Mia slept soundly for the first time in months.